SECRET DANGERS

and

LETHAL SILENCE

by John Preston

The Alex Kane Missions
Books 5 & 6

ReQueered Tales
Los Angeles • Toronto
2023

Secret Dangers
Lethal Silence

by John Preston

The Alex Kane Missions, Books 5 & 6

*For more information about current and future releases,
please contact us:*
E-mail: *requeeredtales@gmail.com*
Facebook (Like us!): www.facebook.com/ReQueeredTales
Twitter: @ReQueered
Instagram: www.instagram.com/requeered
Web: www.ReQueeredTales.com
Blog: www.ReQueeredTales.com/blog
Mailing list (Subscribe for latest news): https://bit.ly/RQTJoin

Praise for the
Alex Kane Missions

"If a book can be judged by how quickly you turn the pages, *Sweet Dreams* is a winner. You may not agree with Kane's methods, but you can't quarrel with his sense of purpose. After such an auspicious debut, the future bodes well for Alex Kane and his creator."
— *Washington Blade*

"The Alex Kane adventure novels expand the boundaries of family constructions. Alex, his young lover Danny, and Joseph Farmdale, his late lover James's father, unite to exact justice for hate crimes directed toward gay men ... Preston's theme in these works is literature's most enduring: the conflict of good and evil – this time with homosexuals being the good guys."

— Jane D. Troxell,
Contemporary Gay American Novelists

"It's here that John Preston brought together his talent as a genre writer and his lifelong commitment to healthy, fearless gay pride. Read these novels for the delicious entertainment and for a reminder of how far we have come as a queer tribe."
— Philip Gambone

"The books provide pleasure on several levels. They acknowledge the harsh world in which we live, and they appeal to our need to think someone is standing up for our rights. They embody a set of values that we can emulate because of their continuing validity. ... The books provide pleasure on several levels. In a vision of the way things could be, gays and straights thus work together to make a better world."
— Drewey Wayne Gunn,
The Gay Male Sleuth in Print and Film

By JOHN PRESTON

THE ALEX KANE MISSION NOVELS

Sweet Dreams (1984)

Golden Years (1984)

Deadly Lies (1985)

Stolen Moments (1986)

Secret Dangers (1986)

Lethal Silence (1987)

SECRET DANGERS

and

LETHAL SILENCE

by John Preston

The Alex Kane Missions,
Books 5 & 6

Table of Contents

SECRET DANGERS

by John Preston

Author's Note

Every gay man has to fight a battle for individual dignity. The forces of ignorance can make that battle doubly hard for those of us who are not white or who love men who aren't white. The face of racial prejudice has no place in our playing fields and shouldn't have to be one of our fighting fields.

Black and White Men Together is a grassroots organization dedicated to overcoming the divisions that poison our community. You can be part of the solution and join this cause. Write and get more information:

National Association of Black and White Men
Together
584 Castro St., Suite 140 San Francisco, CA 94114

www.nabwmt.org

Alex Kane would be proud of your support.

I

Alex Kane stared at the Boeing 727 standing on the main runway of the Lichtburg Airport. It looked to him like one of those poor birds that are always getting caught in oil slicks. There was this machine that was designed to fly, to soar in the skies while it carried people to their dream vacations, or to visit their friends and relatives. Instead, it was grounded. Just like those waterfowl were always having their ability to fly ruined by the foolishness of people who'd pollute our oceans and lakes with their chemical spills, this big bird was being crippled by people who made a living out of messing up the world with their hatred.

"You on assignment?" Alex turned to see who was speaking to him. He recognized the face from countless television broadcasts. He even remembered the name of this man who was constantly showing his "humanistic" concern while he reported the great human tragedies of the world to the American public. Rip Stallion. That wasn't important. No one cared about this asshole's name anyway. They probably thought he was just another character in just another soap opera.

"You could say that," Alex retorted. He went back to staring out the window at the airplane on the tarmac hundreds of yards from the terminal where he and the television news star were standing.

The broadcaster stared at this strange, informally

dressed man. He was certainly handsome enough to be in media and he had a body, that was for sure. A good face and decent physique were increasingly required for success in this field. It had taken Rip and some of his cohorts a while to realize the body part of it. After all, they were only used to standing on camera in their suits and ties. Why would they need to have a torso?

But then he'd been studying the morning news programs. They all did that. Anchoring CBS Morning News, Today, or Good Morning America was the one great goal that all American journalists aspired to these days and Rip had to know what was selling to the network execs.

On this one day, Bryant had to do gymnastics with an Olympic star; Forrest was sitting poolside in a bathing suit at a Tampa hotel where he was doing an on-location bit; and David was part of a fashion show featuring the new see-through look. Hell, they would have never carried those off if they hadn't had bodies.

Rip had always wanted to be a broadcaster. That's why he'd changed his name. "Martin Sackowitz" just wouldn't have made it. But "Rip Stallion" – that was a name that the American public could have confidence in. He'd read a study that showed that network news success depended on audience trust of the newscaster. It had gone into his feeble brain as part of his repertoire. He'd also studied up on being sincere. If the audience wanted sincere – and they kept on saying they did – he'd give it to them. He got to be so good at it that one producer had to scream at him to smile during a humor segment.

In any event, Rip couldn't place this guy. If he didn't know who he was, he couldn't be anyone important. Probably just a go-fer in one of the competing news organizations.

Rip looked out at the plane. The damn thing had been there for two days now without any change in the situation. It was getting more and more difficult to come up with a new angle on the story. It burned him. He knew the high and mighty officials from the State Department were holding back on them. There was something going on in that plane that was the biggest part of the story, but Rip was damned if he knew what it was.

Hijacking was a hot beat. The public ate it up. But it could drag on and on. Rip just wished that the government of this operetta country would do something. At least the Maltese had let the Egyptian commandos go for it. That had been a great story. Dozens die while heroes attempt their rescue!

Sure, the 'Gypts had fucked it up pretty badly, and, later, it looked as though they had been the ones who had killed most of the civilians who had died on the plane. But the headlines and the air time!

Air time was the all-important thing for an up-and-coming young broadcaster like Rip. His progress was measured by how long he got to have his pretty face shown on the American television screen. That was bothering him. Every day the network had cut down on his appearances. It was bad enough that the authorities weren't telling the public just what was going on out there; it was inexcusable that they were keeping Rip Stallion from standing in front of his beloved television camera. There had to be a new story in this ...

"Say," he turned to Alex Kane suddenly, "who do you work for?"

Alex smiled. Rip noticed the way those green eyes were lighting up. They were fabulous. There was an electricity to them. They'd look great on camera. Maybe this guy was a relative of one of the victims. God, that would be great television – if he'd cry it'd be even better. He just didn't look the type to do that though. But if he'd get angry and those green eyes would light up like this while he talked, then Rip would be in high ratings heaven.

"I work freelance," Alex said.

"You're a writer then?"

"Oh, no," Alex smiled more broadly. "I don't do anything like that."

Great, Rip thought. "Well, what's your connection with

the situation? You don't have any family on that plane, do you?" Rip tried to ooze his most gushing sincerity.

"You could say that," Alex's eyes lost their luster. He seemed to be momentarily sad. Then he stood up with even more rigid posture than he had before. Rip realized that the man was much stronger than he had expected. He was wearing a shortsleeved shirt and it seemed that every move he made created a different form of living sculpture from the muscles in his exposed arms. That was some heavy-duty Nautilus work the guy must have been doing to get that build.

"I know this is a moment of private grief," Rip continued with his most empathetic tone, "but if you'd be willing to share the story of your agony with the millions of Americans who watch my reports, you'd be able to give them a sense of pride and hope in the face of ..."

He really didn't doubt that the guy would do it. It was amazing how easy it was to get even a mother to go on camera only minutes after her baby had died. There was something about the way that Americans just loved the idea of being celebrities that made them forget the basic tenets of human decency as fast as the television reporters themselves. Andy Warhol had told the public that they could each be a star for fifteen minutes. Not many passed up the chance.

"You put a camera on me and I swear you'll end up wearing it as a suppository for the rest of your life."

Rip stood back for a moment, shocked at the violence that was clear in the man's threat. "Now, now, I understand what you're going through ..."

"You don't understand shit," Alex turned on him. His fists were clenched tightly and his face was cut into deep frowning lines. "The last thing I want is some dim-witted voyeur watching me while this is going on. The whole bunch of you should be sent to reform school so you can have a crash course in manners."

Rip backed away from the man. He held his hands out straight in front of him as he moved. This man was crazy. Those eyes that he'd admired before had changed their complexion completely. They weren't the eyes of a sane man. They carried with them a threat of something much more than a simple fist fight. Just what that was, Rip wasn't going to explore. After all, he wasn't getting combat pay for this assignment. Lichtburg was considered a plush job.

"I could have made you a star." That was all Rip said when he felt he was far enough away from the crazy man. "You're the one who gave up the chance."

• • •

Alex stood alone and kept on watching the jetliner. There were over one hundred people trapped on the plane. They were innocent tourists, just a bunch of hardworking Americans who were taking their big European vacations. They'd probably saved years for this chance. Some were older people who'd probably denied themselves any luxuries at all while they put their kids through college. He knew there were some honeymoon couples as well. There was a group of students from a college in Missouri who were just coming back from a year abroad.

And there were the twenty members of the Red River Social Club.

So far as the rest of the world was concerned, the Red River group was a fraternal organization from the Fargo, North Dakota, region. There had been some confusion about it. The carnivorous network news programs hadn't been able to get much information on the club when it had gone to Fargo to try to get the "human interest" stories they loved so much – the grieving families and friends of the trapped hostages hadn't been very forthcoming.

There was a reason for that. A simple one. It was the same reason that Alex Kane stood here and watched some ridiculous private army holding civilian lives hostage in a vain attempt to resolve a political conflict that hardly anyone in America had ever heard about.

The members of the Red River Social Club were all gay.

The people in charge of the hijacking represented the

White Army of Bosnia. As Alex understood it – and he didn't really think he could follow the twisted logic – the White Army members were the descendants of the old nobility of a part of the former Austro-Hungarian Empire that was now a part of Yugoslavia. He closed his eyes and tried to remember just exactly how this went. Yes, he thought that was right.

Now, somehow these yo-yos thought by hijacking a plane full of civilians who didn't know what Bosnia was, they were going to get the anticommunist American and Lichtburg governments to convince the communist Yugoslavs to miraculously free ancient Bosnia and give it back to the grandson of its long deposed king.

Sure, they were. Of course. Good old Ronnie was going to ride his horse back out of the sunset and get those Reds for the Whites and everything was hunky-dory. What a pile of shit this was.

It was so stupid it might have been funny. But like the fanatics on the Left who had made a holiday out of bombing airports all over the world and whose idea of a Christmas present was to booby-trap London department stores, these people had one thing going for them that kept any hope of humor out of the picture: They were proven killers.

They'd blown up a train as it was crossing the Swiss border into France once. And they'd even helped out some very unlikely Palestinian allies in the assassination of an Israeli cabinet minister. It seems that the only thing the White Army hated more than Yugoslav Reds were living Jews.

And fags.

What the hell would a bunch of bozos like that do if they ever discovered that those ordinary looking men from Fargo, North Dakota, were gay?

The sweat was flowing from Alex's body. He hated this sense of impotency. If there had been any way that he could have gone out and taken on the whole group of them, he would have. But there was no way to do it.

The plane was rigged with explosives. If any one of the White Army members thought the Lichtburgers had allowed commandos on the scene they'd have blown up everything. It hadn't taken much research to find out that the threat of killing themselves along with their hostages was a real one. Every other action they'd taken had led to the "martyrdom" of at least one of their members.

You could have all the resources of the United States and you could have all the courage of Alex Kane and it wouldn't be worth a damn when a group of fanatics discovered the vulnerability of unarmed civilian air transport.

Damn! It made Alex mad. He slammed a fist into one of the bulletproof windows that the Lichtburgers had installed as a defense against terrorists when the threat had become severe a few years ago.

Lt. Bart Conner saw the strange man pound his hand into the glass. Then he saw the glass shatter. He stopped short and shook his head. As the security liaison for the American embassy, he knew the specifications for those windows perfectly well. No person should have been able to do that.

Conner knew the implications. It had to be another instance of a defense contractor ripping off the government and substituting inferior goods in a contract. Well, he'd see to it that the files were searched and that the government got some money back on this one. But not right now. He was on too important an assignment.

"Mr. Kane?" Conner spoke to the man who didn't seem to even care that he might have shattered the bones in his hand along with the glass window.

"Yeah." The guy certainly had a surly voice. Conner put it down to a lack of discipline in the United States. It certainly seemed to Conner that the guy could show a little more respect to an American uniformed officer.

"Secretary Bartlett will see you now."

Alex Kane stood up and nodded. Conner led the weird man down the aisles of the terminal. They'd tried to clear the building as much as possible. All the civilians were supposed to be gone, but there seemed to be more new people here than there would have been travelers on a regular day.

There was CBS, NBC, ABC, CNN, CBC, their counterparts from the United Kingdom, France, Sweden, Germany, Spain, Italy, Japan, and god knows where else. There was also the army of print journalists and their photographers. AP, Reuters and a host of others. Conner couldn't help but wonder at the extraordinary amount of equipment they'd all brought with them. Conner thought back to his lessons in strategy at West Point. The complex problems of supply and transportation had always been a great burden to the military. But these journalists and their personnel and materiel would have inspired Napoleon with their mobility.

Conner had thought he'd be the first to get to the Lichtburg Airport when the first alert got through to the embassy days ago. He was wrong. The local correspondent for the Washington *Post* and a newscaster for International Network News had both beaten him by a yard.

Conner led Alex Kane into the offices that stood unnoticed behind the ticket counters of the airport. They'd been commandeered by local officials for the duration of the ordeal. One suite had been set aside for the Americans and the cabinet member who'd been sent from Washington as a symbol of concern for the U.S. citizens who were the crew and most of the passengers of the hijacked plane.

Conner knocked on the inner door of the offices. A gruff voice answered, "Come in." The military man stepped aside and let Kane enter.

Secretary Bartlett was sitting with his back to Alex. He was staring out the huge picture window that gave him a perfect view of the jetliner on the tarmac; he seemed to be hypnotized by the scene in front of him.

"I have the strangest orders to speak to you. I don't know who the hell you are or how you got the kind of pull in Washington that a member of the President's cabinet is suddenly supposed to be at your beck and call in the middle of an emergency of this size, but I'm not stupid. You're here. So what do you want?"

"I know your son." That was all Alex said.

II

Charlie Bergen was one of the millions of Americans who were glued to their television sets. There was something excruciating about turning on the damned thing and seeing that vulnerable plane sitting on the runway – still. Wasn't there anything that could be done?

A booming singing voice broke through and overwhelmed the TV announcer. Charlie smiled when he heard his lover Tom's rendition of "The Triumphal March" from Verdi's *Aida*. That production had been one of Tom's own triumphs.

The Philadelphia Opera Company had put out a call to local bodybuilders who were known to have theatrical training. They had needed extras to act as spear carriers. Tom and Charlie were both awed at the chance to take part and had signed up as soon as they'd heard about it. They were both – to put it mildly – physically qualified for the roles as guards. The casting director had snapped them up right away.

They'd made their prized appearances on the stage of the Philadelphia Academy of Music. Charlie had worn coats of "Texas dirt" – the full body makeup that's used to create the impression that the actor is African. Tom had that coloring naturally; he didn't need to play at being black. Their gay friends had loved it. Not only were they excited that the couple had a chance to live out their dream of being a part of the world of opera – no matter how slight – they'd also been more than a little appreciative of the stir that the two men's bodies had made among the audience.

"Honey, the women swooned and the men just fainted away," their friend Marco had declared at the very private and very gay opening night party. "As soon as the two of you walked out with those tiny, tiny loincloths on, I thought the place was going to need a medical evacuation!"

Well, they did look good. They had both been working out since they were in high school. It was even the way they met. They had both been entered in one of the many physique contests in the Delaware Valley during their college years. They'd looked at one another and sensed that they shared more than an interest in dumbbells. That had been the beginning of an awfully good life together.

Tom came out of the bathroom with a towel wrapped around his waist. Even if Charlie did know that his own body was just as developed as Tom's, it always came as a shock for him to look at his lover's huge and well-defined torso and to realize that it was the gift he had to share his bed with every single night.

Tom came over and kissed Charlie. They'd been together for seven years now and the affection – and the erotic interest – were as strong as ever in their relationship.

The television announcer came back on the air after a commercial break. Tom's attention was drawn away from his lover. "That's still going on?" he asked.

"Yes," Charlie answered. He shifted back to watch the television screen again. "It's terrible. You think that you live in a civilized world and then this kind of thing happens. Can you imagine what the poor people inside that plane must feel like?"

"Shit. That's what they feel like. The world's going crazy. I don't think there's anything you can count on any more except you and me."

"Don't add that you're worried about me," Charlie said jokingly.

"No, baby, I'm not at all worried about you." Tom sat

beside Charlie on the couch and put a mammoth arm around his lover's shoulder. He squeezed it a little just to show that he meant his statement. "But you just can't do anything about the insanity of the world nowadays. The most you can do is try to stay out of it. Just pull back to what you know about.

"I've given up all my high ideals about changing the world and creating any kind of better place. What you see is what you get and what you see more and more is the inability of the government to protect you."

"Fine thing for a high school teacher to be saying." There was an edge to Charlie's voice now.

"Sometimes I feel that's a reason I am a teacher," Tom answered, refusing to respond to the hint of argument in Charlie's voice. "I think I might – I just might – be able to reach the kids in my class a little bit. If I can do nothing more than convince them that Spanish is a fine language with a rich literary tradition and that the people who speak it aren't less than human just because that's their native tongue, then maybe I'm making my contribution to things.

"It's like the wise men of every culture say: The children are our only hope. It makes a lot of sacrifices worthwhile."

Now Charlie sat up straight and pulled himself free of Tom's arm. The allusion to their ongoing battle made him angry. Everything for the sake of educating children!

He didn't have to verbalize his thoughts. They'd been around and around about the issues for the past three years. It was a constant stress on an otherwise fine relationship. They had been committed to their shared ideal of being educators since the very beginning. But when they made that commitment, Charlie, at least, hadn't really understood what they'd be giving up.

When they'd started out it was a simple question of two masculine and very muscular men who just happened to like one another a little bit more than males were supposed to. They never talked too much about it. They hadn't even really applied the word "gay" to themselves. They were separate, a unit apart from the rest of the world. But then that world had begun to intrude. They weren't allowed to forget that they were an interracial couple, for one thing. There were constant references to their being "salt and pepper" on the bodybuilding circuit. The little jibes had taken their toll after a while and they'd both learned to be angry about them.

The fact that they were doing sexual things together would have only made the racial slurs worse. So they'd taken extra pains to hide that part of their relationship. There were some things that Charlie wouldn't give up. He had demanded that they live together after they'd left college.

That was the beginning to the drawing of the battle lines. They had both taken jobs in the same prestigious suburban high school and they were both doing graduate work at night to get the necessary credentials to allow them the option of entering school administration. It was too risky to let anyone know that they had a thing going on, Tom had said. Their career plans could go down the drain.

Charlie had insisted and, finally, they had agreed that the way to overcome the fears was to live in another town. No one would have to know. Tom had even bought the idea with a little bit of enthusiasm. They had begun to be braver about a lot of things once they had that physical separation between work and home. They'd make occasional excursions into Center City and go dancing at the DCA Club or have brunch at Key West.

Then AIDS hit.

As they watched the news stories build and build in intensity, the two men had known that there was as much danger from the horrible plague of ignorance as there was from the disease. They cared about AIDS, of course they did. But it didn't get to them in the usual way. They'd been monogamous for so long that they couldn't imagine themselves to be at risk in terms of catching the virus. But the hysteria was certain to present a danger to them.

It only took one newscast of the reaction of a group of parents at a school in New York City to convince Tom that they had to go all the way back into the closet they had only so tentatively left. If anyone found out that they were lovers during the epidemic, then they'd really be in trouble and they'd surely lose their jobs. All the fine human characteristics of the school administration could melt away just the same as they had in New York. "If the man wants to get you," Tom had said, "the man's going to get you." It was something he'd learned the hard way growing up black in America.

Tom had even gone an extra step and rented a post office box for himself so they'd have different mailing addresses. He'd also demanded that they each buy his own car and do the drive to work alone so no one would notice that they arrived together.

They were still in their mid-twenties and they were still climbing up their vocational ladders. They not only had earned their masters degrees, they had taken on endless extracurricular activities at school. Some of these even involved extra money. Charlie had won the position as an assistant coach to the football team and Tom was coaching the growing number of students who were taking up weightlifting. The work was exciting and the rewards of teaching and knowing that he was doing it well were important to Charlie. The fact that they had little spare time had only made them manage what they had more carefully. They still found ways to do things like volunteer as extras for the opera and they had their summer months for extensive travel.

What they had also precious little of was time with gay people. They'd found some like Marco when they started working in the Opera Company. Charlie had been delighted by the turn of events. It had led him and Tom to be introduced to the fascinating people who worked in the local gay theater company and they'd learned that there was a whole network of gay cultural groups that held performances and concerts throughout the Philadelphia area.

But as Charlie dove into the activities, Tom had begun to get more and more frightened. They couldn't go to this occasion because there were going to be cameras; they couldn't go to that because there might be people from the graduate school there. All Charlie ever got from Tom was a constant series of roadblocks.

"It shouldn't matter," Tom would insist. "This is our private life and it shouldn't have anything to do with our jobs as teachers."

"Then why does it rule our lives? Answer me that," Charlie would shoot back. "If this is our private business and no one should bother us because of it, then why are we constantly living in fear that someone's going to discover it?"

The arguments were only getting worse. That was the really bad thing about it. It was part of their getting older and their discovering that there was more to their lives than they had thought. The truth was that Charlie was more desperate for a well-rounded gay life than he could have known he'd want back when they'd started. And he wanted Tom to share it with him.

As Charlie had discovered that their sexuality wasn't something unique to them, but something that made them a part of this fascinating group of people out there, he wanted to join it. AIDS didn't even make him hesitate. On the contrary, the idea that this group of people with whom he now identified was under siege only made it more important to him that he take part in all of its life. He was furious with himself – and with Tom – that they had only made token donations to the AIDS groups in Pennsylvania and that they hadn't taken part in the work that he knew was so necessary. They had special educational skills that could be invaluable. But they didn't volunteer those skills.

If the only problem was Tom and himself, he'd be able to handle it. He'd be able to fight and argue and make Tom see the reasons for them to take some chances and risks.

There was one flaw in the whole picture: Tom was right. They were teachers. There was no way for them to come out and be gay and still be able to stay in the classroom that they both wanted to lead. There was no easy answer to the dilemma. There was only the frustration and the anger and the sense of impotency.

"We've been hijacked!" Charlie burst out. "That's the only way to put it. The whole goddamned world has hijacked us with their terrorism and their stupidity and their fear!"

Tom looked at his lover and didn't quite know what had gone through that head of his tonight. He put his arm back around Charlie's shoulder and drew him back to him on the couch. "Is this the terror you're talking about?" he said as he pulled the towel off his body and groped himself playfully. "Or are you worried about the tryouts for *Attila* next week?"

Charlie tried to keep a hold on his anger. But he couldn't, not with the warm nakedness next to him. He reached down and pulled Tom's hand away from his crotch and replaced it with his own. "*Attila,* no wonder you were singing Verdi in the shower."

"Verdi, hell. Babe, I got other songs I want to sing with you." He pulled Charlie over and they began to kiss. While the hijacking drama played itself out on the television screen, the two lovers moved back into that private world of theirs where Tom was so certain they could never be harmed.

III

Joseph Farmdale would have loved to be hijacked. He would have paid someone to do it. If he had to listen to one more Sousa march he thought he would never regain the use of his eardrums.

He moved awkwardly in his chair in the main theater of Boston's Wang Center. At least that should be the end to the Sousa section of the program. What could possibly follow? *Oh, god,* he groaned to himself as the opening strains of music sounded through the auditorium, *not another rendition of "Stout Hearted Men!"* He put a hand on Danny Fortelli's arm and looked at the younger man with a beseeching expression.

"Great, aren't they?" Danny said over the din.

There was no hope for his rescue in Danny's enthusiasm. Joseph would have to endure. He sat back in his seat and crossed his arms over his chest. The Farmdales had been tortured by native Americans when they had first set out to establish their personal empire decades ago. They had lived through the agonies of wars in Asia, Africa and Europe. They had suffered indignities and they had persevered. He would do no less.

But those ancestors had never had to face anything quite so appalling as a joint concert by every gay marching band in the United States. This was incomparable torment.

He understood that there were people in this country

and elsewhere who enjoyed this common music. There were also people who enjoyed watching television and who went to public movie theaters regularly. It hurt that Danny was one of them, but then the boy was still young.

There were few people who would have called Danny Fortelli young if they knew what he had gone through in his nineteen years. Farmdale closed his eyes with regret. He blamed himself for part of it at least. Of course he had had nothing to do with the real beginning, when the blackmailers had found an even younger Danny and forced him into prostitution and drugs. But he had much to do with what happened after that. It was Joseph Farmdale, after all, who had set Alex Kane in motion in the first place. And it had been Alex Kane who had truly altered Danny's life forever.

Farmdale had seen it coming. He had even looked forward to the time when his own deceased son's lover would finally find another mate for himself. But sometimes he wished that it had been an older person than Danny. Then he wouldn't have to feel so guilty about the boy's youth having been stolen.

He looked over at the Fortelli boy and forced himself to realize once again that he was really extraordinarily good looking. Danny had joked about some of the stares they had received when they had walked in. He'd said that the crowd had assumed that he was being kept. Of course, then the on-lookers must also have assumed that Farmdale had a fortune as large as he in fact did. If there was a price tag on the utter beauty of Danny Fortelli, then the sum written on it would have to be astronomical.

Would James have had a lover like this? Farmdale wondered. But he dismissed the thought. James had made it abundantly clear that he had already found the lover of his life: the strange son of Greek fishermen from Portsmouth, New Hampshire, Alex Kane. Joseph had to admit that James had never been as happy in his life as he had when he had fallen head over heels for the Marine recruit who had shown up in his command. There was the meaning of his life, there was a reason for living and going on. James had been delirious and joyful and ...

Joseph told himself to stop doing this. This was not the way that a Farmdale should carry on. The family had not built its place in America by indulging in maudlin emotions. A slight twinge of regret, that was all he should allow himself after all these years.

He was enough of a Farmdale, though, to have added a good dose of revenge to his initial dismay over his son's death. Joseph had known little about the rampant homophobia that poisoned the country. He had seldom even thought of the issue of homosexuality. After all, he was the person who had to remind himself that Danny Fortelli was so strikingly handsome. Joseph would never have really noticed. Nor would he have noticed it if a woman had been equally as good looking. He had proven that with the total lack of passion he'd shown all of his many wives.

He had never been attracted to men – or women – himself. Still, Joseph had learned about the depth of anti-gay hatred in America – in the world. He had forced himself to as soon as he had learned that it had been the cause of his son's death. James had been murdered in Vietnam where he and Alex had been stationed during that damnable war. A spiteful redneck, jealous of the favors he thought James was showing Kane, had shot the young Farmdale from the back.

Joseph had no means to seek vengeance for that single act. Alex Kane had already extracted it. Alex had turned around as soon as he had understood what had happened and he had executed the murderer where he stood. There was no need for a trial or jury in the matter so far as the young Alex Kane was concerned. When the wheels of military justice tried to argue with his logic, Joseph Farmdale had stepped in and used some of his most valuable trading chips to secure the freedom of his son's lover.

That was the real beginning. That was when Alex Kane had been unleashed to fight against all the forces that would dare to treat gay men as anything less than worthwhile. One of the first of Alex's missions had put him and Danny into one another's arms. They had never really parted since that time that Alex had seen Danny's innocent and sweet dreams ruined by mobsters. He had brought Danny into his own dreams then. Now they were a pair, a couple, lovers whose entire relationship was based on the never-ending battle against the enemies of gay men – anywhere.

Joseph was deep in thought about the many dangerous battles that the two of them had undertaken. He was especially concerned about the one that Alex was taking part in now. Danny would have gone with his lover if there had been any reason to. But there hadn't been; there was no action that could be taken. Farmdale's usual intelligence network – carefully controlled by a computer system that was the envy of every private and public corporation in the world – had sent the facts to Alex and Danny's home in the New Hampshire mountains. The two had studied the data and realized that all they could do was monitor the situation and make sure nothing was done that would unnecessarily expose the gay men on that plane to harm.

Danny still would have gone, but Farmdale had finally gotten them to listen to reason. Danny had classes to attend and schoolwork to do. After all, the Fortelli boy was enrolled in a public university near their home now. But even that thought bothered Farmdale. With the money that Alex had inherited from James – the younger Farmdale had made Alex his heir – they could have afforded to buy Harvard for the boy. But Danny had insisted on going to the state school.

That, *Farmdale suddenly decided,* was the cause for the love of Sousa. I knew I hated public education!

They were suddenly relieved of the agony of the concert. All around them the gay men in the audience were jumping to their feet and applauding wildly. But none of them did so with the enthusiasm of Joseph Farmdale once he understood that their actions signaled the end of the concert. It was over! He might have been well past seventy years old, but the end of the concert brought about a remarkable surge of athletic excitement in him. To Danny's amazement, Joseph Farmdale wasn't just clapping, he was yelling: "Huzzah! Bravo! Hooray!"

The crowd quieted down and Farmdale was horrified to see that someone else was coming out onto the stage. It was a quite properly dressed middle-aged man who made an appeal for funds for the bands.

Farmdale was mortified. They shouldn't be encouraged!

But baskets were being passed through the aisles by ushers. Joseph looked over and saw that Danny was writing out a check. He saw the sum. Danny was writing out a very *substantial* check. Farmdale groaned. There was no way the young man would let him do less. He could just hear the persuasion Danny would use on him if Farmdale tried to get out of the theater without contributing to the "arts." He reached into his jacket pocket and dragged out his checkbook. He reached over and took Danny's pen when the younger man was done using it. The baskets came their way, and the two signed documents were dropped in it.

Perhaps they'll use the money to travel, Farmdale thought. *To Patagonia.* That idea appealed to him greatly. While they made their way through the surging crowd that was leaving the theater, Farmdale had a broad smile on his face.

As they walked out onto Tremont Street, Danny finally had a chance to make a comment to the older man: "I didn't know you were having such a good time. You certainly gave a generous donation."

Farmdale smiled. "1 have never had such a visceral reaction to the end of a concert in my entire life! I couldn't do less than show my appreciation for it," he said as he entered the waiting limousine.

Danny followed him into the car and the chauffeur closed the door. "Sometimes I think I underestimate you, Mr. Farmdale."

"Never do that, Danny, never do that." Then Farmdale rapped on the glass that separated the passenger compartment from the front seat, "Drive, to the South End."

• • •

"I can't help but worry about Alex," Danny was saying as he ate the chicken which was one of the specialties of the restaurant where they were dining. It was evidence of the superb kitchen that they were able to make such a simple dish a gourmet treat. But Danny didn't seem to be enjoying it much.

"There's constant danger in the lives you and your lover have chosen, Danny. This, actually, is probably one of the less hazardous tasks that Alex has undertaken. What can he do, really? He's simply standing by and watching the Lichtburg army as it surrounds that plane. He can – and he will – do everything he can to protect the lives and rights of the gay men on board. But he knows all too well that there's no way he can challenge the terrorists' hold on an exposed 727."

Danny knew that was true. He and Alex had called their pilot friends in Minneapolis as soon as they'd heard the news about the hijacking. They had studied the blueprints for the jetliner and they had gone over all the most detailed reports of other commando raids on hijacked aircraft. There was no hope. It was one of the reasons that terrorists were so attracted to planes in the first place.

"Please, son, enjoy your meal. The chauffeur is monitoring the television in the car and he'll report to us if there's any news at all. Let's talk about more pleasant things."

"Wasn't that a great concert!" Danny said, picking up Farmdale's suggestion.

The older man sighed and sipped his Sauvignon Blanc. This was not his idea of more pleasant topics of conversation. But he luckily wasn't called upon to comment at any length. Danny kept on talking, "Alex says that it's just this kind of thing that we're fighting for."

Farmdale felt the first twinges of a heart attack. He knew it would come to this. There was only so much that a cultured soul like his could take. To think that there was any connection between the ideals of the Farmdale tradition and the desecration represented by that group of barbarians who called themselves "musicians" …

"Not just the band –"

Farmdale relaxed once more. "Oh," he said, trying to be subtle, "what else?"

"The whole thing, that gay guys can have all these community events – bands and choruses, volleyball leagues and discussion groups, all the things that he says makes up a community. If gay guys can't fit into the stuff that society gives to everyone else, he says, then we should just go out and make our own. We're the protective curtain that lets the others do just that.

"He says it's especially important because of AIDS."

They both stopped talking for a moment when the hideous subject was brought up. Danny eventually continued, "Alex says that everyone needs the kind of strength they can get from one another even more during the epidemic. He says he even needs it. Have you ever talked to him about it?"

"Only a little bit. We've discussed the large donations he's made to research, of course. He tried hard to find the most underfunded parts of that budget. Not only do the actual fund transfers go through my office, my staff also helps him make the decisions about where the money could be best spent."

"Right, he's told me that. But have you really talked to him about it? He hates AIDS. I mean, we all do. But he really hates AIDS. I don't want to be with him again if he finds any more people like that man in Houston who use it politically. Boy, Alex just goes crazy about it."

Farmdale had nothing he could add. He hated that damned plague as well, and never more than when he was sitting across from Danny Fortelli – about whom he already felt guilty because of the boy's life as the partner to Alex Kane – and thought that this life, this precious life, could be …

"But the community-building activities help make sure that people band together to try to work out the problems with one another. That's why Alex thinks they're even more important than they were before.

"There are all kinds of things, he says, that were only

beginning to be born into our lives. We have to make sure that they don't get thrown out by the disease, not when we need them more than ever."

"Admirable philosophy, Danny. As usual, Alex is full of that. I only wish he could be full of a means to get rid of those bandits on the airplane."

"Oh, he'll handle it some way. I only hope that he calls and gives me a chance to join him. Don't think that Alex is going to let this go with what happens at that airport, Mr. Farmdale. You should know by now that there'll be another chapter in the whole thing. I don't think this one will require one of your red leather books, either. I think Alex will write this one himself."

The red leather books were the collections of information and data that Farmdale and his staff put together for Alex Kane. The memory of them saddened Joseph Farmdale. They were his responsibility; he was the one who had them compiled and he was the one who had them delivered to the small house where Alex and Danny lived. Each time it meant that they would go out again and fight once more. And each time it meant that Joseph Farmdale was responsible for taking away a little bit more of Danny's youth.

"Will you have dessert, Mr. Farmdale? The chocolate cake's dynamite."

"No, Danny. I think there are more than enough explosions around for me as it is. More than enough ..."

IV

Secretary William Bartlett wasn't used to letting total strangers know the foreign policy plans of the United States government. He certainly wasn't used to telling those secrets to avowed homosexuals. He looked across his desk at the man who had told him that he was … gay. The word didn't come very easily to Bartlett. He closed his eyes and ran a hand across his forehead as though the action could erase the term from his vocabulary.

But it wouldn't be eliminated that readily. "Gay" wasn't a sociological fad word any more so far as Bartlett was concerned. It was something that applied to a member of his own family. It was the word his oldest son Josh used to describe himself. That meant it involved William Bartlett himself, not just some strange group of deviants.

He pulled himself up in his chair, hoping a firmer posture would help him out of this situation. "I really can't answer your question, Mr. Kane. I am, after all, a member of the President's cabinet. I'm pleased to meet any friend of Josh's …"

"I'm not just a friend." The man stood up and walked to the window that overlooked the stranded jetliner from an even closer vantage than the other one had. He stood and stared out at the 727. "I'm the one who saved his life. Do you remember the trouble in Houston?"

Bartlett froze. Of course he remembered that nightmare,

how could he ever forget it? There had been unbelievable violence unleashed against the homosexuals in the Texas city. Bartlett had looked on with only a slight worry that his son, a student at one of the medical schools, might get caught in it. He had never suspected that Josh was actually one of the targets.

When he did finally understand that Josh was a leader of the gay group on campus and that the hate-mongering daily newspaper had singled him out for persecution, Bartlett had been hit by the greatest emotional storm of his life.

His son was a homosexual! No, no, he had to push that out of his mind. The fact of Josh's sexuality had been one of Bartlett's least concerns at first. He was more worried about the reality that people were trying to kill his child. That was the most pressing and unbelievable issue. He and his wife had pulled themselves up by the bootstraps to make sure that their offspring would have every advantage possible in this world. His own rise in American politics was really a series of rewards for his business success. To find out that there was one small item – a question of private sexual behavior – that could divest his child of all the power and prestige that he had accumulated had horrified Bartlett.

When peace had finally been restored to Houston and Josh had come back home to Washington to describe what had gone on, Bartlett and his wife had been so overwhelmed to know that the boy was all right that he hadn't even talked about the issues of homosexuality at first. Instead they had heard about a heroic gay man who had organized the community to defend itself against the marauders who had threatened their lives.

Bartlett recalled all the details of Josh's stories. The man had been powerful looking. He had about him the air of a professional soldier. Then Bartlett remembered Josh's one comment about the intensely angry eyes that had been so distinctive about his champion.

Yes, this was that man.

What do I think about him now? Bartlett wondered. The

reality that Josh's confessions had included the news of his homosexuality had finally caused the family great problems. This man had saved Josh's life, there was no denying that. But he had also made Josh even more comfortable and, yes, even proud of his sexuality. There was even less chance that Josh would consider trying to change – if there ever had been any.

The one thing that Bartlett understood was his own deep disappointment that his son hadn't felt willing and able to come to him and talk about something as important as this. He had spoken to his father only when events had forced him to.

So this man, Alex Kane, was part of it. Bartlett hadn't met any of Josh's friends. He hadn't felt capable of doing that – yet. But here was one of them.

"I honestly appreciate what you did for Josh, Mr. Kane. I really do. But I can't simply ..."

"Do you know that there are twenty gay men on that plane?" Alex Kane still wasn't looking at Bartlett.

Men like Josh ... "No," the Secretary admitted, "that information hadn't been given to me. But the government certainly wouldn't treat those citizens any differently ..."

"The hijackers will. The White Army of Bosnia isn't exactly one of the great cheering sections for gay liberation. There's an army of newspaper people out there, desperate for a story. You know damn well they're wondering why they can't find out much about the social group from North Dakota. Now you understand. As soon as they get their paws on that little tidbit, it's going to be broadcast all over the world. We know the hijackers are monitoring televisions and radio broadcasts to make sure they're getting good coverage. They'll hear it. As soon as they do, we'll certainly know who they're going to sacrifice first."

Bartlett felt sweat beading on his forehead.

Now Alex Kane turned and faced him. Alex spoke firmly, "I want to know what they're really demanding. By now they know they won't get the prisoners from Yugoslavia. So they must have another series of demands. Right? What are they asking *for*?"

"The Lichtburg Prime Minister is on his way here to discuss them with me."

Kane slammed down on his chair. "I want to be in on the meeting."

Bartlett studied the man and felt himself being swayed. Perhaps it was the memory that he owed this man something for saving Josh. Maybe it was his own sense of powerlessness that resulted in his being willing to grasp at any straw. But, he realized suddenly, it was actually something much more. He trusted Kane. He honestly trusted him to come up with a solution.

At that moment Lt. Conner opened the door to the office they were sitting in. "The Prime Minister," he announced. Bartlett and Kane both stood up. The Secretary could see the Army officer look at Alex warily.

"Your Excellency," Bartlett greeted the old aristocrat as he walked into the office. The men had met many times before, both officially and socially. They shook hands with an authentic greeting. "May I introduce you to a special advisor from Washington, Mr. Alex Kane."

While the old Lichtburger took Kane's hand, Bartlett gave Conner a withering glance, "We need to be alone now, Lieutenant."

"Yes, sir," the military attaché said with something close to a sigh of resignation. Then he closed the door and left the three of them alone.

"Mr. Secretary, we have had one final series of negotiations with the White Army members." The Prime Minister reached into his coat pocket and brought out a scrap of paper that seemed strangely informal in his cosmopolitan grip.

"They demand safe passage out of the airport with volunteer hostages from the Lichtburg police force. That, we can give them. We already have volunteers. They demand a ransom of five million dollars. That we will not give them. Finally, they insist on a formal admission of war crimes from the United States Government."

"War crimes!" Bartlett stood up and pounded his desk. "When did the United States ever ..."

"They insist that the United States' refusal to come to their aid when the communists took over Yugoslavia was a war crime." The old man said quietly.

"But we could never ..."

"Give it to them."

The Prime Minister and Bartlett both suddenly looked over at the casually dressed man sitting near them.

"Lichtburg gives them passage; the U.S. gives them their fake apology; I'll give them five million dollars."

"You can't be serious," the Prime Minister responded.

"I am. You already said that you'd give them passage."

"Yes, to end this nightmare we would go that far. But if we give into their other demands we set a dangerous precedent that could encourage other terrorists in the future."

"You have no idea how many precedents you could be setting." Kane seemed to withdraw into a dark brooding that made the other two men uncomfortable. He suddenly broke out of it. "Give them everything they want. I'll get them for you. We'll make an example of them, you better believe we'll make an example of them."

Bartlett seemed lost in his thoughts. He shook his head. "Mr. Prime Minister, I think we should follow Mr. Kane's advice."

"You are willing to go on television, worldwide, and apologize to these monsters? They were allies of Hitler in the war. They were responsible for atrocities that haven't even been revealed yet."

"I trust Mr. Kane. I've seen his work before."

"I'll go get the money." Alex Kane picked up the phone. He turned to the Prime Minister, "What's the biggest bank in the country?"

"It's after office hours."

"Then give me the home phone of the bank president. I have a sneaking suspicion that he'll talk to me."

• • •

Alex watched the debacle from a distance. While the Prime Minister presided over the exchange, hundreds of television cameras were trained on the humiliation. The White Army members filed into the special cars they had been promised to transport them. They were keeping only a few hostages with them, Lichtburg police who were their assurance that the authorities wouldn't interfere with them as they melded into the city.

They had kept their heads covered with hoods that concealed everything but their eyes during the entire operation. They had purposely worn loose clothing that had no markings. They were smarter than most; Alex had known that. They weren't as flashy or as interested in personal fame as other terrorists had been. They would drive around, pick up other cars, then just disappear into the mass of people in the European capital. They had to be awfully confident of their ability to do that. There were friends waiting for them somewhere who they trusted to be not only loyal, but also capable of carrying off the next step in their plans.

Alex could feel the presence of people approaching. He turned and looked as a dozen young men came up to him. "We know you," one of them said. He was no more than twenty-five. He reminded Alex of Danny. Like Kane's lover, this guy moved with grace, a dancer probably, or else a gymnast. He was blond – that was different – and he wasn't in a good mood. But it was apparent that his anger wasn't directed towards the American.

"How do you know me?" Alex responded.

"You were in the bar – The Underground – the other night. Some of us saw you there. I've heard about you, from America. You are the one."

"The one?"

"The one that helps us."

"Us?"

"We are all in the gay liberation front here in Lichtburg.

We suspect you have something to do about the people on the plane."

"What do you know about them?" Alex couldn't imagine that this group of young men could have gotten information that had escaped the omnivorous American press.

"From the same place, The Underground. They came there the night before they were supposed to leave for home. They were happy and friendly. We talked to many of them. We like to meet American gays. We knew as soon as the word came that the plane was hijacked that they were on it and in great danger. I told you, I have heard of you. I knew you'd be here. We want to help. What do you need? Cars? Drivers? Guns?"

"No guns. Not yet." Alex took in the group that stood in front of him. They were young and they'd be inexperienced. But they'd also know the city inside and out, maybe even better than the police. A new plan quickly formulated in his mind. "But there are plenty of things you can do for me."

V

The young blond's name was Bernhardt. But Alex wouldn't have recognized him as the same person. His yellow hair was covered by a black watch hat. His pale complexion was smeared with burnt cork. Only his blue eyes betrayed him. When Alex had first seen the two piercing circles that broke the dark plane of his camouflaged face, he had suddenly realized what others meant when they always talked about his own green eyes and their effect on people. Bernhardt did look eerie, just as Kane must have.

They were with a friend of Bernhardt, Jan, a street-hardened tough. Like Bernhardt, both Jan and Alex were dressed for their special nighttime work.

They had found the lair. A network of unseen but all-seeing gay men in the capital city of Lichtburg had been mobilized. No police force in the world could have been so efficient. There had been hustlers patrolling the red-light district; hairdressers watching the happenings of high society; truck drivers monitoring the highways that led in and out of Lichtburg. Nothing had moved without their knowledge.

Finally the terrorists had been found. Their locations had come as only a small surprise to the organizers. It was the mansion of Duke Ehrlich, an embarrassing cousin of the titular ruler of Lichtburg.

The duke had been active in church politics. He was a

rabid opponent of modernization of religious institutions; he ranted about the change in nuns' dress and raved against any alteration of the Latin mass. His fanaticism had been an annoyance, but had also marked him as a harmless crank. That obviously had been a mistake. They now knew that he was at the center of the conspiracy to hide the White Army terrorists.

Alex, Bernhardt and Jan were racing over the rooftops of Lichtburg in their dark disguises. In their hands they each carried a Karlsrupa automatic rifle. There was no time to worry about the ethics of armed conflict; not when the enemy was as serious as this one.

They stopped suddenly. Most of the houses on the block had been joined together, wall to wall. But there was a slight break in the buildings at this point. Bernhardt pointed down through the small opening to a window on the top floor of the ducal palace.

They could see four men playing cards. They were un-shaven, slovenly dressed. A bottle of cheap-looking liquor was between them. As Alex watched, one reached for the booze and drank right from the container. Good, he thought. It never hurt to have an opponent drinking and losing what-ever sharpness he might have.

This was a moment when Alex really wished that Danny was with him. Not just because he missed his partner terri-bly – he actually hurt at night when he would reach across the bed and find that the younger man wasn't there – but because of Danny's extraordinary gymnastic skills. Someone was going to have to go down through that window and sur-prise the guards.

While they'd discovered that security in the duke's man-sion was tight, Alex also knew that the people inside would be expecting any assault to come from below, through the doors and other ground-level entries to the structure. Few would ever worry about trouble coming from up above.

Jan was moving. Alex looked over as the young man jumped across the narrow space onto the mansion's roof. He had rope wound around his chest. He was quickly unraveling it now. He tied one end to a chimney and tested it. He waved to the other two to come across and join him. Before they could even get to him, Jan was rappeling down the front side of the house.

Alex knew instinctively what Jan was doing. He was stealthily maneuvering until he was parallel to the front windows. Alex prepared himself, ready to follow as soon as he heard a signal. Suddenly, there was the sound of the window breaking. There were some muttered curses, a chair turned over, a glass dropped to the floor.

Alex quickly took hold of the rope and went over the side of the building. He moved much more quickly than Jan had. Speed was more important now than anything else.

Kane flew through the open window. The four men were all standing, their hands already clasped behind their necks. They were staring down the barrel of Jan's Karlsrupa. It was something they weren't about to argue with.

Bernhardt was next. He was the least trained of the three gay avengers, but had insisted on taking his part in the risk of the attack. As soon as Jan was sure both of his comrades were in the room, he told the four captives to keep their hands where they were and to get back in their seats.

"Quickly," he said, "tie them up."

"With what?" Bernhardt asked.

"Use their belts."

As soon as Bernhardt had taken off the belt of the first one, his baggy pants fell to the floor.

In a flash the four men were secured to their chairs. Their shirts had been torn off and used as gags. "A noise from any one of you and we'll be sure we make our exit through this room," Alex warned. "You won't like being caught in that shoot out, believe me."

The three men made their way down the stairs of the opulent house. There were more guards on each floor. But, like the others, they weren't really expecting trouble and certainly not any coming from above. They were quickly taken and bound up.

"They're the worst dressed bunch of creeps I've ever seen," Bernhardt said with disgust.

"They should have listened to their mothers," Alex replied.

Finally, the trio was on the ground floor of the building. They still hadn't found the hostages and they had no indication that any of the men they had taken already were the leaders of the plot.

They were in a formal hallway that led through the center of the house. They nearly stumbled into the room where the real action was taking place. Only a quick motion from Alex stopped Bernhardt and Jan from moving too quickly.

A banquet was in progress. At the head of the table sat a man in an old-fashioned officer's uniform. He was lifting his glass of champagne to the other dozen or so who were seated along the length of the table.

"To the return of civilization!"

As soon as the toast had been given, the rest of the assembly had stood and raised their own drinks towards the man who was obviously their host, Duke Ehrlich. It hardly appeared to Alex that this was a gathering of nobility. The others in the room were in dumpy clothes that spoke of pot bellies caused by too little work and too much beer more than anything else.

But they were certainly not going to refuse to drink, that was obvious. "To the return of civilization!" they all cheered.

Alex thought about their vision of 'civilization' and grimaced. He knew enough about the White Army's dream world of old time nationalism and racism and about the duke's vision of a militant and unforgiving Roman Catholic Church to understand that Alex Kane and his kind weren't going to be welcome in anything these bozos were going to come up with.

Kane had warned the others that when they got to a part of the house where any leadership activity was going on, they were to listen and try to discover more about the activities these people might be involved in. Jan and Bernhardt had remembered their briefing and were stationed on either side of Kane, their Karlsrupas poised and ready to fire if they were discovered.

"The White Army's victory over the decadent government of Lichtburg is a sign of great things to come," the duke continued after the others had taken back their seats. "This is the first in our efforts to show the god-fearing people of the western world what can be accomplished by family-loving patriots of our great countries.

"Our next steps will be even more drastic."

What are they? Come on, asshole, tell me what you're going to do next!

"When our allies begin their move in the United States itself, it will be the most dramatic event in our joint undertakings. By attacking those elements in America that are making the most important force against communism and atheism weak, we will be doing the greatest service we can to the world.

"The American President has been kept from acting on his own instincts by the stupid restraints of 'democracy.'" The duke spoke that word as though it was the greatest obscenity of all. "We will help him act as he would want to."

"Why didn't we know about those ... people in the plane?" The voice that asked the question was almost plaintive. Alex knew just what they were talking about. As soon as the passengers had been released the media had discovered exactly what the Red River Social Club was and had played it to the hilt. The pictures of male couples grasping hold of one another in their moment of relief from the agony had made great copy and assured even more publicity for the event.

"It's unfortunate that our American colleagues hadn't been clear about that," the duke admitted regretfully. "They had used American jargon that we simply didn't understand. A great opportunity to put those people in their place was lost. But we should consider that minor compared to the victory that we've achieved. The publicity we've gathered has shown that the democracies are unable to protect god-fearing people.

"We also collected all that money! We now have five million dollars at our disposal for our next ventures. We will be better prepared and better equipped to continue our reign of revenge on the forces that are trying to weaken the west and make it so effeminate that our enemies can simply walk over us."

"We'll get those faggots out of Washington," one man sneered.

"And those women out of politics," another joined in. "And those communists out of Bosnia," said a third.

A wave of toasts went around the table as each of the men found a new object of hatred that he was anxious to see eliminated from the 'civilized' world.

Alex had heard enough. He nudged Jan and Bernhardt and gave them a silent signal. In one motion, all three men burst into the dining room with their machine-guns blazing harmless – but astonishingly loud – rounds of automatic fire into the ceiling.

The duke's ornate candelabra came crashing down in a cloud of plaster dust that made the attack seem as though it involved three battalions instead of three men. The conspirators who had been so full of brags and threats only moments ago were terrified.

Most froze, their hands going straight up over their heads. One and then another couldn't control their fright and wet their pants, long lines of urine running down their legs leaving dark stains along the trail.

A couple of men tried to race for another door, but Bernhardt blocked their way. Another pair had gotten out small handguns, but they were smart enough to realize that they were no match for the bigger Swedish-made weapons. They dropped their arms on the floor and grudgingly lifted their own hands in the air in defeat.

"Where are the hostages the Lichtburg government gave you?" Alex demanded.

"In the cellar," the duke admitted with what little dignity he had left. "They are unguarded."

"Good. Now, why don't you all line up here and spread your legs, put your hands up against the wall and don't even think about moving."

"Shall I call the police?" Bernhardt asked when all the men were in place.

"No, not yet," Alex said, "I have a better idea."

• • •

Within an hour the duke's house was surrounded by media. The lights brought by the international contingent of television cameras were so bright that it seemed to be daytime. The journalists went crazy with delight as the captured terrorists and the duke were all brought out of the building, one by one.

"Can we show that? It's disgusting," one cameraman asked a reporter. "They've all got piss stains all over their shorts. The yellow's going to show up on camera."

"We'll say it was acid rain," Rip Stallion responded. "My problem is can we show the other ones?"

The other ones were a contingent of the Gay Liberation Front of Lichtburg. Some, like Jan, were dressed in black motorcycle jackets and tight faded denim jeans. A few were dressed in student outfits like Bernhardt's, but the real problem for the journalist was those who had been chosen by the group's leaders to publicly present the captives to the chief of police. While only a couple of them were in actual drag, there was no doubt that the rest of them were quite effeminate homosexuals.

"They sure as hell don't look like freedom fighters," the journalist complained.

"Oh, thank god," the cameraman exclaimed. "There's one with clean underwear."

The duke hardly looked ducal as he was led down his stairway in his boxer shorts with two skinny queens on either side of him. He had his jaw held up high, but there was no way even he could have made this a dignified event.

"Who's going to believe that these jokers were the ones who had the whole world on edge for days?" the cameraman asked. "Airplane hijacking is sure going to get a bad name out of this one."

Alex Kane just smirked when he heard that. He would have liked to talk to Secretary Bartlett about some of the things he'd overheard in the ducal mansion. But he had a plane to catch as soon as he recovered Farmdale's five million. He had some ominous information that had come out of the operation. He needed to get back to the U.S. and get Farmdale's computers working.

And he wanted to go home to Danny.

VI

The images on the television infuriated Jack Vance. He threw his empty can of Coors beer at the offending screen. "God damn those foreigners!" Jack stood and paced up and down the room. "How could they have fucked up that way? They didn't get anything right and then they go and they get caught."

Stu Manger watched his boss getting more angry with every length of the room he walked. Stu got up and pulled another Coors for Vance from the refrigerator. "Here, Jack, have a brew and let's talk this out."

Vance took the cold can and, still frowning, took his seat. Manger had enough sense to turn off the television and remove the scenes of Duke Ehrlich from his boss's view. The room was suddenly quiet. The broadcast had drowned out the sounds of target practice that was going on outside the house. The regular explosions of the .30-.30 rounds seemed to soothe Vance a little bit and reassure him that he hadn't really lost everything.

"Jack, you tried hard. But this idea of an alliance just isn't going to work the way it was set up."

"It was Reagan's idea," Vance argued. And it had been inspired by the American President. A year or so earlier Vance and his friends had seen a ragtag collection of right-wing guerrillas brought together in Angola for consultations by an

American conservative group that hoped they'd find ways to act together against such common foes as Cuba and Tanzania, Marxist regimes that had a habit of supporting their own left-wing terrorists.

There had been some minor embarrassment in Washington when reporters did their usual snooping and discovered that most of the right-wing leaders who had gone to the Angola meeting were stooges of South Africa. Still, Jack Vance was only one of many Christian conservatives who had heard a message that they should align themselves with other countries to do the work that the wishy-washy Congress wouldn't let the government do: Wipe out communists and other undesirables and anti-American forces wherever they could.

Vance had thought that the international alliance aspect was brilliant. He'd been the one who'd gotten in touch with Duke Ehrlich and, through him, with the Bosnians. It had been Vance's use of intelligence that had picked up the particular flight that was hijacked.

"We should have gotten to the networks ourselves," Vance muttered just before he took another swig of beer. "Then they would have known that the fags were on board."

"Jack, they also would have figured out that there were some connections between us and those people over there. Look, I know I've said it before, and I don't want to say I told you so, but ... I told you so. The only way for Americans to deal with those foreigners is to lead them. We have to be stronger in what we do.

"Getting hooked up with some of those crazy sons of bitches isn't going to do us any good. We can start the whole thing our own way, real direct. Forget their national quarrels and stop dealing with chicken-shit countries like Lichtburg. Hell, I never even knew where that piece of dried turd was until this whole thing started."

"We've got to do our work though," Jack insisted.

"Of course we do. And we have to do it right. We figured out some stuff in that hijacking they did. We have the means of discovering information from the airlines now. We know more about how to get things and our people on planes. I think we also know a secret – the one thing that the right can do that won't get people so upset.

"I think we should go on with our plan, but do it ourselves here in the good old U. S. of A."

"What do you mean?" Vance hadn't always trusted Stu. He was awfully slippery sometimes, and sharp. Almost too sharp in ways. Manger was one of the few professional types that Vance had met who understood the politics of the real American people – at least, one of the few who wasn't a preacher like Jerry Falwell.

Manger had gotten into the Organization only a couple years ago. But he'd come up with great plans, lots of contributors and recruits. The gunfire on the practice range was proof of that. He also never seemed to be interested in trying to take over Vance's position – that was very important.

"Go after them, Jack. That's what I mean. The gays, the ones that no one cares for. Get them scared so they either go back to their closets or else come out fighting – and lose. Make them give up all this crap about laws and publicity. Scare the shit out of them."

Vance watched Manger as the other man's enthusiasm built. Jack had listened to guys talk about blacks and get excited, and others talk about pushy women who needed a good fuck to get them back into their place, but no one ever got as riled up about anything as Stu Manger when he got on the bandwagon about homos.

"Why do you care about them so much?" he asked Manger.

"Because they're the soft underbelly of all those creeps out there that ruin American families and make the Army soft and leave the United States vulnerable. They're the ones that we can get and use to tear apart the whole communist conspiracy to destroy American life. Dirty, filthy people like them … Everyone really knows they're after our kids. Everyone knows what they do with them." Manger actually shuddered when he made that last statement.

Something really got to this man, Vance thought. But he wasn't about to play shrink to a guy who was as hot on the trail of the Organization's plans as Manger was. From the day Vance had begun to think about the Organization, he knew that there would have to be thinkers near the top. He, himself, had watched dozens of decent groups fall apart because they didn't have smart people to help them do their planning. The Klan was splintering into so many factions that Vance couldn't keep track of them. The Order in the Northwest must have had infiltrators to have let themselves be busted the way they were by the FBI.

Vance had been sitting here in Pennsylvania and he had watched it all. His own commitment to the right cause came when he watched his home torn apart by the stupid things those bra-burning lesbians who called themselves feminists taught his wife. She walked out after a little fight and got custody of the kids too – just because of a couple times he happened to have slapped her around when she had gotten uppity. Hell, a real man always did that to his woman when she needed it. Jack was still nursing a grudge against the black-commie magistrate who'd called him an animal just on his wife's say-so about their spats. He never understood how a man like Reagan could let a good American like Vance be judged by a jigaboo.

'Battered Woman!' Hell, the bitch had worn the label like it was a rosary or something. Manger had to have something like that in his own past. But he didn't talk about those things much. He just listened to Vance and the rest of the guys in the Organization as they told their stories and he got excited. He explained over and over again how it was faggots' fault that it was all happening.

"So what do you think we should do next? I got two dozen men signed up here full-time and another one hundred trained and in reserve, just waiting for the telephone call to come to arms. The Organization has been in place for months. Everyone's getting awfully antsy about it, just sitting around.

I thought this foreign thing would help us out, you know, give us some action.

"These guys want to fight. You don't always seem to understand that. They want to get into it. They don't want any more indoctrination speeches. They don't want to rob banks and pull the shit that The Order did out west."

"Then we'll give it to them," Manger's eyes went glassy as he thought. "We'll give them some of the biggest stuff they ever dreamt of. No, no more alliances. Instead we're going to have to lead the way for the whole world. We're going to start soon, Jack, really soon."

"Where?! Damn it, where?" Jack was done with this Coors as well. He went to the refrigerator himself while he waited for Manger's answer.

"We've got the key. I've thought it through. That little tour group in Lichtburg wasn't a bad idea. But it wasn't big enough. We have to make it very, very dangerous for homos to travel in the United States. And we have to make sure that it's no little accident that the planes they fly are the ones that have ... problems. But that's just the beginning. We're on to the real thing that can force this country back into a posture of strength and manhood."

"I'm listening." Vance had to. His speech about the men becoming restless was true. They were. There was nothing worse than putting together a group of guys and telling them they were going to get something and then not coming through. It might be great to be a part of the team. And it might seem entertaining to be able to shoot off endless rounds of ammunition in the Organization's camp. But there had to be something more if he was going to keep them in line for any considerable length of time.

There were really only two things that the men that Vance had recruited wanted: Money and action. The money from Lichtburg was supposed to help keep them going. Manger might have done wonders with fundraising, but not enough to feed the hungry treasury that was keeping the men's pockets full. The big bucks were pulling out.

Their backers wanted the same thing the men did: Action. They had been just as anxious as Vance had been in the beginning about making sure that this was truly a working force and not just a bunch of idiots with rifles in their hands. But the word had come down: Do more. And do it now.

If Vance couldn't show some real results soon, the whole thing might go down the drain. He couldn't let that happen. He wasn't going to lead just another right-wing group into oblivion the way so many others had. There were people out there who understood where the country should be going, but they didn't have the guts to take it there.

Ever since he had been a sergeant in the Army, Jack had wanted to be more. He still believed all his promotions had been blocked by the brass's insistence on letting blacks get preferential treatment when the list came around with news of who had gotten new stripes. The reasons they gave when Jack had complained were just excuses.

After all, Jack Vance had been the martial arts champion of the entire service. He'd won all the belts and all the medals that there were. There wasn't a man he couldn't take, even many years and many cases of Coors later. That was a disappointment, too. That there weren't worthy opponents. He was tired of taking on and humiliating the recruits. Even the ones who thought that they were such hot shit never really got his blood flowing.

"We still have our contact with the tour operation, Vance. The guy over in Reading can tell us where the fag groups are going. We're going to give him a call, Jack. We're going to start a new operation – one even bigger than the Lichtburg thing."

"Yeah," Vance said idly. *Maybe I can get a decent fight out of this one.*

VII

The Spartans was one of the few gay groups that Charlie was ever able to get Tom to take part in. For one thing, it wasn't public at all. The organization of gay athletes had insisted on privacy from the very beginning. For another, these were men who didn't threaten Tom too much. He wasn't as comfortable around the less masculine men at the opera and he certainly had never felt too good about the political types who were always lecturing them on why they should be willing to go to public demonstrations.

Those people never seemed to understand the dilemma that the teachers were in. It took an awful lot of self-esteem to believe that gay was so good that you could stand in front of your students and understand that you were presenting them with a role model that you honestly believed was a good thing for them. It had even taken Charlie a long time before he believed that was something he could feel good about doing.

But even more, there was the problem about jobs. There were hardly any public school systems in the country that would let gay guys in the classroom, and not many more private ones. Tom was right about the dangers involved in coming out. Charlie couldn't deny them. It was just that he was equally worried about the dangers of not doing it.

Once he understood that his original reluctance to stand

in front of a class of students and let them know about his own sexuality really displayed his own ambivalent feelings about himself, then he began to question everything else around him. If this part of himself that led him to love Tom was so wonderful – and the fact of their love for one another was certainly proof of that – then how could it stand to be hidden away?

Well, the Spartans let him avoid some of those questions for a while at least. The group met in a private gymnasium in Center City Philadelphia every week. The two teachers didn't make every meeting, but they went to as many as they could.

They would have enjoyed a gay weightlifting group if one could have been formed as a part of the Spartans, but they so far outclassed the others that they knew they couldn't find any real competition here. Instead they took the role of teachers and coaches. They left their own heavy workouts for their own gym hours. Charlie had offered to help set up a small-scale football team for the Spartans, but so far not enough of the men involved had expressed interest.

Still, the two of them enjoyed the group a great deal. This physical world of males involved in sports was their milieu, after all. This is where they felt comfortable and where they fit in the best.

There were numerous activities on any night. A volley-ball game was going on in one section of the gym; a basket-ball game was happening in another. Right now, Charlie was explaining the art of free weights to a young acned teenager who seemed incapable of paying attention. He was staring so intently at Charlie's enormous pectorals that he didn't seem to be able to concentrate at all.

"Can I have those if I do this?" the young man asked.

"Well, sure. You can develop pectorals in many ways. Perhaps you should consider going to a gym with Universal equipment."

"How long did they take?" His eyes were moving back and forth between the points where Charlie's nipples were pressing against his t-shirt.

"Well, I've been working out since I was in junior high school."

The young man sighed, "I should have known. Years. Just years to get tits." Suddenly he looked up into Charlie's eyes. "Hey, do you know any guys who've gone to a plastic surgeon to get them? Girls do that. You know that song in *Chorus Line?*"

"I'm afraid it's not quite the same."

"I should have figured that." The teenager reluctantly went back to the free weights.

Charlie watched his form for a short while and then left him to struggle alone. He went over to where Tom was working with a more advanced student. Rusty was twenty and had been going at it long enough that he was really able to do an impressive routine with the weights. He wasn't even as interested in coaching nowadays as he was in getting advice from Tom about the possibilities of entering into bodybuilding seriously enough to enter competitions. He was always after advice – and a chance to be alone with the black behemoth with whom he was obviously infatuated.

Charlie stood by while Tom carefully went over the size and shape of some of Rusty's muscles. The redheaded man was hypnotized by the sight and feel of Tom's hands as they made their clinical exploration of his own pale body. Well, Charlie thought, I'm certainly not going to worry about this. After all, if I can't trust Tom after all these years, there's no hope left.

And Charlie certainly did trust Tom. "Well, Mr. Thomas Bolan, it looks as though your latest flame hasn't lost any of his interest in you." Charlie used Tom's last name and a formal tone of voice to communicate the humor in the situation and – he hoped – his lack of concern in it.

"Oh, he's a good guy." They watched as the redhead walked away from them over to the volleyball game. "More than I can say for some people." Tom's expression clouded over as he watched a new couple walk out of the dressing room and onto the gymnasium floor.

Charlie stiffened, not because he was as offended as Tom,

but because he knew that the presence of Terry Draper and his young lover, Andrew, infuriated Tom. They represented everything that was bad about homosexuals to Tom. It wasn't just a question of discomfort the way it was with effeminate men either. This was something much more profound.

The whole group knew the story about Terry and Andrew. Tom wouldn't ever even discuss the situation with anyone. It was a simple and obvious breach of the most basic and most important elements of the teacher/student relationship.

Terry had been Andrew's English teacher in high school. They had started their affair when the younger one was only fourteen and had continued it behind everyone's back. Terry was at least forty – at least. Andrew couldn't be more than sixteen.

The couple wasn't well liked by many others, either. But no one felt like saying much. The politically active members of the group insisted that the love between a man and a boy had to be recognized as legitimate. Maybe. Charlie could see other sides of the issue. He only wished that Andrew looked ... happier. The kid always seemed to be in a dark mood.

But it wasn't just the age difference that got to Tom. It was the fact that Terry had been in a position of trust and power and had still gone to bed with the teenage boy. It was inexcusable to Tom; there could be no justification.

Charlie had made the mistake once of trying to find a rationalization for the way things had happened. Both of them knew perfectly well that teenage boys can come on to their teachers; it had happened to Charlie and to Tom. They also knew that the rate of maturation differed tremendously between individual kids. There were some twelve-year-olds who were obviously adult; and there were some eighteen-year-olds who were clearly barely into adolescence.

Those arguments never went anywhere with Tom. Andrew was a student in a high school and Terry was a teacher in the same school. There couldn't be any excuse for their having a sexual relationship.

"They shouldn't be here. We're leaving." Tom turned

and walked away from Charlie. He was careful to avoid even coming close to the other couple. Charlie wasn't going to go through this argument again. This was one fight that wasn't worthwhile. Besides, the club night was nearly over. Terry and Andrew could only be here to meet someone. It was far too late to really get into any of the activities.

Charlie went to his locker and stripped off his gym wear and his jock. He grabbed a towel and went into the shower room. The water was cascading down Tom's wonderful body when Charlie walked in. It looked like a perfect piece of sculpture, a kind of classical nude placed in a fountain.

There were rivers of the shower water that flowed down between the huge muscles of Tom's back and then seemed to fall off his large, firm ass. Charlie walked up behind his lover. He had a bar of soap in his hands. He calmly began to lather up Tom's back. The simple touch of his hands seemed to relax Tom. He sighed and let the sudsy palms move over his torso.

Then, Tom turned around. He was smiling now. He took the soap out of Charlie's hands and began to reciprocate. He lingered when he came to his lover's prominent chest. "Some kid wanted to know if a plastic surgeon could give him pecs like mine," Charlie laughed.

"God, gay life would never be the same if it was that easy!" Tom joked back.

Charlie took the humor as a good sign. He decided to take advantage of the opening. "Marco called before we came here tonight. He wondered if we'd go out for a drink with him when we were finished. Can we?"

Tom frowned a little bit, but the evidence of the electricity between the two lovers was all too apparent in the arcing cocks that were both rising as though they wanted to meet one another in the space between their bellies.

"Well, since we can't take care of the obvious for a while anyhow, I suppose we can go and see Marco. He's an okay guy. So long as it's not a gay bar."

"Promise," Charlie said. He leaned over and kissed his lover on the lips, something Tom only allowed him to do in private. "But I think we better rinse off with some cold water soon, before anyone comes in here and finds us defying the laws of nature and the rules of the establishment at the same time. And we better make that very cold water."

• • •

They met Marco in the bar at the Garden Restaurant on Spruce Street. "Well, even this place can't charge that much for a Perrier," Tom grumbled. Charlie just smiled. There hadn't been any complaints about the bill for the extravagant anniversary dinner they'd had here earlier in the year.

Marco was used to Tom and didn't pay attention to his comment. "It always makes me feel good when I know I've rescued you two from the clutches of suburbia. I have nightmares about your eating in Ponderosa Steak Houses and going to movies at the mall."

He waved over the bartender and ordered himself a gin and tonic while the two weightlifters kept to their regime and only asked for mineral water.

"This is an event," Marco said when they were alone again. "I have an announcement to make."

"What?" Even Tom picked up on Marco's obvious excitement.

"I am the new conductor of the Philadelphia Choral Society."

"The what?" Charlie hadn't even heard of such an organization and thought he would have.

"It's been in the works for a long time. I hadn't mentioned it because I was afraid it would either not happen, or else be so wretched that I wouldn't want to admit I was involved. But neither is the case. It's actually pretty good. And I'm proud of it."

The drinks arrived. Charlie waited anxiously for the bartender to leave so he could find out more about the new group. "When did it start? How did you get involved? When are you going to perform?"

Marco held up a hand to stop the flood of questions. "It's actually been ongoing since Christmas. I told you that a few of us did a quick and easy *Messiah*. Well, it was only the beginning of something much bigger than that, it turns out. We had so much fun that we kept on practicing. The others found out I was involved with the opera, so they asked me to take more and more responsibility for the program and administration.

"It's so big, in fact, that I'm going to start drawing a salary soon. We've gotten some pretty big backers and the whole thing is growing so large they're going to need full-time staff."

"That's wonderful, Marco!" Tom said, and he meant it. Marco had been struggling to find employment in the music world since they'd first met him. He'd been willing to take on any task that had anything to do with his artistic interests. Both Tom and Charlie liked the Italian man quite a bit. He wasn't as butch as Tom might want him to be; maybe it was the fact Marco was so very good at his music that allowed Tom to overlook his effeminate characteristics. In any case, the congratulations were heartfelt.

"As to when we start – we actually have already. We've been performing at a number of gay clubs as fundraisers and we had a couple performances ..."

"Why didn't you tell us?" Charlie was astonished that he hadn't known.

Marco only looked at Tom and shrugged. The message was received: The performances must have been in obviously gay contexts where he knew Tom would have been uncomfortable.

"In any event, all that is over. We have a chance to sing in a group concert in Chicago. It's our real debut. We've raised the money to charter a flight and everything. It's all set. And when we come back I'm going to make you come to one of our concerts – gay or not, closeted or not."

Tom looked away from the other two. Charlie ignored his lover's discomfort. "When do you leave for Chicago?" Marco gave the date of the flight and the rest of the information. "We'll take you to the airport – won't we, Tom?"

To Charlie's surprise, Tom reacted quickly, "Of course we will. We'll send you off with flowers and champagne."

●　　●　　●

Tom seemed to brood while they drove back to the suburbs later that night. Charlie knew that this kind of silence was dangerous if it was allowed to go on too long. He took a chance and asked Tom just what was wrong.

After a moment's thought, Tom answered: "It's all the stuff that you always talk about. Marco's the one gay guy I like the best of all the ones we've met. Something this important has happened to him after all the time he's tried to get his music act together. But he didn't even think we'd care."

"Of course he knew we'd care."

"Well, he didn't think we'd care enough to take part in it. It's what you feel about me sometimes, too, isn't it? That I'm so closeted that some very important things can't be shared between us? The way that Marco just assumed that I wouldn't share his success."

"Would you have?"

"I don't know. I'm just feeling blue that I've made such a mess of things that he didn't even think he could ask me if I wanted to go hear his group play in a gay bar because I'm such an asshole about not going into those places. Something's fucked up about it all."

Charlie didn't say another word. He only hoped that this was the beginning of something that would change their lives – finally.

VIII

Alex and Danny sat with Joseph Farmdale in the dining room of the Ritz hotel in Boston. The report that Alex had just given obviously disturbed the old man. He was sipping his cognac and clearly thinking hard about the information.

"So far," he observed, "terrorists have mainly been out after money and attention. They've played the mass media that the electronics age has given us as though it were a fine violin. One of the grave concerns of governments around the world has been that these people might actually undertake a sustained and coordinated drive which utilized their joint strengths. If they were to take their abilities and apply them to a campaign directed at the civilian population ..."

"But they have," Danny said. "Look at what the IRA did with the bombings in London, they killed all those shoppers at Christmas time a while back."

"Yes, but even they backed off when faced with the public outcry that followed," Farmdale replied. "The actual vulnerability of our cities and our economies has not yet been the target of any of the terrorists. They either haven't recognized that vincibility, or else they understand that governments would have to act with extraordinary methods if they thought their very foundations were being assaulted."

"Well, they are," Alex fumed. "When they go after aircraft

with tourists on them ..."

"Then they are approaching those limits that no state can tolerate. The first rash of air piracy is a perfect example of what I mean by the states being willing to undertake extraordinary methods. They began with all the hijackings of American domestic flights to Havana. Certainly you remember that. In order to stop them, the United States and Castro were actually willing to join together and the Cubans even announced that no skyjacker would ever receive asylum in their country.

"That certainly must qualify as an extraordinary event, especially since the two countries had no diplomatic relations with one another at all. But, to protect the trade routes of the world, even a communist fanatic like Castro and a conservative Republican like Nixon were willing to work together."

"It's that important?" Danny asked. "I mean, it's that important to me – I care about the people on those planes and the danger they're in. But what motivates the governments so much that they'd put aside their battles to stop it?"

Farmdale nodded to indicate that he understood the question. It was a good one. "The governments of the world were established to protect commerce, Danny. That is their reason for being. They were able to organize and collect taxes only because they could promise to make trade routes secure. If they failed, they collapsed. It is a simplistic answer in some ways, but surprisingly accurate in others."

"And if those same governments can't protect today's trade routes in the sky ..." Danny said.

"Then those governments will fall. Perhaps not the way the ancient regimes fell, but they will be intolerably weakened. What would happen if we lived in a world where our most important forms of travel were ruled by anarchistic elements? It can't be allowed to happen."

"That's not what it's really about," Alex said. He was clearly angry over this conversation about trade and early governments. "The reason we have a society is to protect human life."

Farmdale didn't argue. "Your position is an even more fundamental one, Alex. The original coming together in tribes was to do just that. The creation of governments came about when those tribes wanted to trade with one another. The point only emphasizes the importance of free and safe passage for innocent people in every day and age. In this century, that means air travel.

"If someone were foolish enough – insane enough – to want to really disrupt the world, then that person only had to go after that one link in global communications. The birth of air transport not only created a new form of trade carrier to be protected, it multiplied the number of people who were exposed to its disruption. Millions of people around the world get on airplanes these days. If they are systematically attacked in their unarmed flight, then there will be mass panic and god knows what the consequences will be."

"So that's why Alex's report is so horrible," Danny said. "The right-wing idiots are talking about doing just what you said. But he got those people – or the Lichtburg Gay Liberation Front did."

"Can you imagine what those yo-yos in Washington must have been thinking when they watched that on television?" Alex asked. His smile was dancing over his face while he contemplated the idea.

"I doubt that my ... colleagues in the District of Columbia were especially pleased to have seen that image." Farmdale said. He had to work to suppress his laughter. Alex Kane had a concept of what the powermongers of federal government were like under the current administration. Joseph Farmdale had actually gone to prep school and Harvard with many of them and he knew first hand how embarrassed and upset they would have been when they had to acknowledge that a gay guerrilla organization, and not some NATO military force, had bested the White Army.

"In any event," Farmdale drew himself together, "what we know now is that the right-wing terrorists have gathered themselves into a network. They're sharing information and they're sharing resources. This government of ours can only understand terrorism as something that comes from the left. We know that this terrorism comes from the right. You two, in particular, know that all too well. If right-wing groups are getting together on an international scale –"

"Then we're all in big trouble," Alex finished the sentence for him.

"Precisely. I'm going to get to my computers and I'm going to start tracing the money transactions of some of the more unreasonable conservative philanthropists in the country. I might be able to discover something that way. If I can, I'll contact you immediately."

"I hope you can come up with something and that the something is right," Alex said. "What if the targets are more diverse than just airplanes?"

"I can only work on this one assumption at the moment," Farmdale said. "If they alter their strategy in any way that we can see, I only hope we understand it quickly enough."

•   •   •

Alex Kane woke up in his own bed the next morning. He stretched, wanting as much of his body as possible to touch the welcome feel of the familiar sheets. When he'd collapsed back onto the mattress, his first thought was to realize that Danny wasn't with him.

He sat up quickly, then forced himself to relax. As soon as he did, he could hear his lover moving around in the kitchen. There had been so many nights in Europe without Danny that Alex had for one moment thought that perhaps he had only been dreaming that he was back in New Hampshire.

He didn't think he could have taken the sorrow if that had been true. The weight of being alone so far away had been more onerous than he would have thought possible. For the past couple of years the two of them were hardly ever separated. Just how important that had been was more than passingly clear to Kane now.

He wanted to get up out of bed and run downstairs to grab hold of his lover and hug him tightly. But he knew what Danny was up to at the moment. Danny loved the small rituals of life together, the little gifts that housemates in love with one another can give. The subtle smell of bacon frying and coffee brewing made their way up the stairs and Kane knew that he was about to be feted with his breakfast in bed.

He rolled over onto his side and smiled to himself. This was the stuff that made life worth living. This and the yearning erection that was rubbing against the sheets where Danny had slept last night. He put his head into Danny's pillow and smelt the odors that had been left there. They were so uniquely Danny's. They were the best perfume that Kane had ever known.

Every ounce of himself wanted to just leave his face buried in the down and take his hard cock in his hand and masturbate to the image of Danny. But he fought off the urge. Why do that when the real thing was right downstairs?

Danny brought up the tray a few minutes later. It was loaded with eggs, meat, breads and orange juice as well as a pot of coffee. Hardly the best training breakfast, but this was a celebration and Alex wasn't going to insist on anything that would interfere with it.

But there were some things that would have interfered with any meal. Alex's cock hadn't softened in the least. When Danny put down his tray and stepped back, his whole nude body was standing there for Alex's inspection. There was the fine coating of dark hair over the tight chest and the ropy, muscled thighs that Alex had dreamed about so often. And, of course, there was Danny's own cock nestled above his fur-coated balls.

"How about an appetizer?" Alex asked playfully.

"What, and let everything get cold?" Danny answered with just as much fun.

"Trust me, there's not much around here that has a chance of getting cold, not the way I feel."

"Good. Then we can pay attention to the food first," Danny answered. He took a piece of toast and jokingly shoved it into Alex's mouth.

"Since when are you into S&M?" Alex mumbled as he sat up and yielded to the obvious insistence that they eat first.

"I'm not," Danny answered. "I'm just concerned for your health. I don't trust you to eat enough when you're away from home."

"Great, just what I need, a dietician." Alex may have appeared to be angry but, ignoring the bulge under his sheet, he was digging into the eggs and bacon on his plate with gusto.

Danny reached over and patted the hard mound of flesh that was pressing against the percale. "Don't worry, you don't have just a dietician. I'm a renaissance man of many talents. I'll prove it as soon as you finish your meal."

Alex acted as though he were hurrying even faster to polish off the breakfast.

But Danny was finished with the jovial mood. There was something on his mind that he wanted to talk about. "Alex, what do you think about all this stuff? The hijackers and all?"

Kane slowed down. He looked over at Danny with a serious air about him now. "It's as bad as the worst we've seen. What Farmdale said is true. But there's something else in what those guys in Lichtburg were saying. They're after that vulnerable part of society all right. But the thing is, they're using us – gay guys – to get at it. I don't think Farmdale understands that yet.

"You know the way that everyone's so crazy about AIDS? One of the things that they do is say that gay men caused it. Instead of understanding that we're the victims – the ones who were so deadly unlucky that the virus got to us first – they think we produced it. It fit all their foolishness about the evils of sex and the fear that certain kinds of sex can actually manufacture disease.

"Well, what if these right-wing assholes can convince people that gay guys are making it unsafe to travel? What if its our fault that there are so many hijacked planes? When people get scared they start to think in ridiculous ways. The impulse to survive is more important than anything else they can feel.

"Just the way that people ignore all the medical authorities and start to want to have gay waiters fired and then they won't go to stores where gay men are clerks – all because they think they'll get AIDS if they even stand near one of us – if they start putting danger in travel together with gay men ..."

And if Farmdale's theories about the importance of commerce are true ..." Danny continued.

"Then what if they won't fly on a plane with one of us? What if they won't get on a plane unless they know that the pilot and the stewards and all the rest are certifiably straight?"

Danny put aside his plate. He was finished eating. He took Alex's as well and then placed them both on the table beside their bed along with the tray and the rest of the food and condiments. Then he put his head down on Alex's chest. A hand trailed down over Alex's hairless stomach. It didn't stop at the sheet, but went underneath it. Danny's fingers traced the hard and firm muscles of his lover's belly until he came to the thick and sudden bush of pubic hair.

Their conversation had been the one thing that was finally able to scare away Alex's erection. But as soon as Danny's hand went around the familiar flesh, it began to fill up again.

It always amused Danny that so many people thought that Alex was such a frightening forceful man. Here, in their bed, he was a warm and thoughtful lover. What was it that their friends in Texas had called him? Vanilla. At first Danny had thought they were just talking about the easy way that Alex Kane and Danny Fortelli made love with one another.

Vanilla. It made Danny think about ice cream and milkshakes. With a smile on his face, he decided he shouldn't just dream about those things. He should go about making his own.

Slowly and erotically, Danny let his head make the trip

down over his lover's wonderful chest and belly until his lips touched the once again hard cock of Alex Kane.

IX

"Marco, Chicago's only a few hundred miles away and you're only going for a weekend. How could you possibly need all this crap?"

The weight of the two suitcases that Charlie was carrying seemed enough to qualify this trip to Philadelphia International Airport as a workout session. They made their way into the terminal while Marco shot back his answer: "I have to have formal wear for the banquet, tails for the first concert, cowboy outfit for the second – it's a western theme. Then, there's leather for the bars, casual wear for the hotel, a suit for the dining room ..."

"Don't you dare say anything about stereotypical faggots," Charlie snarled to Tom as he dropped the bags in front of the ticket counter.

His lover stared back at him blankly. He didn't have a clue what Charlie was talking about. He was standing here just where he'd been told to meet the other two. A late conference at the school had kept him from doing the whole trip into the city to pick up Marco and then bring him out here.

Then Tom realized what must have gone on. Charlie was rubbing his own biceps to get the circulation going in them. "We had to park miles away and I had to lug all of this stuff here."

"That's not fair," Marco protested. "I told you I would have paid for a red cap."

"It seemed pretty stupid to do that when I'm supposed to be such a jock that I can ..."

"Hey, hey," Tom said to calm Charlie down. "It's not like you to get yourself so worked up. It's cool. There's no problem."

There really wasn't. Charlie had put so much into this simple act of taking their friend to the airport that he was just too nervous about it. Tom studied the other big bodybuilder who was now standing in front of him as anxious as some teenager on a first date and once again he had to realize just how much his own fears had poisoned things between them.

Those fears were real – especially for a black teacher like Tom who had to begin the whole profession with a lot of strikes against him. But their cost had become real as well. Charlie was one of the most easy-going men Tom had ever met. That had been one of the attractions he'd felt when the two of them had first met. Unlike most of the others on the bodybuilding circuit, Charlie wasn't terribly competitive. He had actually started the whole thing only as a weightlifter.

That had begun because of his football career at Temple. Charlie had been a good back, but had started out too small for the big-time football circuit. He'd started in with weights to add to his bulk. The fact that he was sculpting a fabulous body hadn't really occurred to him. It was simply something he enjoyed. He'd started going to the physique competitions just as a lark.

He enjoyed the football field much more. Nothing gave him as much pleasure as the game. It had been such a safe thing for Tom to go and watch his new friend play during college. After all, who was going to say that anyone who was a starter for the collegiate gridiron team was a fag and who was going to question the fact that his workout partner went to watch him play?

When Tom had realized that Charlie also enjoyed the idea of teaching children as much as he did, then he realized that he was someone he could spend his life with in a relationship that was built on a lot more than sex.

But the past few years had begun to tell on Charlie. Tom could look back and see the signs now, even if he hadn't been able to understand them at the time. There was the way that the guy ate up every piece of literature on being gay and gay politics there was. There was the frantic manner with which he responded to every gay-themed movie on television. Charlie was like a deprived child, looking on at people who had all the things that didn't exist in his own world and having to get them second-hand because he couldn't have them to live himself.

It wasn't the same thing as his disappointment over never having gone into professional football. That world was too heavy for Charlie and they had both known it. He really wanted to teach when he graduated and was realistic enough to realize that his chances of getting into pro ball were slim. Charlie handled that easily, without any emotional scene. Possibly the only other thing Charlie really had wanted out of life that he hadn't gotten was a victory over Penn State. He'd come close once; Tom remembered the game well. But he hadn't won. Tom couldn't help that chapter in his lover's life. But, he wondered, did he really want to be the cause for that kind of frustration in an even more important episode?

They got Marco checked in and Tom thought more about the strange situation they'd gotten themselves into. He wished he had other teachers to talk to – especially black ones. Maybe they'd be able to share some of the experiences they'd each had and talk out some options. That was one of the big problems for Tom: He didn't know what his options were. He didn't know at all what might happen if he took this risk or that one. He had no role model ... Tom stopped short on the walkway that led to Marco's gate.

"Is something wrong?" Charlie had come back to where Tom stood and looked worriedly at his lover.

"Yeah, yeah," Tom waved away Charlie's concern. "Just a little heartburn." Then the three of them continued on. *It was just a little heartburn.* Tom realized he hadn't lied. It was a burn that flared up when he recognized that he held himself up to such high moral standards about so many issues precisely because he was a role model for his kids. Except for this one very particular example. Whenever he thought about letting down on his training, or sloughing off on his preparations for class, he would discipline himself by remembering how important it was for all those kids to see a black athlete and teacher who wasn't a fuck-off.

It had suddenly sunk into his skull that it might make a difference if they also saw that there was a gay teacher who was still a moral, physical person as well. If he didn't take the role, then it was his own fault if the media kept on focusing on those other types that always got the attention.

Tom was thinking it all through as they approached the gate. Then he realized that Charlie was the one who was standing stock still all of a sudden. He followed his lover's expression and he immediately understood why.

There, just handing in his ticket to the agent to get a seat assignment and a boarding pass, was Terry Draper. Off to the side was his "lover," Andrew. All of Tom's new thoughts were erased as soon as he saw the two of them. This was definitely something that was never going to make it into his classroom. Never!

Tom nudged Charlie to move on – and also to let him know that he wasn't going to make a scene. He never had and it wasn't his style, certainly not in a public place like an airport.

Tom and Charlie focused all their attention on Marco. Terry and Andrew were over on the other side of the waiting area and there was no need for the couples to cross paths. Finally the charter flight to Chicago was called for boarding.

When Marco was safely on board and the area was almost cleared, Tom realized that Andrew was still there. He had assumed that the kid was going on the trip with the others. That obviously wasn't the case. He wondered about it, but wasn't about to investigate.

Charlie had insisted on watching the plane take off. He

was like a kid, himself. They stood by the floor-to-ceiling window as the plane taxied away from the terminal and went down to the end of the airstrip in a line of others. Charlie had always loved planes and loved any trip to the airport that gave him an excuse to watch them, a sight he always insisted was one of the beauties of the modern age. Tom wasn't going to deny him such a simple pleasure.

When the gay chorus flight was poised for take off, Tom realized that Andrew had moved over near them. Theirs was the one vantage point where you could best see the craft. It began to move up the runway, picking up more and more speed. Then Tom heard Andrew talk. He wasn't really speaking to anyone, he was making a passionate statement so honest and intense that he probably wasn't even aware that anyone could hear him.

"Thank god he's gone."

Tom didn't have time to figure out what that really meant. The plane was hurtling forward now and had begun to lift off the ground. Its wheels were being pulled up into the fuselage and ...

When they were finally able to talk about it they would comment that the strangest thing was there hadn't been any noise. The distance and the thick glass of the airport terminal building had muffled it and all they were aware of was the sudden bright light. It was nearly blinding. After a single second – probably not even that long – there was a huge, billowing cloud of smoke where the flare had been. Then there were only tiny pieces of debris falling with obscene lethargy to the ground, the only evidence that Flight 551 to O'Hare had ever existed.

"I did it." Andrew moved back away from the window as soon as his mind had been able to comprehend the tragedy that he'd just witnessed. "It must be my fault."

Tom stared at the teenage boy. He was obviously in a state of shock. It was something Tom understood all too well. He'd like to retreat into it himself right about now.

"Shut up, Andrew," he said. He moved to the adolescent.

His own mind was reeling from the awesome sight of destruction he'd just seen. The people on the plane – what had they felt, thought? Nothing, he realized. They hadn't had a chance to even know what was going on. Tom put an arm around Andrew's shoulder, glad to have this immediate problem to deal with and to grasp the escape it gave him.

"Andrew, you didn't do anything. Stop talking. Someone might overhear you and misunderstand. It had to have been an accident. How could you have done it?"

"I wanted him to die." The boy spoke with conviction. "I wanted him to die and now he has. Oh, god, I killed him and all the rest."

Tom tried to get his thoughts under control. There was a voice coming over the loudspeakers and talking in code. The calm female tones were obvious signals for the airport employees to go to emergency stations. There were people running madly up and down the corridors of the building. There were screaming and crying people standing around the gate – the rest of the people who'd stayed behind to watch friends and relatives board the Chicago flight.

Charlie was just standing there, frozen as he watched the scene on the tarmac. There were fire engines speeding out towards the wreck. Tom could feel himself losing what control he had. They had to get out of there. Watching the useless attempts to rescue the obviously doomed passengers was a waste of time.

"Marco ..." Charlie whispered. "How could that have happened to someone like Marco."

"Please, Charlie, keep cool. Try, baby, just try. Let's go." He took Charlie and Andrew by the arm with his hands and started to guide them down the long hallways of the airport. "Let's get home. Let's calm down a little bit and we can talk it out. Don't either of you try to say anything right now.

"We have a lot of work to do and we have to keep our heads about us."

X

Danny had started packing for both of them even before the phone call had ended. There had been no doubt in his mind what the message was. The way that Alex's posture had stiffened while he talked to Farmdale told him all that he needed to know. Alex understood what was going on when he came into the room. He simply began to help Danny with the task.

"They got a plane in Philadelphia," he said. "There was a gay group on board. They're all dead. They used enough explosives to have done in an aircraft carrier. There are hardly any pieces of the passengers left big enough to use for identification purposes. The authorities are saying it was an accident. They're scared. They should be."

Danny was closing one of the suitcases. "What leads?"

"None. Not a goddamn one. There may not be anything in Pennsylvania either. It might just be a wild goose chase. But it's all we have right now. I can't sit up here in the mountains and wait. I want to be there."

"Of course."

•   •   •

The last suitcase was closed and they carried them downstairs and out to their car. They only had to drive a few miles to get to the private airport. Passing tourists assumed it

81

was just another small landing strip for sightseeing planes. The locals knew better. The manager let a very few people – almost all of them year-round residents of the town – use the all-weather facility. It was good cover for there to be some regular planes on view for passersby who seldom noticed how very long the runway was.

But what looked like a rural airport – one of dozens in the country where little Cessnas and Beechcraft could land and take off – was capable of handling a lot more than that. Alex looked at his watch after they'd been waiting a short while. He obviously trusted the pilot to be on time. In a few seconds they could hear the sound of jet engines above the clouds. Then the DC-9 broke through as it made its approach to the field.

The jetliner landed as smoothly as always. Its engines braked and, when the craft had slowed enough, the plane made its way towards the hanger. As soon as the DC-9 was stationary and its stairway had been lowered, Alex and Danny took their bags and went up into its body.

Their old friends Mike Anderson and Tim Ranson were waiting for them. The two Minneapolis-based pilots shook hands with the others and saw them to their seats. The men knew that this wasn't the time for a chat. Whenever the red alert call came to tell them that they should make one of their emergency flights to New Hampshire, small talk was ruled out. They'd have to wait for another trip to sit down to dinner and memories with Alex and Danny.

"Philadelphia International's about an hour and a half away. No turbulence, no hassle. Last we checked, there was no hold-up for landing either. You'll be in Center City by dinner time."

"Thanks," Danny said to Tim.

Alex wasn't talking. He was already leafing through the red leather-bound book that had been waiting for them on the plane. It was much thinner than usual; Farmdale's research department hadn't been as lucky as it sometimes could be. After a quick scan, Alex realized that there simply wasn't much to go on.

They made the flight in silence. Access to a private jet was only one of the many advantages available to Alex and Danny. But this was one time when all the high tech aids they could buy wouldn't do them any good.

They said a fast farewell to the pilots after they landed in Philadelphia and gathered up their suitcases. A car was waiting for them on the tarmac outside the Butler Aviation terminal. One more useless symbol of their wealth. Alex and Danny climbed into the Mercedes coupe and followed the directions they'd been given to Center City Philadelphia.

They were staying at the Four Seasons. "This is starting to get to me," Alex complained as they walked into the luxury hotel.

Danny tried to calm him down. "You know it's going to happen whenever you let him make our reservations for us." The Four Seasons was the most ostentatiously luxurious hotel in the city. It was new, though not as splashy as some places could be. It was typical of what Farmdale thought was a decent place for the duo to lay their heads at night.

They checked in and went to their room. The call and the travel had interrupted their daily routine. They hadn't done their usual work-out. Farmdale had even anticipated that. There was a message waiting for them that they had visitors' privileges at the Delaware Club.

They'd already parked the car. Instead of retrieving it and trying to manuever the unfamiliar streets of Philadelphia they hailed a cab and went to the Society Hill address they'd been given.

The Delaware Club was one of those private men's fraternities that had been established in the last century as a symbol of its members' ascendance over the rest of the society. In more recent years it had become a sanctuary where the now fragile and anachronistic "status" of its fellows was something that they could affirm at least to one another.

The Club had begun as an athletic organization. In order to keep up that pretense, it maintained a wonderful gymnasium. But that was hardly ever used by the regulars, most of whom were well into their fifties by the time they joined or else were sons of members, a group of heirs for whom cocaine use was their major sporting activity.

Alex and Danny had the whole thing to themselves. They slipped on their jocks and then the gym shorts that they wouldn't have bothered with back in their own home and, after putting on running shoes, went out onto the hardwood floor.

"Not an easy one," Alex said.

"That frustrated?" Danny asked.

"Yeah. That frustrated and that mad."

"Then get ready." Without any more warning, Danny went into a fighting stance. Alex barely had time to get himself ready before one of the young gymnast's feet went speeding through the air only inches from his head.

Physical work-outs for the lovers were most often careful and loving studies in synchrony. Their shared routines were physical ballets that allowed them to display their forms to one another in the most graceful and peaceful fashions possible. But there were times when the pressures of their work built up too much, when they had to move into a different plane of activity to ease their tensions. This was one of them.

They sparred with more reality than usual. The style was a mixture of various oriental martial arts. It allowed them to use their feet – to Danny's great advantage. It was based not on brute strength, but rather on sharp, accurate movements. It was an exhausting match of ability between two foes who were nearly equal.

They were most used to working together, in the arena as well as on the fighting field. They were wondrous to see those times. Often the attendants at gymnasia would be awed by the sight of masculine beauty they projected when they were with one another. Then their movements and their bodies – as wholes and in the various parts – would be delicately balanced.

But when they needed to hone themselves and their

skills to the maximum degree, taking on one another was the most effective practice they could have. There had been a time not too long ago when it would have been too unequal a fight. Danny, though trained for years in gymnastics, had never practiced the martial arts. But he'd learned a lot – and quickly. Now he could take Alex occasionally.

They moved around the mats with a dark intensity. Their arms and legs would dart out towards one another. It seemed as though neither one could get the final grip on the other nor deliver a telling blow. Their legs bent, their arms raised in defensive positions and their attention totally focused on the task of their competition, they were soon sweating profusely.

The liquids ran down Alex's body. They would run in rivulets that were diverted and directed by the sharp ridges of his highly muscular torso. The whiteness of his skin and the almost total lack of body hair were two of the reasons people so often thought that he looked like a statue – he reminded them of an ancient Greek sculpture. It would have had to be one of the gods that they recalled; Alex's physical perfection was seldom approached by mere mortals.

As Danny danced around and delivered or avoided the blows of their physical combat, his own body's near perfection was just as apparent. He had trained it since he had been old enough to understand what pleasures physical work could bring to youth. His chest and belly and legs were covered with a thick matting of hair. After a short while, the exertion had produced so much perspiration that it was plastered to his skin, letting his own hard definition show through.

Two of the old members of the club were in the gymnasium while the two young men were going through their paces. Pomfret Atwater III couldn't help but notice the way the youngsters were so very well built. Miles Adams-Smythe IV was his partner in a not-too-invigorating game of passing the medicine ball.

Pomfret tossed the ball to Miles once more. "Reminds me of prep school, don't you think?"

Miles caught the ball with an *oompf!* "We're too old to be

remembering those days."

He passed the ball back to his partner and was rewarded with Pomfret's own *ugh!* when it hit. "Those were good days though, playing fields and all that."

Miles tried not to let out another loud expulsion of sound when the ball was returned, but he couldn't help it. He tried to ignore the conversation and the ball began to go back and forth between the two men with only the sounds of their exertion as punctuation.

Alex and Danny had begun to slow down their pace. With an unspoken signal, they changed their rhythm. Now, as was more usual for them, they began to mirror one another's motions rather than try to offset them. They began something that seemed strangely like an erotic dance. They had started a particular exercise that they had always enjoyed together, a form of tai chi.

With amazingly fluid moves, their legs and then their arms would flow through the air. Their eyes were locked now. But they almost seemed to be trying to compensate for their indulgence in competition. They were attempting, instead, to discover how closely they could cooperate.

"'Tis like prep school," Miles said when he turned and saw the couple now. But what could possibly have gone on at Groton that even approached the erotic dance he was witnessing now? Certainly there hadn't been anything on the football field ...

"Remember the summer of '36?" Pomfret said with a teasing sound to his voice.

Miles looked at him suddenly. A flash of memory did come through from fifty years ago. "My god, Pommy, you mean that summer you and I ..."

"Quite the best time I ever had with a chum, you know." As though he wanted to avoid having said that, Pomfret threw the medicine ball at his old schoolmate.

Miles caught it, but wouldn't throw it back. "What a rum thing for you to bring that up now, so much later. Hell, Pommy, we're married and have children and grandchildren!

We're pillars of the community, we have position ..."

"Not nearly as much fun having all that as we had that summer though."

Miles couldn't help but grin. When he and Pomfret had been schoolboys they had spent the summer with a family on Mount Desert Island in Maine. They'd played so many games ... So many! They'd spent their days in the tall forests of the island pretending to be wild Indians and wearing mock loin-cloths while the bright sun bore down on them and turned their skin into a healthy tan that was uncommon for such sheltered city boys. And they'd explored themselves and one another as much as they'd charted the unknown island.

Now Miles turned to watch Danny and Alex once more. The two had escalated the overt eroticism of their motions now. They were actually touching one another, subtly, to be sure, but the way their chests were rubbing ever so slightly so that their nipples would barely graze each other's ...

"It was a damn good summer, Pommy."

"Ever think of going back?"

"What? And playing Indians at our age?" Miles laughed out loud at the idea. But there was something about being so close to those other men and remembering things that had been pushed back in his mind for so very long ...

"We could play something, I suppose," Pomfret said. "Don't know that it has to be Indians."

Miles just laughed and finally returned the medicine ball hard enough to receive a whopping good *thump* as a reward. It was a foolish idea. Actually, though, he didn't have any plans for July as of yet. And that had been an *awfully* good summer.

XI

"That miserable son of a bitch," Tom said between clenched teeth.

Charlie turned over in bed and put a leg over his lover's thigh and an arm over his chest. He could feel the tension and anger that gripped Tom. He didn't wonder at it. He felt it himself.

Once they had gotten Andrew home, the kid had spilled his guts; the whole story was gotten out between tears and sobs. It had been a horror, all of it.

He'd been brought up in an abusive family with a father who'd beaten him regularly. The father was convinced that the Bible was right: Spare the rod and spoil the child. He'd been even more upset when he discovered that Andrew was involved in some sex play with other boys in the neighborhood. He'd terrorized the boy by threatening to castrate him. Andrew had gone for years with none of the pleasures or joys of childhood. Among many other things, the father thought that after-school activities would erode his son's character and forbade Andrew to take part in anything that might have allowed him to create a normal friendship network.

Terry Draper had read the signals. He had seen the lonely kid's needs. Andrew had been a walking sore by the time he'd gotten to junior high school and Draper had been there to suck the blood out of him.

He'd paid special attention to the kid, giving him a sense of worth that he'd never had before. Then he had let Andrew know the price for all that attention. The boy had been so abused in so many other ways that the sexual coercion Draper used on him hadn't even seemed to be a bad thing at first. After all, it involved some physical touching and affection. He'd kept on going to the after school meetings that Draper had arranged.

He had been too young to realize what was happening when Draper had taken nude photographs of him. He knew too little about sex to question anything that Draper wanted. Like a refugee starving for food and happy to get even a rotten potato, Andrew had gone back over and over again just to have a chance at even a minute in the teacher's arms. If it cost him a spanking to get it, the price wasn't too high. If it meant that he had to pose in obscene stances, that was nothing in relationship to the payoff he'd receive afterwards.

Andrew never figured out how his father got hold of copies of the pictures. But one day, when he was just fourteen, he'd gone home and his old man was waiting for him. Draper had beaten him regularly as well, but he'd at least put it in the context of play and there was the affection afterwards. His father wasn't interested in little games and he wasn't going to make it feel all better when he was done. The belt had slashed into Andrew and when it was all over he was unconscious. He woke up on Draper's doorstep, left there by his own father.

Draper had been delighted by the turn of events. He took in Andrew, who didn't think he had any other place to go. He also made it perfectly clear what the rent was going to be if the boy wanted to stay in his house.

Andrew had been paying it with his body and his spirit for more than two years. That's why he'd been happy to see Draper leave. The bastard had presented himself to the gay community as a fine upstanding member who was "caring" for his younger lover. The lover was a terrified boy who was trapped by Draper's sick desires.

"Andrew just didn't know what else he could do. He lived

outside the city. He hardly ever even saw a gay newspaper, how could he have known about the gay youth groups? It's not as though they're publicized on television."

"Don't rub it in," Tom snarled and moved away from his lover.

Charlie was shocked by the statement. Rub what in? He thought for a minute that Tom was still reacting to the way that Andrew had assumed that he had to have sex with the two bodybuilders if he expected to stay in their apartment even for one night. It was, after all, the only thing of worth he'd been taught that he could offer an adult.

Charlie rubbed the back that Tom had turned on him. He had no way of knowing that the one thing Tom was reacting to the most strongly was his own sense of guilt. He had only just realized that his unwillingness to present himself as a strong role model had left kids without any kind of gay man that they could look up to and now, with Andrew's story of how he was trapped by the invisibility of his own options, Tom had the proof of the damage that his own inaction could cause.

It pissed him off. At himself.

•   •   •

Tom wasn't in bed when Charlie woke up the next morning. He got up and put on a robe and went into the kitchen. Tom and Andrew were already up. Somehow both of their sour moods had disappeared and the two of them were laughing out loud.

"Morning," Charlie said. He didn't dare say much more than that; he might break this magic moment.

"Hi," Tom said and then got up and kissed Charlie on the mouth. Something was up. Tom never would do that even in front of other gay friends. The lovers embraced for a beat more than necessary and Charlie realized that this was at least a little bit of a show for Andrew. Well, if Tom wanted to play happy gay couple at home, Charlie wasn't about to pull the plug on the screen for this plot. He liked it too much.

"We have a cheering section for our meet the weekend after next," Tom announced. "Andrew's going to come and be a spectator. I made him promise. It's a down payment on the lessons he's going to get."

"Lessons?"

"Yeah, from you and me. I'm the weight coach and you're in charge of football. Full time, all brakes pulled out until next fall. The kid's got two more years of football eligibility – he stayed back a year when he had that trouble with his parents. He's always wanted to play sports but there was no one to teach him. Always wanted to try out stuff with the weights, too, but ..."

"Terry wouldn't let me. He said I'd get too big, too much like a male." Andrew suddenly blushed after he'd admitted that. "That's why he shaved me – down there. So I'd look like a real kid all the time."

Charlie could see Tom's face wring into a field of anger. This must have been just one more piece of information that he hadn't heard before and it was one more piece of evidence of the abuse the boy had taken over the years.

"Well, looks like you have good bones, you're tall enough. It'll be hard work, but we can get you into shape."

Andrew smiled. It was the first time that Charlie had ever seen him do that. The kid looked good when he did it. He looked more natural than Charlie had ever seen him before.

"Just one question: What is this competition we're entering? The next one I know about isn't until ..."

"Mr. Gay Delaware Valley. I filled out the forms in the *Gay News* already. It looks legit, not just one of those beefcake things. There was a poster for it at the Spartans, don't you remember?"

"I remember, but I don't quite believe that you and I are going to enter a gay bodybuilding contest."

"Why not? We're gay and we sure as hell have worked on our bodies. If we can do all the other competitions, why not this one? Might be a little unfair; we've had more experience than most of the others I bet. But it's a logical thing for us to do.

"Now, who wants what for breakfast?"

•   •   •

The next ten days were a roller coaster of emotion for Charlie. They must have been for Tom as well, but he was so wrapped up in Andrew that he never let it out.

There was Marco's funeral to go to and the friends and relatives and lovers of the others who had died on the plane had to be sent heartfelt consolation messages. Charlie and Tom did more than go through the motions on all that. The sorrow that swept through their lives was real and they were glad to have even a few gay friends to share it with. It seemed that all of gay Philadelphia was in mourning over the tragic crash.

But as sincerely as all that affected them, the intrusion of Andrew into their lives left them no time to brood over it.

Tom had become a whirlwind. Their charge cards had burnt up as the boy was given a new wardrobe. The old clothes were at Draper's house. The dead teacher's family refused to acknowledge that Andrew had any rights to anything that was in the place. Everyone was just as happy to forget the bad memories that were stored there and the three of them had used the excuse to go on a shopping binge.

It turned out that Draper had never made his "adoption" of Andrew legal. The kid was without any standing. Tom had gone to their lawyer and had him begin the process to declare Andrew an emancipated minor. The attorney had been shocked to hear Tom declare just what relationship he had with Charlie. Not that he was surprised, he'd assumed all along that they were lovers. He simply had come to never expect them to use the words. He was pleased though, since it gave him his own chance to let them know that he was gay as well. He'd assumed their closet was so ironclad that they'd never want to discuss gay issues. Now he was happy to invite them to dinner at his house to meet his lover.

And there was more.

As part of the façade that Tom had insisted on presenting to the world, they'd always lived in a two-bedroom apartment. The spare room was needed for Andrew now. There was a massive moving of clothing in and out of rooms, a rearrangement of drawers, and even more money had to be spent to get the boy his own desk.

"You're not just going to ease out a little bit, are you?" Charlie finally asked one day. "You're going to start the whole thing off with a bang."

• • •

Even though the situation that had brought Andrew into their home had been a difficult one – to say the least – the transition was made with surprising ease. In less than a week the legal technicalities had been handled. Tom had applied his sense of organization and had constructed a schedule and order to the life the three of them lived together.

The timing was tight; they were all so busy. It also meant that there wasn't much leeway for social considerations. Andrew's teachers had to be informed of the new living situation. Tom and Charlie lived in the right district so luckily Andrew didn't have to change schools. But there had to be a conference with his instructors.

Mrs. Marabell Sweet wasn't used to talking to such large men about a student, especially when she was forced to consider them as a couple and Andrew's "parents," but she actually warmed to the men who were so much younger than she was. "There's no doubt that you two have accomplished something in Andrew's life," she said at the beginning of their conference. "His moods have become much less severe in a very short period of time. I had always wondered about ... But that's not important. I am still concerned that this is only a transitory situation, that he'll revert back to his previous behavior.

"You two are teachers, certainly you know as well as anyone how much damage to the boy must have been done in
all these years. You can't take a sixteen-year-old and remold
him, erase all of his memories and relieve all of the damage
he's suffered overnight."

"We can try," Tom had replied. And Charlie knew he
meant it.

• • •

The day before the Mr. Gay Delaware Valley contest, the three
of them were at home watching television. Charlie had made
popcorn and they were all drinking iced herbal tea. Andrew
had a hard time adjusting to the health food addiction that
the bodybuilders espoused, but he was trying awfully hard
to fit in and peppermint tea was one of the least bothersome
of their tastes.

The local news was on. The three of them had gone
through a long day. Charlie was grateful that it was over and
that he could enjoy the sudden new home life that had rev-
olutionized his and Tom's existence. From the closet to gay
nuclear family in one easy step. What a life!

Then he sat up in the chair and leaned forward to listen
to the announcer who was suddenly much more animated.

"This just in: A major explosive device has just been
set off at Amtrak's 30th Street Station in Philadelphia. Our
Action News Team is on the spot and we're going to them
right now. Sam, what's the story there?"

The screen was filled with the familiar sight of the huge
old train station. Smoke was billowing out of its portals and
the streets around it were jammed with police cars and
ambulances. A reporter stood in the foreground and began to
talk quickly as soon as the signal reached him:

"Mike, the carnage is unbelievable. A bomb was evidently
planted on a chartered Amtrak train bound for New York.
It went off just as the special was moving out of the station.
Dozens have been killed according to first reports and many

more are injured."

An off-camera voice asked: "Any clues as to who placed the bomb?"

"There have been phone calls to our station and to the major newspapers. They've only said ..." the announcer seemed worried about what he was going to report, "The calls were obscene. They claimed that the bomb had been set to help rid the city of Philadelphia of deviants and disease."

"That makes no sense," the off-camera announcer said.

"Mike, the train had been chartered by a gay group that was going to New York City for a special event to raise funds to fight AIDS this weekend. To the best of our knowledge, all the immediate victims were homosexuals. There have been other non-fatal injuries, but those seem to be uninvolved people who were simply caught in the cross-fire between the homosexuals and their attackers."

"There can't be any connection between this and the plane that exploded at Philadelphia International ..."

"Mike, Action News has been told by the same obscene phone callers that the authorities have been lying about the plane incident. They insist that they wanted to prove themselves once more before they went to the media with their boasts. I've talked to the mayor's office, Mike, and there's something going on. There are only adamant 'no comments' being made about the allegation that the airport incident was misrepresented.

"Mike, it appears that there are terrorists who are after the gay men of Philadelphia and no one has a single clue who they are."

Tom stood up and slammed the television off. "What the fuck do they mean: 'Caught between the cross-fire of the homosexuals and their attackers'? They make it sound like those guys on the train were active participants ..."

But Charlie was thinking about something else: "This means that someone murdered Marco. It wasn't a tragic accident the way they claimed it was. It was planned. Jesus, what's going on?"

XII

Alex Kane looked out of his hotel room window and saw the statue of William Penn standing over City Hall. For decades the statue had been a reminder to all that this huge metropolis had been founded on the best instincts of the colonial forebears.

This, the City of Brotherly Love, was founded as a refuge from the prejudice and intolerance of another, older country. Here, in this very city, the settlers decided that even the most tenuous ties with the Motherland were too much for a free people to stand. It was only a few blocks on the other side of City Hall that the Declaration of Independence had been signed.

"I want to go there."

"What?" Danny asked from the other side of the room. He was actually pleased that Alex had said anything. The idea that the Amtrak bombing had happened so very close to their hotel had made his lover's sense of impotence all the more enraging. They had actually heard the blast. They, too, had seen the television broadcast that described the non-gay dead and wounded as people caught by a battle in which the gays were presented as active participants.

There had been a flurry of late night phone calls to Farmdale's home in California. The computers had been run and emergency conferences had been held over the long distance wire. But there was nothing to be learned from the content of the phone calls that had been made to the Philadelphia authorities and media.

Farmdale had been even more anxious than usual. His original thought that the airways were the prime target were evidently incorrect, though the basic assumption still held: The vulnerability of the country's transportation system was still the target. Train stations made even easier marks. They didn't have the security checks that airports did. They simply allowed people to board and go on their way to their destination. Now the question was: Would the terrorists go after any other part of the transportation network that held the country together?

The mayor and the governor were caught in a bind. They couldn't shut down the railroads and airports that held the region together. But neither could they deny the possibility of massive destruction and loss of human life.

Some group out there, in this city built on the principles of peace and liberty, was trying to murder its gay population. They had to find out who those idiots were. They were going to have to answer to Alex Kane for a lot – a whole lot.

Alex had been silent all day after a fitful night's sleep following those conversations. They knew nothing more now. But at least he was willing to talk and he wanted to go out. That was fine by Danny. It seemed to be an awfully good sign, in fact.

The harsh reality of the situation couldn't be avoided, though. Danny watched while Alex got a leather satchel that he strapped around his shoulder. It looked something like an elegant man's bag, the type of thing that so many men in New York were using these days. But Danny knew that it wasn't a pleasant looking substitute for a briefcase. Inside, ready to be clipped together, were the parts of the deadly, compact Uzi machinegun that Alex had brought with him.

They walked the length of John F. Kennedy Boulevard. After they'd passed City Hall, they went down the busy Market Street retail area. Long distances meant little to men in as good physical shape as Danny and Alex. They kept up a fast pace until they finally arrived at Independence Mall.

The walk had eased Alex's mind a bit. The bustling crowds and the clear spring day had made the city seem to be alive again. The images helped him get rid of the memory of the smoke pouring out of 30th Street Station – smoke that he knew marked the death of so many gay innocents.

Now, suddenly faced with the graceful and well-maintained grounds of the historic district, he was able to sense some of the good of the country and remember that the evil was an aberration, not the norm.

There were crowds of tourists who hadn't yet become so frightened as to leave Philadelphia. There were school children and tour groups lined up to go through the buildings. Alex and Danny enjoyed the sights of the people at play.

"My god," Danny suddenly muttered. Alex had seen it, too.

In the middle of the longest line, the line leading into Independence Hall itself, was a group of men, all of whom appeared to be in their twenties or thirties. They had the usual tote bags that tourists use to carry their goods during the day. The bags' markings showed they were from Great Britain. But, no matter what their nationality, Alex and Danny both knew they had to be gay.

They quickly looked around the open area around the building. They moved quickly to get closer to the group. There couldn't possibly be any way that they could overreact to the situation. Not after the airport and the railroad terminal bombings.

For there to be an identifiable collection of gay men standing out in the open ...

"Alex, look!"

Danny didn't wait for an answer. He was racing at top speed across the grass. A park employee was yelling at him to use the sidewalk, but he wasn't paying any attention to those kinds of rules today.

Alex saw what had caught Danny's eye. Four men who had been standing near the entrance of Independence Hall had moved to the side of the building. They were trying to look as though they were gathered in a circle to have a conversation. But their body posture and their air of conspiracy made them stand out from the crowd of pleasantly chatting tourists. They were deadly serious about something and that something had little to do with American history – at least not the past history of the American people.

Alex threw down his satchel and pulled out the parts of his machinegun. He began to run after Danny as soon as it was ready.

"Rambo, Mommy, there goes Rambo!" one little girl yelled when she saw Alex speeding across the Mall's grounds. The child's alert spread two immediate and contradictory waves of sensation through the throng. Half of them thought that Alex was part of the festivities, an actor playing out the role of modern-day freedom fighter in the ancient context of the old buildings. The other half only saw the gun and its deadly reality didn't allow them much time to fantasize about super-human heroes.

The crowd surged and ebbed, pulled in two ways as some tried to get closer to Alex while others tried to move as far away from him as possible.

Alex sped up, pushing himself as fast as he could. He didn't dare let many civilians get between himself and the group of men he'd seen. He muttered under his breath about the very idea that people would equate him with that asshole, anyway. Rambo! God, couldn't they find a better man to compare him to?

Just then, there was a blur in the air. It rose at least eight feet up. It was spinning so fast that there was only a hint that it might be a human form. It was catapulting towards the suspicious men.

The missile landed; its shape was suddenly recognizable as it arrived at its destination in a sweeping motion, feet first, no longer tumbling. Danny. Each of two feet landed squarely on the back of the necks of two of the men. They cushioned his fall, taking most of the force of the impact themselves. Too bad for them, since the thumping they got left them unconscious and sprawled on the ground.

For one quick moment, Alex realized that Danny was actually standing on their heads. The younger man's gymnastic skills knew no bounds. He wasn't finished with his trade secrets. He seemed to dip his knees only a slight bit. Then he was airborne again. The leap wasn't as high as before, but the effect was just as great. He turned over twice in midair. During his descent, the hard heels of his shoes made contact with the faces of the two other men. They collapsed backwards, their heads bouncing off the brick walls of Independence Hall with a sickening thud.

By the time Alex had arrived, the four conspirators were totally incapacitated and Danny was going through their pockets. Alex only muttered, "Show-off," and then went to work ripping open the bags the men were carrying.

Police were running towards them now. "Stop!" "Freeze!" and other orders were screamed out at them. But the two kept up their search.

When the first officer got to the scene, Alex simply handed him two of the open bags he'd gone through. "They had M-16s set on automatic. That enough proof for you?"

The policeman stared at the ugly and deadly weapons he knew only too well from his days in Vietnam. He raised a hand and stopped the next cop from interfering with the work the two gay men were doing.

"They're on our side," he said with a sudden conviction.

"What about that fucking cannon the joker was carrying?" the second officer asked.

"Forget you ever saw it."

"What? Are you crazy?"

"Do as I say. Get the other men back to the crowds and calm everyone down. This situation is under control."

Danny looked up at him with a silent question. The policeman said simply: "My lover was on that train. That's what you're doing, isn't it?"

Danny nodded, yes.

"You have two minutes, tops. By then the real brass will be here and I'll be outranked. Hurry up. And get that damn gun under cover."

He turned his back as if to protect the scene while Danny left his search and quickly dismantled the Uzi and replaced it in one of the bags they had emptied.

One of the men began to moan. Alex scurried over to him. He pulled him up by his hair. The sudden pain brought with it a sharp dose of consciousness. "Who are you? Who sent you here?"

The man's eyes opened wider. "You can't stop us. The Organization knows what's best for the country."

Alex couldn't understand how the man was using the name. "What organization?" he demanded. "Who's the head of it?"

"Slime, they're all slime that are weakening us and making us lose our manhood."

"I swear to god, I'll tear your balls off with my teeth if you don't answer me."

"Their muscles are just camouflage," the man didn't seem to be speaking coherently. "There's nothing to their muscles but cover. They're not real men. We'll show them tonight when they try to deceive the world. Their strength is the devil's ..."

Then the man passed out again.

"Get going. Fast!" Their friendly cop was talking now. "The squad cars are starting to pull in. You have to split. Try to merge with that gay group. Hurry."

XIII

The crowd had been much too large for the original contingent of Philadelphia police to handle. They kept themselves occupied talking to those many people who were offering eyewitness information.

"There was a huge man, twice the size of a normal person ..."

"A gang of at least ten of them attacked those poor innocent ..."

"I saw Rambo, just like in the movie. I swear it was Rambo. He lives here in Philadelphia, doesn't he?"

The stories got more outrageous and the lines of people who wanted to give their version only grew. There was no way the officers could see the two men moving away from the throng.

Alex and Danny caught up with the British tourists on the other side of Independence Hall. The Englishmen were horrified by the open violence of the American city. They had been warned at home that Americans were prone to that kind of thing, but now that they'd seen evidence of it, they wanted some peace and quiet ... and a drink.

"Where can we get a bloody pint around here?" one asked.

Danny remembered his map of gay businesses and quickly said, "This way, I'll show you where there's a gay bar."

The place was glad to get so much business in midday. The manager happened to be there doing paperwork when the crowd of twenty-five men piled in. He joined the bartender and they got out lots of beers and drinks in record time.

"What a thing to see! What was it that was going on?" one man asked Danny. The tension and surprise about the afternoon events had made him more talkative than he would usually have been with a near stranger. "Bombs and guns everywhere you turn, I think it would be a damn good idea to climb the next British Air home."

"What," one of his companions said, "and take a chance on still another bombing? Hell, I feel as badly put out as those poor sods who get hijacked, I do. Don't dare to move nowadays, do you?"

Danny made small talk and did everything else he could to calm down the tourists. Over in a corner Alex was going through the current *Gay News*. When the crowd seemed to be adequately interested in their beverages and comfortably involved in the business of retelling their own individual recollections of the earlier events – none of which included a recognition that Danny was the human missile that they'd seen – he went to Alex to discover what he was reading that was so important.

"Finding anything?" Danny asked when he'd sat down beside him.

"I think so. It's all we really have to go on. We'll never get in to talk to those guys the police have on the Mall. But the one who I got to talked about 'their muscles.' There's a gay bodybuilding thing tonight. I'm afraid it might be the target. It's close enough, a long shot we have to take."

Danny nodded agreement and looked over Alex's shoulder at the advertisement for the Mr. Gay Delaware Valley contest.

•   •   •

Stu Manger was furious when he heard the report from one

of the men who had witnessed it all. He'd been a look-out for the team that was supposed to take out the Cockney tourists.

"You failed and you've fucked up the whole thing! Those guys will talk …"

"My men don't talk," Jack Vance said with a hard voice. "They know better."

"The police have four of them in custody. If only one of them …"

"I saw Elmo speaking to one of those weirdos that got them," the witness said. "He didn't seem in his right mind. He might have said something …"

Vance sat back in his chair and thought to himself. That was always a possibility. Just the way you had to assume that a decent interrogator might use truth serums to make the best and hardest man talk, you had to worry about what a guy might say in delirium. *Damn.*

"We'll break up the camp. It was part of the plan to move on anyway. We'll just do it ahead of schedule. I've already set it up for us to join with a group of the Klan in Virginia. It's not too far from here …"

"But our plans for Philadelphia!" Manger was clearly upset by the idea of leaving the work in Pennsylvania undone. This was his personal priority. This was where he wanted his vindication.

"Damn it, Stu, we got the plane, we got the train, what more do you want?"

"The subways. The interstates. The bridges. Bring the city to its knees. That's what we said we'd do. It's so easy. I showed you how. American cities are the easiest strategic targets ever made. They're overdeveloped and overly concentrated. We can show the American people just how unprepared they are. They'll be screaming for a military to take over to protect them if we follow through."

"But what's the difference? I mean, hell, we can get the subway in Washington just as easily, and the freeways in Baltimore and …"

"No! You have to listen. They haven't seen a major city

paralyzed the way we can do it. If all we do is random acts of terror ..."

"What we've done is a hell of a long way from random acts of terror, Manger. We've got over four dozen of the fairies and we've crippled Amtrak while traffic at Philadelphia International is down fifty per cent since the news finally broke that we bombed the plane, it didn't just have an 'accident.'"

"I want Philadelphia!" Manger slammed a fist down on the desk and leaned over it. For the first time Vance could remember he was actually threatening the leader of the Organization and had left behind his calm, managerial façade. The man was mad – Vance was actually relieved to discover that.

Vance thought it over. "I'm moving the main force to Virginia. There are too many men here. If anyone's actually looking for a group like ours, we're too obvious. But I'll stay behind – you too, Manger – and we'll keep a few of the best men with us.

"After all, tonight's already set up and there's no good reason not to go through with it. None at all. You might be right about the rest of it, too. Maybe just a few more bombs and we can really get people going. It'd certainly make them concentrate their attention here and make them sure that this is the only target. It'll make Washington all the easier when we're ready for it."

XIV

Andrew had never seen anything like it. He was standing backstage in the dressing room. Around him were over a dozen of the biggest gay men he'd ever dreamt of seeing. They were all huge – and they were all naked or almost so.

While he stood and watched, Charlie and Tom were oiling one another up for the contest. They'd explained that this was a sort of beauty thing, where the men were judged on the visual impact of their bodies. So it was necessary for them to put themselves in the best light.

It had been strange to watch them shave their chests, underarms and legs this morning. Terry Draper had done it as an act of humiliation when he used to shave Andrew. But the two lovers did it for the sake of the contest. They did lots of things for different reasons than Draper had done – like the way they were taking care of Andrew these days and the way they treated one another.

He'd only lived with the men for not quite two weeks. But he could already see so many things about them that made him realize that his years with Draper hadn't been the only way that gay men acted. He could find an example right in front of him.

Draper only cared about Andrew's cock and his asshole. But Charlie and Tom each cared a lot for every single part of the other's body. Tom was rubbing the glistening oil onto

Charlie's enormous back right now. He was paying careful, slow and erotic attention to every single inch of his lover's flesh. The way he was doing it seemed almost ... not obscene, but too intimate for other people to be able to watch.

Andrew had wanted someone to pay that kind of attention to him when he'd been younger. Someone who'd touch parts of him and not expect to get something orgasmic back would have been awfully welcome in his life. Charlie and Tom had both tried to give it to him the past few days, but he was so tortured by his memories of what Draper had done and how he'd treated Andrew that the boy had automatically moved away whenever one of the bodybuilders had tried to put an arm around him.

As Andrew watched the two lovers change places and Charlie now put the oil on Tom's back, he had a sudden desire to be handled in that affectionate fashion.

Could these two really be that different? Would they really come through on all the promises they'd made him? To teach him how to play sports? To help him with his school work and to introduce him into a gay life that included more than sex? If they would ...

But Andrew understood as he watched the sensual rubdown going on that he was going to have to make his own contribution if it was going to work. He would have to learn to do his own trusting and his own risk taking in the whole operation. They had been trying, that was for sure.

A sudden wave of guilt came over him as he remembered the last time that Charlie had attempted to put an arm around his shoulder. Andrew had shirked away as though the other man were some animal. He was sorry for that, very sorry. He made a silent vow that he wouldn't ever let that happen again.

"Got some more, champ?" Charlie asked him. They'd given Andrew the duty of carrying in some of their supplies, including the oil. He went into the gym bag and got another bottle. Charlie let Tom have the one they'd been using to oil up his legs. He used the new one to do his own.

"Not very glamorous, is it?" Charlie asked as he went about his task.

"Oh, yes it is!" Andrew said without thinking. Then he blushed. The men around him were all obviously used to this kind of thing. They were going about their exercises to "pump up" – that's the phrase Charlie had used to describe the quick torture they each suffered to force blood into their muscles for the maximum visual effect – or else they were oiling up like Charlie and Tom. They might be used to the idea of seeing so much male muscle in one room, but Andrew had never seen anything like it.

The odors were wonderful. The oil and the sweat combined in a thick way that seemed to almost have physical substance in the air. Andrew was fascinated by so much of it, but also unable to take full advantage of the possibilities the situation offered. After all, he was only sixteen and full-fledged voyeurism wasn't quite expected yet. But when that dark-haired man in the corner who was still nude bent over to retrieve something he'd dropped on the floor and the huge, hard mounds of his ass ...

"Are you okay, Andrew?" Tom asked. "Your mouth's wide open."

"Sorry," Andrew muttered as he tried to regain control of himself. "It's nothing."

Someone came into the changing area and told the contestants to hurry up. The crowd was getting restless and the judges were ready. Andrew shook his head. If the crowd was getting restless now, just wait!

When it became obvious that the event was really close to beginning, Andrew said good-bye to Tom and Charlie and went out front. They'd reserved a seat for him in the very first row by the stage. The contest was being held in the ballroom of the Hotel Hershey. Andrew thought that was funny. He doubted the Mr. Gay Delaware Valley contest was the usual kind of event that took place here.

The edge of the stage was actually rounded and, while he'd have a wonderful view of what went on, his place also let

Andrew see most of the rest of the crowd because of its angle.

The organizers of the contest had considered cancelling after all the recent tragic events. But they'd decided that the best thing they could really do was let life go on as usual. They didn't want to give in to the forces of fear that might grip people. They opted, instead, for a brief memorial for the victims of the two major disasters at the opening of the judging.

A man got up and began a speech that Andrew thought was too long and too depressing. But he realized that it really wasn't. He was just still reacting to the relief that Draper was gone. One of the two evil forces in his life had been eliminated. He couldn't help but feel grateful for that. Tom had told him that it was okay to let those feelings come when they did. There would be some grief later, but it wasn't healthy for him to feel guilty that Draper was gone.

That was the conversation the two of them had that first morning when Charlie discovered them. Andrew hadn't been able to sleep at all and he was sure that his anger and hate had murdered the old teacher who'd misused him so much. Tom had convinced him that it wasn't true. His hatred wasn't so powerful that he could kill people.

Andrew tried to get all those thoughts out of his mind. This wasn't the time to be worried about those things. He had too much future to plan. These days with Charlie and Tom had been a dream come true for him. Their house, the way they loved each other and the way that they both took such a special concern for him had made him feel better than he had ever felt in his life.

Some day he could grow up to be like them. That was a pleasant thought. He idly scanned the audience. *Maybe I'll grow up to be like those two.* He was looking at a couple that had just walked into the room. One of the guys looked as though he wasn't really that much older than Andrew was. Maybe a few years, but not many.

He had dark hair and a complexion that looked as though it wouldn't recognize a pimple if one stared it in the face. His clothes seemed molded to his body, not because they were elastic, but because the young guy's chest and legs were so obviously well built and were pressing against the fabric. He didn't have a physique as huge as Tom and Charlie, but there was no doubt there was just as much power there as he'd ever need. There was no doubt that he was hot, either. He was very hot.

He deserved a lover as attractive as the somewhat older man who walked in beside him. This guy was tightly built as well. He had on a pullover shirt that clung to him and showed off some very nicely etched muscles in his chest and his bare arms. They seemed to create a new form every time he moved, they were so compactly developed.

He reminded Andrew of something – oh, yeah, a statue he'd seen in a book that he'd seen once. It had been pictures of Greek statues, that was it.

The couple took their seats and Andrew kept on looking around the room. It was going to be fun to be gay! He was just now being able to realize that. Draper's bullshit about the loneliness of older life and the way that gay men could never have real relationships was just that: bullshit. Tom and Charlie proved it. And so did this other couple, and the many other people in the room. There were hundreds of them. Unlike the dirty old men that Draper used to bring to the house, these were people that Andrew wouldn't mind growing up and being like.

Then he saw him.

His whole body went tense. There was a quick flow of sweat down the small of his back that soaked through his shirt. What was *he* doing here?

Andrew was frozen to his chair. He didn't want to do anything that would call any attention to himself. He wanted to melt into the background as much as possible.

The lights went down and he breathed more easily. At least in the darkness there was less chance that the man would see Andrew. The contest began now that the ceremony was over.

One by one the men came out on stage; those tiny and revealing briefs were the only things that covered their bodies. And they didn't do a very good job of it, either. Andrew wished that he could look more closely at the show. His seat was so wonderful that, if he'd wanted to, he could clearly make out the lines of the various men's genitals under the fabric. They weren't wearing any kind of supporter to flatten out the details, that was for certain.

But Andrew couldn't take his eyes off that part of the ballroom where he'd seen ... him. The question still burned in his mind: *What's my father doing here?*

The one answer that made any sense at all was the worst: That his father knew Draper was dead and had come to claim him. In one wave of nausea, Andrew remembered what life had been like and he recalled why he had agreed to Draper's "arrangement." Two years ago, Draper was a lot better than the only other option the boy thought he had.

The memory of that harsh leather belt ripping away at his flesh made the light spankings that Draper had used in sex seem like foreplay. And that's what he had thought of them for a while.

But he didn't want to leave Charlie and Tom! He just couldn't let that happen. A new surge of emotions came over him. Panic was at the top of the list. There was no way he could get out of his chair and out of the hall without making himself obvious. Nor could he get backstage; that path was now blocked by standing members of the audience and they would probably object – perhaps loudly – if he tried to make his way past them.

He worried and worried about the situation. He kept his eyes on the place where he had last seen his father's form at the very back of the ballroom. Since he wasn't looking at the bright lights that were trained on the stage, his sight was adjusted to the dim of the audience.

Tom was being announced. Andrew felt vaguely disloyal that he didn't just watch the black man's routine. But he couldn't get over the sense of dread ...

Then he saw that his father reaching into his coat to get something. There was another man he didn't recognize there beside him as well. They had something in their hands.

"Stop them!" Andrew screamed at the top of his lungs. "They have bombs!"

The crowd screamed and began to try to move out of the auditorium. The lights suddenly went up and the effect blinded some of the men and made them even more afraid.

From the stage, though, Tom and Charlie were used to the bright illumination. They stared at Andrew. He pointed to the back of the room where his father and the other man were getting something ready.

The two lovers bounded off the stage and ran towards the men. The center line of the seats were empty, abandoned by the fleeing patrons who were jammed into the exit doors. Clad only in their skimpy briefs, Tom and Charlie leaped from chair to chair.

The other couple were making their own way to the back as well. They got there first. The younger, dark-haired one delivered a crushing blow to the head of one of the bombers. His package fell to the floor. But Andrew's father's was still safe. Before the statuesque man could get to him, he had thrown it into the middle of the ballroom.

Charlie caught it! Years of football had given him the edge. He looked at the strange plastic coated bundle for a split second, and then began to run across the rest of the chairs towards the fight that was going on between the four men – the two bombers and the other pair were at it with a viciousness that startled everyone.

• • •

Charlie saw the fight. He hadn't even stopped to wonder if the kid was telling the truth. This wasn't the time to figure out if Andrew was having some psychotic incident. Bombs! After the past few days in Philadelphia you had to take that seriously in a gay event.

As he hurtled through the floor, Charlie realized that the physical battle that was going on had one advantage for him: It had scared away the rest of the onlookers and left that exit clear. He jumped over the last of the chairs and saw the other parcel on the floor. Was it activated? He didn't have time to ask politely.

He grabbed it up and bolted into the lobby of the hotel. There was pandemonium there. At least it wasn't as packed as the ballroom and there was room to maneuver. He suddenly realized that he could feel a ticking in the packages he was carrying.

He had to get rid of them.

His mind flashed back to his days of football at Temple. There had been one time when his team could have beaten Penn State if he'd connected for one long pass in the last quarter of the game. Well, this glorified jock strap might not measure up as a uniform, but Charlie put himself back into the memory of that game.

Make up for lost glory, man. Do it!

He hefted one of the heavy parcels back over his right shoulder and sent it screaming through the air. It was perfect! It would have gone fifty yards on the field! But here it only did what it had to. It hit the window that looked out over Broad Street and shattered it on contact. The second parcel followed through the hole with just as much behind it.

Just as the second package was in the air over the pavement of the street, on its way to join the other on the asphalt, there were twin explosions. The force of them threw Charlie back against the wall behind him as hard as if he'd been hit by the whole Penn State line. But it didn't matter. He'd thrown his touchdown pass this time. He'd won the game.

XV

At least that part was done. Charlie put down the stack of paper that signified the end of the legal adoption process he and Tom had gone through to make Andrew Manger their son. It had been touchy, but the courts had luckily understood the complex dynamics at work in this case and had decided that good adult gay role models were the best thing for Andrew after all he'd gone through.

There was also the obvious fact that Andrew's father was incompetent to take the boy. Stu Manger had been utterly psychotic. They'd finally put together the pieces. He had been a student of Terry Draper's as well and he, too, had been sexually seduced by Draper when he was a boy.

Draper had been even more malevolent than anyone had suspected. He had purposely taken the obscene pictures of Andrew in order to send them to the father, his former victim. Stu had been overwhelmed by guilt over what had happened between himself and Draper. That's why he had eventually ended the affair, something Draper had never forgiven him for. The older man was used to being the one to discard his boys. He hated having been the one tossed aside.

It didn't make any difference that Stu Manger had been plagued with neurotic memories of his childhood fling. Draper had always planned to get back at him. Seeing Stu's lonely and mistreated son available to him was just what he needed to push Manger over the hill. It had worked. Not only had Manger been convinced that the "disease" of homosexuality had been passed through his genes to the boy, the fact that Andrew had been in those photographs had so enraged Stu that he couldn't stand to have the living evidence of his own past in the house.

He'd given in to Draper's sick demands and had taken the boy to him, abandoned him to a hell that he couldn't forgive himself for having once inhabited.

Once that was done Manger had gone on in rage and with a need for visceral revenge. He'd joined the Organization and had been one of its most successful and hard-working recruits.

To think that one man's sick sexual needs could have started such a long series of events in motion! Charlie knew that there were still other questions as well about the Organization: Where had they gotten so much money? Who else was involved? But those were things that other people were going to have to get the answers to. Charlie had his new job as a high school principal to keep himself occupied along with the new role of father.

He loved them both.

The Federico Garcia Lorca Academy was a long way from the suburbs. But as he sat at his desk and went to work on a pile of test exams that had to be graded, Charlie Bergen couldn't remember when he'd had more enthusiasm for education.

They'd decided to name the high school for the famed gay Spanish poet and playwright who'd been killed by Franco's secret police. A martyr seemed appropriate for a gay and lesbian institution in Philadelphia after the recent events here in the city. Besides, there were so many Latin students in the program, everyone had agreed that they should name the high school after someone of Hispanic descent. Charlie frowned, remembering the response their benefactor had when he heard what the academy was going to be called: "At least it isn't Souza!"

Mr. Farmdale was obviously a ... unique person. He'd arrived in Philadelphia after the carnage had ended and immediately went into a long and private conference with Alex Kane. The two of them must have had some enormous personal problem. They'd screamed and yelled at one another for hours. But it had all been behind closed doors.

Danny Fortelli had simply entertained Charlie and Tom and Andrew and ignored the occasional sounds of broken vases and furniture that came from the other room of the suite at the Four Seasons.

"Don't worry," Danny had said sweetly, "They're just discussing the size of the endowment."

That remark hadn't made any sense until after the two men emerged. Alex had been glowering and Farmdale was just as obviously displeased with whatever had gone on. But their moods didn't change the size of the check that Mr. Farmdale had written out and handed to the two teachers.

"There is only one stipulation," he had declared ominously. "There must never – ever – be a marching band at this school."

"If they want a goddamn marching band ..."

Danny only had to lay a hand on Alex's shoulder to cool off the situation. It was just as well. Charlie and Tom were so freaked by the amount of money they had just been handed that they couldn't have taken much more excitement.

They'd all gone out for a celebratory dinner at the Warsaw Cafe after that. Danny paused over his exquisite pierogies – the special appetizer the restaurant was famous for – and explained that they wanted Charlie and Tom to use their skills in the gay community.

"There are too many kids like Andrew who are forced out of their homes and who can't find a way to get a complete education. A couple of schools have been started – there's one in New York – for them and we think it's a great idea. I certainly know all about it." Danny seemed to be suddenly sad. Charlie and Tom both knew that some painful memory of his own youth was coming back to him. But he shook off his depression.

"You two have had so much publicity that it's going to be rough for you to simply go back to teaching as though nothing had happened. Especially after all the news photos of Charlie in the posing strap after he got those bombs out of the hotel.

"We just thought you'd be great candidates to start a gay school here in Philadelphia. You're obviously qualified and it's what you guys say you want to do with your lives. The money we've given you is enough; you can use some to get going and the interest on the rest should give you a foundation. All we ask in return is that you teach the kids well and help them learn."

Charlie had been in heaven. But he didn't dare say so until he and Tom had been alone. He was worried that the transition would be too much for his lover. True, Tom had been coming out with a passion these days, but to become full-time staff at a school for gay teenagers was a lot to ask.

But there had only been one concern: "Will there be enough other boys the right age so Andrew can play football? That's what he said he wanted."

"But, Tom, what about us?"

"Us? Hell, Charlie, we're going to be able to design the progressive school we've always dreamed of working in. And the set-up is perfect. No more hiding. No more lies. We'll be able to live the way you've wanted us to."

"The way I want to?" Charlie didn't like the sense that this was all his responsibility.

Tom came up to him and hugged him. "The way we both want to live."

Then they went to work. Andrew had met some other young people at a gay and lesbian rap group in the city. They were excited about the idea of going to a homosexual school. Some of them wanted it for the simple reason that it meant they could escape the torments other adolescents directed at them. Still more wanted to be able to learn in a different climate, one that didn't assume they were heterosexual and, thereby, wouldn't make them feel so alien.

Tom and Charlie had been surprised that so many social service agencies cooperated in getting still more students to enroll at Lorca Academy. There was no doubt in their minds now that their school was necessary.

Now, all the hard work was done and the doors had been open for a month. There were no regrets. Well, just one. There weren't enough other boys old enough and interested enough in sports to field a football team. Charlie and Andrew would have to do without that.

Not that Andrew was that disappointed. He'd adjusted wonderfully to life with the two lovers. He was committed to being the best student at the Academy and the first evidence of his study habits showed that he just might make it. The three of them were such a solid household now that there wasn't much time to be sad about a simple football team that didn't materialize.

Charlie looked at the clock. This was one of his favorite hours. Even if it wasn't very nice of him to want to spy on his lover, Charlie could seldom pass up this opportunity. He left his desk and quietly made his way down the hallway to Room 105.

There was a loud, high-pitched chatter going on.

"Gentlemen, gentlemen!" Tom's voice raised above the clamor. "This is no time to be sharing make-up tips."

There was immediate quiet in response to Tom's command. Then the class began the dreary work of learning English as a second language. The members of this particular tutorial were all Hispanic immigrants who'd been tossed out of one or another of the many schools in Philadelphia, not for their language problems, but because of their effeminate behavior.

There were certainly many other Spanish-speaking boys who were going great guns in the macho department. They were the most enthusiastic participants in the weightlifting and bodybuilding program that Lorca Academy was starting. Some of them were serious, more were only interested in using the expensive Nautilus equipment that promised to give them the pecs and buns they wanted. But there were enough of the effeminate Hispanic adolescents that they'd had to create a special class for them.

It had been the the greatest trial yet for Tom, and he was passing it with flying colors, if a shortened temper. Charlie listened a bit more and then started to go back to the office. He only had another half hour before he'd have to get to the gym and supervise basketball drill.

"Hey, Mr. Bergen."

Charlie turned and saw Bessie Anderson walking towards him. She was an enormous black lesbian who had been the first girl to enroll at Lorca. He greeted her warmly. "What can I do for you?"

"Is it true, what they say? That you're a football coach?"

"Well, yes, Bessie. At least I was before."

"Why doesn't the Academy have a team?"

"There weren't enough boys ..."

"Come on, now, Mr. Bergen. You said there wouldn't be any of that sexist stuff here at Lorca. You promised the girls would have as many opportunities as the guys."

Charlie stared at her blankly.

"Look, me and some of the others, we always did want to play football. How about us getting it on? I mean on the field? Can you put us in shape? I hear one of those fancy prep schools out on the Main Line's got a girls' team now. We could play them. If they dared walk on the field against the Lorca Tigers."

"The Lorca Tigers?"

"Yeah, we thought that was a tough name for a women's football team, don't you think? You know, its the female cats that are the real rough ones. So, what do you say? Can we practice with you? Say, starting next Monday?"

"Well, sure, Bessie." Charlie stuttered out his answer. "I'd be happy to teach you how. But do any of you know how to pass? Anything about the game? Anything ..."

"Mr. Bergen, you find out if any of the other Tigers can do all that stuff. Me? I'm strictly a defensive linewoman. Figure if I start now, there might be pro football for women when I graduate from college. So, we'll see you after school on Monday, right? I'll get the others there, you just trust me."

Charlie watched Bessie's big backside move down the corridor and couldn't help but smile. He was going to have his football team after all! He wondered, would Andrew be happy as a cheerleader?

XVI

They had sacrificed much of their own happiness to make sure that people like Charlie, Tom and Andrew had a chance in this world. They had done it with their eyes open. But there was something in the air that made Alex Kane and Danny Fortelli know that their own lives were about to be made even more difficult. There had been the tone in the phone conversation, the unanswered questions from Philadelphia and now ...

The helicopter circled over the New Hampshire mountains. Alex and Danny watched it lower itself gently onto the ground. The noise was deafening. Even when it had landed and the engines had been cut, the continuing whirling of the blades kept up too much of a roar to allow them to talk to Joseph Farmdale when he'd walked onto the ground and over to them.

They weren't sure what the emergency meeting was about. They'd only gotten a call that said that Farmdale had to talk to them as soon as possible and that he'd make the journey to them.

They walked into the house and all took seats. The couple had never seen the old man look so horrible. Alex suddenly was frightened that he'd come here to tell him that he was going to die. He was always aware of Farmdale's age, but somehow the idea that the man could leave them had never been real before. It was a measure of his condition that the thought now entered Alex's mind.

"I have to talk to you about Philadelphia." Farmdale spoke without looking them in the eye. It was just more proof that something extraordinary was going on. "We've finally discovered how the Organization was funded."

That had been the great mystery. There had been more money in the Organization than quasi-military groups usually ever have. They hadn't been able to get any of the people they'd captured to tell what had produced the wealth that had allowed the group to keep so many trained men on payroll.

Alex and Danny waited. This was obviously difficult for Farmdale. "It was ... my son."

Danny was startled. He sat up in his chair and tried to make sense of what Farmdale had just said. James was dead! And even if he were alive, he had been Alex's first lover. Surely James wouldn't have ...

"You mean Theodore?" Alex Kane asked softly.

"Yes." Farmdale looked as though he might cry. "I have never told you just how angry he was when he understood that James had left his money to you. He became even more incensed when he discovered that I was using the family money to bankroll some of your activities and to fund projects such as the Lorca Academy.

"He would never listen to reason about any of it. I tried to explain, but his selfishness and his ego made it impossible for him to understand.

"Now I've found out that he's using his own money to fight us. He's going to put the most sophisticated weapons and the smartest right-wing brains on the field against us, Alex. This is a man who is evil – but also talented. This is the greatest danger we've ever faced and there's only one thing that you can do about it.

"Alex, you must go after my son and stop him."

The old man stood up and tears rolled down his cheeks. Alex and Danny both stood and walked over to him. Danny put his arms around Farmdale. His body suddenly seemed so frail and so vulnerable.

Alex put a hand on his shoulder. The other two embraced in their pain. But the eyes of Alex Kane reflected much more than the sorrow that still another family was being torn apart by intolerance and hatred. The eyes were glowing a fierce, iridescent green. They were the signal that he was ready for the greatest battle of his life.

LETHAL SILENCE

by John Preston

Author's Note

EDGE (Education in a Disabled Gay Environment) was an organization dedicated to to making our community accessible
to all our members. You owe it to yourself and to the rest
of us to become aware of the barriers — physical and mental — that have been constructed against some physically
handicapped people in the gay world. Alex Kane will stand
for nothing less!

> EDGE
> Post Office Box 305 Village Station
> New York, New York 10014

Since Lethal Silence was first published, EDGE has closed.
A number of organisations, however, support accessibility
programs targeting LGBTQ persons. Please do an Internet
search for an organisation near you to support.

Alex Kane would be proud of your support.

I

"How could you have just sent them away?"

Brian Osborn looked up from his desk at the reporter. He'd been working on the latest budget projections for North Lawn Hospital. Actually, the computer printouts were labeled "Profit Unit #33". North Lawn was owned and operated by the Medical Corporation of North America, Unlimited, one of the fast-growing private hospital holding companies which were taking over healthcare in the United States. It was an important element of MCNA's business plan to keep the usually homey names of the hospitals the company bought. But internally the titles of the various subsidiaries tended to have more realistic titles.

Osborn wondered how his secretary could have let another one past her and into his private office. He'd told her that security had to be more tightly enforced after the recent fiasco. The place had been swarming with reporters and he was tired of them. Now another one. This guy must be from one of the newspapers. There wasn't a video camera following him around.

"Look," Osborn said with a sigh, "I've had enough of you news hounds. If you want a statement, go to the public relations office like the rest of them. They'll help you there. I have nothing more to say."

"You'll talk to me," the man said. Brian felt a small shiver run through his body when he heard the way the guy spoke. He looked at the intruder more closely now. The man was staring out the twelfth story window. Osborn could only see his profile at first. The nose was strong, the forehead was wrinkled as though the man was in pain. The chin was one of the most striking figures on the face that Osborn was studying; it was sharp and protruded slightly, as though it were some kind of symbol of the man's assertiveness.

There was no doubt that the man was pushy. You could tell from his stance, Osborn thought. His back was straight. His legs were spread slightly apart, the way a wrestler's or a boxer's would be when he was prepared for a fight to begin at any moment. Brian could see that the man's fists were clenched. The skin around his knuckles was white from the pressure.

The man turned away from the window and looked right at Osborn.

Was this a reporter? Suddenly Brian found himself hoping that was it. Otherwise, this man could be some kind of psychopath. That possibility seemed even more realistic now that Brian got a look at the guy's eyes. They were dangerous. That was the only word that Osborn could think of. He'd thought they were blue at first, but now he realized he'd assumed that because they were so light in color. But they weren't blue. The hue was green. Just in this one moment that Osborn had been watching, the eyes seemed to become brighter, some inner energy seemed to be firing them.

"Answer my question," the man repeated. "How could you have sent them away?"

Brian Osborn might be the director of Profit Unit #33, but he still had his own bosses. Corporate headquarters was adamant about these things. All public statements about Medical Corporation of North America, Unlimited were made by PR specialists. "I told you," Osborn said, "you have to go downstairs to get a statement." He felt some sweat seeping through his shirt under his arms. There was a tightness in his belly.

The intruder turned again to look back at the nightscape of Chicago. "I want to know how you, a supposedly civilized, educated human being, could have sent four men to their deaths. I want you to tell me."

"You have to go to ..."

The man seemed to fly across the room. Both his fists were lifted up in the air. They slammed down on the top of Osborn's desk with a force that sent papers and pens crashing onto the floor. But it was the man's eyes that got to Osborn. They were on fire. The green in them had come alive. He'd never seen anything like them before. This, Osborn was sure, was madness. This was insanity. He was looking into raw rage.

Osborn cringed back against his chair. He forced it to roll on its canisters until it hit up against the wall behind him. But that wasn't enough distance. He was still too close to this guy.

"I ... I only followed company policy." Osborn tried to swallow, but it was difficult. His throat had dried and he couldn't seem to even perform that simple bodily function. "We don't have the facilities to care adequately for AIDS patients," he said, finally remembering the official line. "We felt they were better off in another operation where the staff ..."

"They weren't here to be treated for AIDS," the man said. The green eyes were still flickering in a way that reminded Osborn of angry, burning flames. "They weren't asking for that kind of help. They'd been in a car accident. They didn't even choose your fucking hospital. They were brought here by an ambulance. There was danger of internal injuries. At least one of them should have been operated on."

"We already had enough of their contaminated blood spilled here," Osborn shot back. He immediately knew he'd answered too quickly. He shouldn't have spoken like that to anyone in this guy's unstable mental condition.

"Their contaminated blood," the man said, speaking the words slowly. Osborn thought he was actually spitting rather than talking. "They were sick young men who had a terrible illness. They'd just gone to a meeting of a support group, to get together with other men and women like themselves and try to cope with this monstrosity of a disease. Then they're rammed by a drunk driver and they have to end up in this place. Of all the rotten hospitals in the world, they get brought to this hole."

Osborn didn't like the term "hole," but he agreed with the rest of the man's statement. He certainly hadn't wanted those four men brought into Profit Center #33. Nor did headquarters. They'd made that clear as soon as they'd heard about it.

"We had no way of knowing that the driver wouldn't be able to operate his vehicle ..."

The man wasn't going to buy Osborn's recitation. "They should have been kept here for observation. You ordered them thrown out in the middle of the night when you found out they were here. The doctors had admitted them. But you overruled their medical judgment." The intensity of the man's look had dissipated a bit. Osborn could see that a deep sadness had overcome the guy. It was stronger even than his anger. *Why was this man going through all of this!* Osborn wondered. *Those four were going to die anyway.* "Look, if we let those bedpan jockeys call all the shots, we'd have half the bums in Chicago in here and never collect a penny from a one of them. There's a county hospital for those people. We're a business. We can't have derelicts and AIDS patients in a facility where the real money's in elective surgery – surgery the patient can have done anywhere he wants, in a hospital surrounded by any kind of person he wants.

"It's just bad marketing to let those others in here with the ones who can afford our special care. It was strictly against the rules. The medical staff had no right to admit them. We got the four men dressed. We would have sent them away in a taxi but they scared the cabbies with all their complaints about misjustice and threatening to sue. Since we had their home addresses, we just had someone go and get another car for them, the original one wasn't in operating condition of course. But this one guy gave us his car keys ..."

"He was barely coherent. He hardly knew what was going

on around him," the intruder growled.

"He knew enough to tell us the make of the car and where it was parked. Hell, we got them the fucking automobile. We didn't have to even do that. We could've made them walk out of here." Brian was losing his patience with all of this. "We sent them on their way. Can we help it if the driver blacked out and got them all killed in an accident?"

"The autopsy showed he'd had a concussion. Your doctors would have caught that if you'd let them work on the patients."

"Those four wanted to leave anyway." Brian Osborn was getting bored with this self-righteousness.

"Anyone would want to leave this dump after the way you treated them. You made them sit in a room with an armed guard to make sure they didn't get into the bathrooms. You made the nurses scrub just to bring them a drink of water and then you made the nurses scrub again every time they'd been in the room with the four men. You called them filthy names. You ..."

"What do you expect? They had AIDS! They shouldn't have been out and around anyhow. They should have been isolated all along." Couldn't this stranger see the obvious?

Brian was relieved to see that the man was evidently finished with arguing. The man stood up to his full height and his body seemed to relax. His hands unclenched and he took a deep breath. "You're the one who should be isolated. You should be isolated for a long, long time. You're the one who shouldn't be allowed inside a hospital. You desecrate the whole idea of a caring institution."

"Look, I've had enough of this horseshit!" Brian finally said in exasperation. "I get directives from headquarters and I follow them. That whole romantic notion of the 'caring institution' is hogwash. Hospitals are big money. They're big time. In that scheme of things, AIDS is just bad public relations. It erodes profits. That's all there is to it."

The man blinked, as though he suddenly couldn't believe what he'd heard. He repeated the words slowly: "'AIDS is bad public relations.'" He made it sound like a question. And then he started to laugh. He laughed so hard he bent over and had to hold his stomach. He moved around behind the desk where Brian was standing now. But the administrator wasn't as worried. The man seemed to have understood his point. He put an arm around Brian's shoulder and lifted him up a bit, guiding him over to the window where he'd stood earlier.

Through his laughter, the man repeated the line once more, "'AIDS is bad public relations.'" He seemed to clutch onto Brian's shoulder a little tighter. Osborn thought the guy was just being friendly. He didn't try to move away from the manly clasp.

"Well, that's what headquarters says. The Chairman of the Board ..."

The man held up his free hand like a traffic cop. "No, no, don't tell me about him. I know all about him."

"You know Mr. Farmdale?"

"I know Teddy real well. Real, real well." Then the man started to laugh again, though not quite so hard. He could speak more clearly than he'd been able to before. Brian looked out over the city. The lights lined the broad avenues of Chicago. The carefully laid out grid of the north side of the city was a clear pattern from this height. Profit Unit #33 wasn't really that tall in comparison to the giant skyscrapers that dominated downtown – they were some of the tallest buildings in the world – but the man seemed to think it had sufficient height for his purposes.

But Brian never would be able to understand that. All he knew was that the arm around his shoulder tightened incredibly; it felt like a vise. The grip was so strong that the man had no problem using it to lift Brian up in the air. Brian felt the excruciating pain only when he hit the picture window with enough force that it shattered open. Then he was sailing through it and into the night air. As he was falling, Brian heard that man's voice once more. He was laughing again, "'AIDS is just bad public relations.'"

If Brian Osborn had kept his consciousness just one

second or two longer, he might have agreed with him. But Brian never had the chance.

II

Alex Kane walked into the suite at the Barchester. He didn't pay any attention to the famous hotel's luxurious accommodations. That sort of thing never impressed him. He would have been happier in a cheap dive. No, that wasn't true. Alex Kane could never be happy anywhere but home. There were no gradations of that elusive emotion so far as he was concerned. There was this thing that was called happiness and it existed in his house, on his land, and, most of all, in the company of his lover Danny Fortelli. Without those elements, happiness did not exist. There was only loneliness and constant vigilance when he was away from them.

Kane sat down at the dining table. There was one other person in the room. The waiters had left after they'd delivered the food. Dinner was being kept warm in chafing dishes on a sideboard. Alex's companion stood up and went over to them now, lifting off their covers and serving the contents onto plates.

Alex sat, silent and brooding, letting the other man go about the motions of preparing the food. Kane was so lost in his own thoughts that he seemed a little startled when a full dinner was put in front of him: Roast beef, potatoes, vegetables. He ignored the second plate, a salad of some sort, and began to eat the main course without any enthusiasm.

Wine was poured into his glass. He watched the level of

the liquid rise in the crystal container and he simply assumed it must be excellent, one of the really expensive ones that Joseph Farmdale liked so very much. Alex could care less what kind of booze it was. He wanted a drink. He took the glass as soon as it was filled and drained half of it.

The wine was good, he could tell because it didn't burn at all when it went down his throat. But the kick of alcohol was still there. He wasn't used to it anymore. He used to drink a lot, back before he knew Joseph Farmdale, and when he had, it hadn't been fine French wine.

Farmdale sat down at the other end of the table. He and Alex usually spent hours verbally sparring with each other. It wasn't that they disliked one another. On the contrary, they loved each other in their own way. That affection was so strange to them, though, that they'd expressed it most often by bickering about everything they could think of – letting the quantity of words express the quality of affection in a sense. Only a few people understood that about the two men.

But Farmdale didn't have it in him tonight. In fact, he hadn't had much spirit to him at all in the past few weeks. That was because of Theodore. Teddy Farmdale was Joseph's son. And right now that son was the most dangerous person on earth so far as his father and Alex were concerned.

Alex wasn't exactly in his best mood either. He wasn't upset or even depressed about what he'd done to Brian Osborn. That was part of the world he lived in. What did bother him was that he'd found no satisfaction in it, none at all.

Alex looked out the window of the hotel. The view seemed so similar to the one from the hospital's penthouse offices. He was thinking about Osborn and about how evil the man had been, but in such a meaningless manner. Alex thought about the trials that'd taken place in Israel when they brought the overlords of the Nazi concentration camps to justice. There was no doubt those had been terrible, horrible people who were put on trial. But they'd been so ... banal. They'd acted with such a lack of understanding of what they'd done. They'd defended themselves by saying they were simply soldiers carrying out their orders when they'd sent power-less Jews to the gas chambers. And Brian Osborn had only been following headquarters' orders when he'd sent the AIDS patients uncared for into the streets of Chicago that night.

Alex thought he understood how strange the prosecutors in those other trials must have felt. They'd known they were dealing with utterly guilty people. But they must have also known that those weren't the personifications of evil they'd expected to find. Those had existed – Hitler, Goebbels, the rest of the Nazi high command – but those men on the docks in Israel often seemed to be nothing but ciphers. They had to be punished. They deserved to die for their heinous crimes. But they'd been so ... common.

"I have news," the old man finally said from the other end of the table, interrupting Alex's thoughts. "I've gotten more information on Theodore. We knew he held the controlling interest in Medical Corporation of North America. The anti-AIDS directives of the company date from his acquisition of the majority of stock."

"No surprise in that," Alex answered.

"I've discovered that he's been attempting to invest in other hospital-holding firms. The privatization of medical care in America is a process few people know about. The public certainly isn't aware of the extent to which it's progressed."

"What are you going to do about it?" Usually a statement like that would have been an aggressive challenge from Alex to Farmdale. But it didn't have any of that weight right now.

"I've made certain arrangements to make sure Theodore has less success with some of his other takeover targets. I've also made certain that various state and federal agencies have been alerted to some of the improprieties of such firms."

"'Improprieties,'" Alex's voice had the usual scorn in it this time. "God, the way those guys were treated, what happened to them ..."

"Please, Alex, don't." Farmdale put down his utensils. The idea of eating any more during this conversation was intolerable. There was pain in his voice, honest suffering at the idea of what'd happened. "The entire country has been outraged by that act. It's become the crystallization of so much anger and so much horror at the entire history of the way the people with this disease have been treated."

"They're already calling them the Chicago Four," Alex said, "as though that makes up for anything, to make them heroes."

"Not heroes, but martyrs. Perhaps martyrdom isn't a state to which people aspire, but at least it means their deaths haven't been in vain."

Alex wanted no more of this conversation. He began to eat again, even though the well-prepared food had all the flavor of sawdust for him.

"At least we've stopped Theodore, at least a little bit, at least for now." Alex didn't answer. The two men finished their meal in silence.

Later, the people from room service cleared the table and left them alone once more. When they'd gone, Alex poured himself a stiff drink of cognac. Farmdale noticed and lifted an eyebrow at the uncharacteristic behavior, but he didn't say anything. He poured himself a more conservative amount of the brandy and then the two men sat and turned on the television. It was time for the late night news. They hadn't said a word about it to one another, but they expected there'd be a story about the death of Brian Osborn and they wanted to see how it'd be reported.

The announcer's face came on the screen. Like most television newscasters, he had two expressions. One, the more common, was a smile as he prepared to entertain the audience. The other – the one they saw now – was an attempt at portraying the serious commentator. Alex wondered if the media were really going to treat Brian Osborn's death so solemnly.

"Tragedy has struck Chicago's gay community once again," the announcer began. "Fire swept through a cruise boat crowded with members of a gay group who'd chartered the vessel for a party on Lake Michigan. At least twenty-eight people are dead. Another twenty-two are missing and presumed dead.

"The Fire Commissioner told us this evening that the tragedy was caused by a collision on the Lake. People searching for their friends crowded the pier on the Near North Side of Chicago, desperate for news ..."

Alex bolted from his seat. "Teddy. He must have done it."

"Alex, Alex, there are accidents in this world," Joseph Farmdale had hold of Kane's arm.

"I have to go down there. Now. I have to find out."

• • •

Over an hour later, Alex Kane stood on the edge of the crowd. Everywhere he could see, men were crying, holding on to one another. Others seemed to be standing in a state of shock, disbelief marking their faces. The familiar litany of tragedy sounded all around.

I was supposed to be on that boat ...

If I had been able to get out of work just a few minutes earlier ...

Not fake. No! Not fake!

Alex showed no emotion. But inside he felt as though some huge weight were crushing down on his heart. Fifty men, fifty men who'd gone on an early summer cruise to celebrate a birthday, nothing more. And now they were all dead.

He felt it was his fault. He was responsible. He'd been a part of the vicious jealousy that fueled Theodore Farmdale's vendetta against all gay men. At that moment, Alex wanted it all to stop. At that one moment, he would have traded his life for all of theirs if it could have convinced Teddy to give up his hatred and his killing.

Alex looked away from the crowd and over to the obscenely even and ordered lines of body bags that were laid out on the pier. The lumps, covered by canvas, seemed so inhuman. It was almost possible to forget that those had been people who'd been living only a few hours ago. But Alex couldn't forget it, not with those voices sounding all around him.

Have you seen Kim? He's got to be okay. He was a great swimmer. He must have been all right. Where's Kim?

Alex had talked to the rescue crews that were still working in the night. The boat had just been launched. It had all the safety equipment required and more. The captain had been competent and able. There was no question about most of the details. Another boat had rammed into the cruise ship which had been sailing along with its happy party-goers. The second boat's fuel supply had ignited with the impact of the collision. The inferno had been too much for the larger craft to tolerate. All of its up-to-date safety features couldn't absorb the explosion.

There was a hand on Alex's shoulder. He looked over, surprised that anyone here would approach him. He was used to being left alone; there was an air about Alex that usually discouraged friendliness from strangers. But it wasn't a stranger. It was Joseph Farmdale.

The two men looked at one another. Alex turned away. "It wasn't an accident."

"But the news reports," Farmdale protested, "I just heard another one on the way over. They said there was a collision ..."

"They haven't found any other bodies, none from the other boat."

"But there are so many bodies lost. It was far out from shore. Lake Michigan is huge."

"The boat that rammed into them had some of the most modern electronic equipment possible. They've found pieces of it, just enough to show how sophisticated it was. That thing was a guided missile on the water. It was aimed at the gay group. It was an act of war."

"Can you prove it?"

"Prove it!?" Alex yelled. Then he regained control of himself. "The Fire Commissioner's men are better than I expected.

They've already caught on. They've begun an investigation. They've called in the Coast Guard.

"But by the time it all happens, they won't be able to find anything. All traces of the ownership will be gone. They won't be able to show just how it happened. Theodore is like that: thorough."

"God, Theodore, again." Farmdale seemed to slump against Alex. No matter how angry he was because of his own impotence, Alex couldn't let Farmdale suffer through this alone. He put his arm around the older man and led him away from the scene. Alex could see Farmdale's limousine waiting on the edge of the pier, standing beside the fleet of ambulances and other emergency vehicles. There weren't any sirens anymore. There were just the lights as they eerily revolved on top of the cars and trucks. They seemed to be beacons in a modernistic hell. And that, Alex thought, was just about the right image for this evening.

III

"God damn it!" Larry Menario yelled in frustration. It'd taken so much effort to build up the courage to come to this fucking meeting and now …

"Can I help you?"

"No!" Larry said without even looking to see who was speaking. He felt suddenly like a fool. He wanted to get out of there, fast.

"Hey, hey, come on. Let me help you."

"Look, fella, I can take care of myself. I'm just pissed off because every building on this campus is supposed to be wheelchair accessible. I come here and there's no ramp. There's no way I can get up there." Larry stared at the thirty steps that led to the entrance of Kennedy Hall. "Damn state colleges were all supposed to make all their buildings accessible. They were supposed to have finished this one over spring break."

"There was a notice in the student paper about it. They couldn't get to it."

"Well, why not?!" Larry tried to calm himself down. He could feel that too familiar urge to cry. He was nineteen and it was time to stop crying. He grabbed hold of the wheels of his chair and swerved around.

Because he hadn't paid attention to the voice that'd been talking to him, he hadn't realized how close the other man was. Larry ran his chair right into him, smashing the metal foot pads up against the guy's shins.

"Ouch!"

"Oh, god, I'm sorry." Larry meant it. The guy was bending over to take hold of his ankle. "I'm really sorry." Damn, what a fuck-up. First the anger at finding the promised ramp to the building still not there. Then the frustration that he couldn't get into the meeting. Now doing something as fucked up as running into someone with his wheelchair.

But, as usual, he thought, all he could do was sit in the chair and watch. He wasn't able to do a thing about it. The guy seemed to be getting past the worst of the pain. He wasn't jumping around anymore, but he still stayed leaned over, rubbing his leg. "Pretty vicious weapon you have there."

"Who are you?" Larry asked. Then he realized he'd put it very rudely. He hadn't meant to say it that way. But the face was familiar, he did know it from some place.

"Scott Gilson," the other guy answered.

"Oh. You." Larry began to move the wheelchair again. This was all he needed, to meet the campus super-jock, the big media star quarterback of Mansford State College.

"What the hell does that mean?" Gilson was walking quickly to keep up with Larry's chair. The slope was downhill here and he'd been able to pick up a lot of speed. "Hey, come on, tell me. What the hell did you mean by that?"

The chair stopped so suddenly when Gilson grabbed the handles that Larry nearly went flying off it. He just managed to take hold of the arms in time. He wouldn't look at Gilson, even though the football player repeated his question still once more. How could he ever tell the guy what he meant? How could this guy understand what it was like for a crip like Larry whenever he had to come into contact with someone as strong and healthy as he was?

"Please, I'm sorry," Larry said. He hated the way he was talking. He loathed that defeated sound in his voice. "I ... I didn't mean anything. I'm just having a really hard time and ..." The tears were coming. Larry fought them back, but they were definitely on their way up from deep inside and he knew he wouldn't be able to fight them off for long.

"Me, too," Scott Gilson replied. Larry wasn't used to having his own self-pity reflected back at him. He wasn't sure how to react. "God, what a night."

"Girl stand you up?" Larry asked. He quickly hoped the football player hadn't heard the sarcasm that'd crept into his voice. But he was also relieved that the guy's unexpected display of emotion had seemed to conquer his own feelings. Scott didn't answer. He looked away and dug his hands deep in his pockets. Then his attention came back to Larry. "Why did you want to go into that building?"

Oh, no, Larry wasn't going to get into that one. "Look, I got to get back to the dorm now." He started wheeling again.

"Why? Why did you want to get into Kennedy Hall at this time of night?"

Scott was holding the handles of the chair again and there was no way Larry could fight against the other guy's strength. There was a freezing sensation of fear sweeping through Larry. This was one of the things that he hated the most. He was so damn vulnerable while he was in this thing!

"Look, please let me go back to my dorm. I don't want any trouble. Can't you see that I have enough already? Let me go. Damn it. Please let me go." And then the tears did come. They began with one big huge sob that shook Larry's chest and once they'd started, there was no way he was going to stop.

"I'm sorry," Scott was saying beside him. It only made Larry cry more when he heard that hated sound in the other man's voice. Which was worse? The pity people gave you when they saw the wheelchair or the powerlessness of needing it?

"Don't. Don't," Larry finally was able to get the words out past the tears. "I told you, it's just been a really lousy night."

"And I told you mine was pretty bad too." Scott's hand was on Larry's back now. The guy probably only meant it as a meaningless gesture, but the physical contact startled Larry. "I really don't want to be alone," Scott said. "Will you come and have a cup of coffee with me?"

Scott's request took Larry by surprise, but there was something that let him know the guy was sincere. To his amazement, Larry realized that Scott was reaching out in some way to him. He couldn't remember the last time another person had looked to him for support of any kind.

Larry took a deep breath and that helped stop the crying. He pulled a handkerchief out of his pocket. He blew his nose, making such a loud sound that both the young men had to break out laughing.

"Sure," Larry finally said. He forced himself to smile. He hoped his face wasn't too blotched by the tears. If nothing else, he was glad to get the conversation away from the question of why he'd been trying to get into the building. "Yeah. Let's go to the Union. I can handle that."

"Want me to push you?"

"No!" Larry yelled. He breathed deeply once more. "I can do it just fine," he said in a softer voice.

They began moving down the walk together. Larry had to sniffle a couple times, but he was able to control himself. God, he hated that. He should be stronger, like this Scott.

Larry was able to turn a few times and look at the figure walking beside him. Larry'd never seen him this close in person before. But he'd seen plenty of pictures of Scott Gilson. Everyone on the campus of Mansford State College had, so had most of America. What would this guy do if he knew that one of those pictures was hanging on Larry's own dorm room wall? It was a good thing it was nighttime and Scott Gilson couldn't see the hint of mischievous guilt on Larry Menario's face. Scott Gilson wasn't just a local star. He was becoming a national sports figure. He'd turned down scholarship offers from all the big-time football colleges. Instead, he'd come here to Mansford, a small campus stuck in lowly Division II. On a team like Boston College, he could have been another Flutie. At Alabama, he could've been so popular they'd have elected him to the Senate the day he graduated.

But Gilson had never allowed himself those chances. He didn't hustle to get the attention he received either, the way some collegiate stars did. He avoided the press even though they'd besieged the Massachusetts campus time and again looking for the special story. There was none. Well, there was none if you overlooked the two years without a defeat or a tie that was Mansford's record in the past two seasons that Gilson had played on the team.

Larry saw something about the way that Gilson walked that showed him just how good Gilson must have been on the field. Scott was a big man. He stood over six feet tall and weighed, Larry remembered from the newspapers, about 190 pounds. But he carried himself with an unmistakable grace. Those legs that were moving on the sidewalk now were the ones that had jumped over defenders, made impossible cuts, powered the rest of him for long runs. Those were the kinds of legs that Larry would never have.

Of course, Larry realized, Gilson's athletic abilities weren't the only reasons for his popularity. The junior back was also handsome. Even though he had that thick bull-neck that so many football players got from their weightlifting programs, the face wasn't lost on that column of thick tendons. It was just the kind of all-American look that the magazines and newspapers loved to photograph. It had one of those broad smiles with white teeth showing through well-formed lips. The dark brown hair framed its fine complexion and the deep blue eyes caught light from the lamps that lined the walk.

The path changed now and the grade was uphill. Larry had to struggle to keep up the pace. "Why do you have to be so pig-headed about it?" Gilson asked. "Why don't you let me push?"

Larry wouldn't answer. He just kept on going, refusing to let up even a little bit, afraid he'd start to slow down. He wasn't about to give Scott the whole lecture on the importance of self-sufficiency right now.

Gilson's next question sounded different. "Or, why don't you have one of those mechanical chairs?" he asked. "I've always thought they were so hot."

That stopped Larry short. "What do you mean? 'Hot'?"

"You know," Scott said, "those electric wheelchairs they have that you can drive with one of those joy-sticks. Varoom! Varoom! Varoom!" Gilson danced around a bit, playing with an imaginary control. "Damn, I think that'd be great. Just powering your way through crowds, all of it!"

Larry nearly laughed at the sight of this big man jumping all over the pavement. "You're not the only who wants to stay in shape," he answered, nearly forgetting to be angry for once.

Larry started the push up the hill again. "I have one of those," he admitted, "but I like to use this one, it builds up my arms. I race." He blushed. The statement was absurd when he was talking to this guy, a real athlete.

"You do?" Scott said. At first his voice sounded questioning, but he got more excited when he went on, "I've heard about that. Those special events they have for people with disabilities, right?"

"Yeah," Larry said, "I've done the stuff like that. But that's not what I'm training for. I'm going to be in the Boston Marathon some day soon."

"The Marathon!"

"There's a special division for chairs," Larry said. "I've always wanted to be in it."

"That's wicked hot stuff, man," Gilson said. There was a real tone of admiration in his voice.

They'd arrived at the Union. It did have a ramp and Larry wheeled himself up it into the building. At least this modern structure had been built according to government specifications about accessibility and Larry knew that he wouldn't face any unnecessary barriers here.

They went through the cafeteria line and collected coffee. The tray fit over the arms of Larry's chair and he didn't have any trouble delivering his own drink to the corner table they chose.

Larry was just as happy that Scott was going on and on about wheelchair racing. It wasn't just that it made Larry feel less like an outcast, it also meant that other subjects weren't being addressed. He willingly gave long answers to all of

Gilson's questions about the races he'd been in and how he trained.

"How did it happen?" The query came out of nowhere and for once Larry wasn't ready for it. He took a drink of his coffee as an excuse to claim some time. He hated this discussion, though it seemed like he'd had it a thousand times before.

"I was five. I barely remember it. A car hit me." The words always sounded so matter-of-fact, a simple recitation given in a classroom or something. But Larry had never found a way to describe that event that'd changed his life forever. And, it was true, he could hardly recall the details of that afternoon now.

"Wicked bad." That's all Scott said. Larry was sorry that Scott seemed to avert his eyes now. They'd been staring at one another intently before. Larry had hoped that Scott wouldn't be so typical when this conversation happened. Maybe it was just something that would always go on. At least Scott had asked about the accident up front, he hadn't played around with it the way so many others did.

"Why are you at Mansford?" Larry asked. He hoped he might gain some ground by grabbing the initiative.

"You a spy from *Sports Illustrated?*" Scott asked. A strange smile came over his face, he seemed to be as used to that question as Larry was about his own.

"They say you could be a candidate for the Heisman next season."

"Not in my junior year. That's too much to expect." Scott's reply was soft-spoken. He obviously didn't find it strange that someone would talk to him about his winning the most coveted college football trophy in the country.

"Year after?"

"It's hard to think someone in a Division II school will ever win it," Scott answered. "And I'm not going to have a chance anyhow."

"Why not?"

"Things." Scott was shifting uncomfortably in his seat.

Larry could see Scott didn't like this conversation. Scott actually seemed sad now.

But the football player suddenly turned and stared at Larry again. He was taking back the conversation's direction. "Why were you going to Kennedy Hall tonight?"

Damn it, Larry thought. He locked eyes with Scott's and he decided he might as well come out with it. That was what he'd wanted to do, wasn't it? Come out with it? Why not? No one in a wheelchair was going to become friendly with anyone like this guy anyhow. Larry had nothing to lose by being honest.

Larry was suddenly shocked when he realized that he'd even had that thought, that he and Scott Gilson might have become buddies. Having friends was one expectation he'd learned to do away with and he wondered why it'd come up now. The surprise made him all the more anxious to get this over with.

Larry looked back at Gilson and told him, "I was going to the Gay Students Alliance. I wanted to go to the organizational meeting for the march on Chicago."

He watched Scott stiffen. That's what they were all going to do once they found this out. Larry tried to convince himself that it was just one more automatic reaction he'd have to learn to live with. But it was hard to keep himself strong about it. His wheelchair was a trap now. He could see the sweat breaking out on Scott's forehead. Would Scott get violent? Larry knew people did that; look at all the things that were happening in Chicago. It could be directed towards Larry. He couldn't possibly defend himself in this damn chair.

People were so often repulsed when they looked at his chair. Now, he could see that every time they found out about his sexuality, this was going to be the reaction he got. And he just didn't want Scott – or anyone else – to hate him. His life was trouble enough without that.

"Me, too."

The pair of them sat there stunned, as though neither one could believe the words he'd just heard come from Scott

Gilson's mouth. Scott swallowed hard and fidgeted with his hands. Larry sat there silently; he instinctively knew he had to let Scott tell this at his own pace.

"It's gotten to be too much," Scott finally began. He seemed to collapse forward and leaned with his elbows on the table. "Those guys, all dead. The way everyone's treating the ones who're sick. It's just too much. You finally know you gotta stand up and say so."

Scott looked back up at Larry and he seemed to be begging for some kind of affirmation, anything. Larry nodded slowly, "That's the same for me. I've never gone before."

"When I do," Scott sat back up and smiled sarcastically, "I think we both know that the Heisman isn't going to be in my future, is it?"

"Why are you here? At Mansford?" Now Larry knew there had to be more to the reasons than any reporter had ever guessed.

"Because," Scott said, "I was always afraid this was going to happen. I thought – I used to think that I could control it, wanting to be with men. But I was unsure of it. If – when – I come out, there'll be hell to pay. But if I'd gone to Notre Dame or Penn State and been good and gotten this attention in one of those places ..." He shook his head silently.

Larry knew Scott was right. He could just imagine what it'd be like if Scott'd been at a national school. "Who knows?" he asked.

"No one, really. There've been times ... you know ... I'd make believe I was drunk or stuff and fool around with guys. But they never talked about it later, neither did I."

"At least you're going about it for a good reason, the march," Larry was amazed by what he was hearing. He was trying to find some supportive way to respond.

"I can't claim that," Scott answered. His voice was heavier now, close to sounding like he was terribly depressed. "I was going to do it anyway. But for my own sake. I'm a psych major, I wanted to understand things about myself more. I'm not all that smart, just enough to get along in those classes, but I thought I'd learn something.

"Well, I did. I learned enough to understand that I was starting to get self-destructive. I've been doing ... more. I've been joking around and saying more things to people and I was picking out the worst ones possible to do it with, the real rednecks who would've beat the shit out of me, or tried real hard."

Larry was amazed to hear someone like Gilson say he worried about physical violence. He thought that fear was his own private preserve. But he didn't want to interrupt Scott's speech, so he didn't say anything about it.

"I was going to do it somehow, I figured, and I just got to the point where I realized I had the power to decide how that was going to be. I could create a big scandal – I nearly did do that a couple times – or I could walk into that meeting tonight and go to Chicago and join the protest. I could do it all with some dignity. I could at least choose the time. But I didn't go in. I couldn't do it."

"But you told *me*," Larry continued his defense. "And you can still go to Chicago. You know you aren't the only one who's stopped himself from coming out. Look at me. That would've been my first meeting too. I haven't dared go before. I've never dared go to any group where I might get to know people in any way.

"In a way ..." Larry hesitated now. Did he really want to admit this to Scott? He had to, he decided. If not now, when? If not Scott, who? "In a way, I've used my chair to make sure people didn't know I was gay. People don't seem to think that we have all our emotions if we don't have all our bodies. They get so used to thinking of us as cripples, they're fine just leaving big gaps in the whole of who we are. So I could have gone for a long time, maybe forever, without anyone knowing the real me. But I couldn't do it, really. I had to try to find out what the real person was like, and I couldn't do it by myself. Does that make any sense?"

Oh, god, please say something Scott, don't leave me out here alone after I've said that.

"Couple of sick puppies, aren't we?" Scott said quickly and quietly. "The real walking wounded of the world."

"We aren't both walking with our wounds," Larry said, surprising himself that he'd ever joke about his chair.

For one minute it seemed that Scott was someplace between crying and laughing. He seemed to be caught between a flood of emotions, all of them contradicting one another. He was embarrassed by what he'd just said. He was scared that he was having this conversation about himself. He was unsure what this all meant to Larry. But he beat back the demons and somehow forced himself to smile. He reached over and grabbed hold of Larry's wrist.

IV

Joseph Farmdale threw down the copy of the Chicago *Tribune* in disgust. Again! Theodore had found still another way to fan the anger and fear that were sweeping through the city.

Joseph stood up and poured himself a fresh cup of coffee from the pot he'd ordered brought up with the newspaper. Alex wasn't around. He must be out on his morning run. The man never seemed to stop working on himself and his body. Whenever there was a moment another person might use for relaxation, Alex used it for exercise of some sort. If Danny were here, the boy would have joined his lover on the jog.

If Danny were here ... They needed young Fortelli's presence now, he and Alex both. Danny could calm them, give them a moment's pleasure. Danny had that power over Alex and Joseph. In a different manner for each of them, of course. Danny and Alex were sexual lovers, joined by emotions and needs that hadn't crossed Joseph's mind in years. Still, Danny Fortelli had a special place in Joseph Farmdale's heart. Another man his age, finding himself so attracted to a younger man, but without any sexual desire, might think in terms of the youth being the son that he'd never had. Farmdale wondered about his own feelings for Danny. Joseph had sons; that wasn't the issue. Perhaps it was even more simple: Maybe, Farmdale realized, he just wanted another chance to start again with a young man. Maybe the ending could be different this time.

"Bah!" he said out loud, angry at his own foolishness. A new start wouldn't change what already was, what already had been, and he had to deal with reality, not fantasies.

But the fantasy was so appealing, he had to admit. He thought about the vicarious pleasure he got watching the relationship that had developed between the two gay men who were so important in his life.

Alex had met Danny in one of his early missions. Kane had freed the boy from an unscrupulous circle of pimps who'd been blackmailing young men in Boston into prostituting themselves. Alex Kane usually walked away after those successes, but that one time he hadn't able to do that simple thing. That one time, Alex Kane had found himself drawn to another man as he hadn't been attracted in years. Now they were a pair, a couple, lovers, partners, the most complete entity Farmdale had ever seen.

That thought alone allowed Farmdale to relax. There were such good people in the world, he realized. It was something he lost sight of at times, especially now when he was faced with the duplicity and malevolence of Theodore's activities.

The article in today's paper that had made him so angry reported that a real estate trust, one which had just recently accumulated vast holdings in the city's most prestigious neighborhoods, had made a blood test for AIDS antibodies a requirement for a leasehold. The demand was patently outrageous, but even so, it slipped through a loophole in the law. It was legal. But who would be willing to accept such an invasion of privacy and volunteer for a blood test?

That was what had gotten the story onto the front page of the *Tribune.* There had been blocks-long lines outside the company's office the day after the policy had been announced. There was no question what the subtext of the offering had been: *In this time of pestilence, we will give you housing where there are no homosexuals.* That proved to be something that an astonishing number of Chicagoans wanted to have.

How could so many people accept that offering? Farmdale wondered. There were so many good people who were out there, common people, only wanting to go about their work and their play and not wanting to harm others. But they would accept this horrible ploy; they would rent housing that excluded others. *But why should I be surprised?* Farmdale thought. *It's my own son who's doing all of this.* He didn't doubt it for a moment. The *Tribune* had reported that the real estate firm involved in the blood tests was unknown to all their sources in the city's business circles. When they dug further, Joseph knew, they'd discover one of Theodore's corporate shells. If they got too close, the company, and its records, would disappear completely.

Theodore had been using his money in these diabolical ways for months now, perhaps he'd been at it for years. His investments seemed to defy economic logic. They were all aimed at humiliating gay men, at the very least. They were often aimed at much more drastic ends than simple degradation.

Joseph sat down and tried, still once more, to find a rational reason for all of this. He would have welcomed evidence that he'd been a bad father to Theodore. He kept searching the past for some incident that might have led Theodore to become this vile creature.

But he couldn't find one. It never worked, no matter how often he went over the past. There was never one thing Joseph could see that he or anyone else had ever done to Theodore which could possibly justify the man's bigotry.

He had not been a perfect father. Joseph wasn't trying to fool himself about that. But he'd been there for the child when he'd been growing up, at least as much as other parents had been. He'd taken great delight in all his children's upbringing and had followed their progress in school.

He'd been a disciplinarian, but never a truly harsh one. He had, if anything, given the children too much. They certainly had never had a moment's fear of going without any material thing. But they hadn't been spoiled the way so very many others of their class had been.

Could it be, then, that there is simply such a thing as an evil person!

Farmdale wanted to hate that being if he could only find the strength to do it. He wanted to hate him with every particle of passion that existed in his own soul. But he could not ever get himself past that one barrier: *This is my son.*

Nor could Joseph Farmdale forget that he'd gone through all of this once before. So many years ago. There had been another time when he'd wondered what he'd done wrong in bringing up one of his children. He would never forget the chain of events that'd begun with a letter he'd received from his oldest child, James.

That letter was crucial to the entire series of events that followed it. What had Theodore thought about it? Joseph didn't know. He could see the repercussions, but he simply did not know what Theodore really felt about the things James had had to say.

The revelations had been too tumultuous in Joseph's own life for him to be aware of the reverberations they created in other peoples' existences.

Communications from James were hardly a surprise. Even when he'd gone into the Marines, that boy had been utterly persistent in keeping up a close relationship with Joseph. The other children would rebel at times, or demand a moment of autonomy, but James would write his weekly letter and expect his answer – and complain strongly if he didn't receive it. This one letter had begun with the routine kind of information James would send his father. There were the usual complaints about the intolerable tropical weather in Vietnam, the terrible food, and the losing battle that was being fought under the leadership of endlessly incompetent generals.

But there had been one paragraph which had grabbed Joseph's attention because it was so unlike anything else James had ever written to Joseph. It was a description of a new recruit in James's company. Joseph had read something between the lines which perturbed him. Or was he simply made uncomfortable by how detailed James had been in describing the new man physically?

The letters continued; Joseph ignored his own distress over the constant intrusion of that Marine into the correspondence. He refused to challenge James on just why an officer was spending so much time with an enlisted man. And he refused to acknowledge that James had taken that Marine on a leave with him to Saigon.

But the avoidance couldn't go on. James had finally written and admitted to his father that he was in love, with Alex Kane, the son of a Greek fisherman from Portsmouth, New Hampshire. This was the only love James expected to have in his life, he'd told his father. When Joseph Farmdale had finally understood that his own son was telling him that he was a homosexual, he had spent days wondering what developmental flaw had scarred James. He damned the boy's dead mother for her weak genes. He wanted an investigation of his preparatory school, sure the tutors there must have seduced him into some kind of contagious state of immorality.

Most others would have recoiled from the anger and the loss that Joseph Farmdale felt over James's confession. But James had stuck by him, walked him through an education on the subject, and finally, with the sheer weight of persistence and passion, had convinced Joseph that, whatever else was involved, his love for this other man was so very strong that it must have been the product of something good. In the end, it'd been almost that simple. Except the rest of the world hadn't been educated, hadn't seen the depth of the feelings, hadn't understood that there are ways in which some people could be different than others and still have worthwhile lives.

Instead, another Marine had been consumed by his own ignorance and his hatred of homosexuals and he'd taken up his rifle and shot James in the back in the rotting jungles of Vietnam.

It all ended then.

James's death was a blow to Joseph. It was all the more horrible because of the advances he and his son had made with one another. By going through the whole process of learning to understand their individual feelings, the man and his son had grown closer, more than ever before.

But, in another way, it had all begun then.

Because, just as Joseph Farmdale had lost James, he had found Alex Kane. The very moment on that battlefield when Kane had discovered that James had not been shot by one of the enemy in front of them, Kane had understood. He'd known what had happened. He'd turned on the murderer and he had extracted justice, there and then, as judge and jury.

Farmdale had heard the story when he'd stormed the Pentagon demanding all the details of his son's death. They'd tried to keep the truth from him, a common reaction in those days of government lies and hidden activities. But Farmdale had found out all about it. And he'd found out that they were going to send Alex Kane through a court martial for the crime.

A man of Joseph Farmdale's position normally accrues many chits in Washington. There are donations made and secrets kept; there are favors given and others held back. Farmdale cashed them all to have Alex Kane freed. Whatever the Marines thought he'd done, Alex Kane had not committed a crime, not so far as Farmdale was concerned.

Besides, Joseph had other plans for Alex. He had one huge master plan, in fact. He'd gotten the young Marine out of Southeast Asia and then tracked him down after he was released from the military. Kane had thought to drown himself in the underworld. Drugs and drink, anonymous sex and self-hatred would all combine to let him forget James Farmdale.

That was not the father's intention. Far from it. Joseph Farmdale hadn't wanted Alex Kane to forget James. He wanted Kane to remember him with a fire in his stomach that would fuel him to avenge James's death. His son couldn't be brought back to life, Joseph had known that. But, dedicated to his memory, Alex could become a one-man army of justice to see that other homosexuals didn't die without cause, didn't suffer without reason, didn't languish without hope.

How long had it been going on? Joseph couldn't quite remember. But he did know that the battle had been going their way – until this damnable virus mutated its way into the bloodstream of America, spawning new levels of panic and blame.

And that was when Theodore had begun to move. He'd used the virus to justify some of his most horrible plots. The real estate scheme was only one example. He'd also picked up on the new romance of conservatism that was sweeping the country. They'd just recently discovered that Theodore had funded a quasi-military rightist group in Philadelphia, one founded on racist and anti-semitic principles as well as homophobia. That group of urban terrorists had been willing to shut down an entire city in order to get to the homosexuals they wanted to slaughter. That had been the first indication of just how far Theodore was willing to go. There was evidence there, in the Philadelphia operation, that hinted at an even greater threat from the younger Farmdale. Alex and Danny had been able to stop them that last time. But, now? Again? Could they come through once more?

And did Joseph even want them to? Did he want them to catch his own son? He knew perfectly well what the probable outcome would be if Alex were to win the battle.

Alex Kane stormed into the suite at that very moment. Farmdale looked up to see Alex in a fury. He had been running, he was wearing a jogging outfit. Oblivious to Farmdale's presence, Alex began to remove the scanty clothing. Many people, Farmdale knew, would love to be here in this room to view this remarkable body. But Farmdale had never, himself, been attracted to men. He could only view Kane the way he judged the finest of his stable of thoroughbred horses.

The lines of Kane's body showed wonderful blood stock. There was hardly any body hair at all to obscure their lines. Now that Alex had stripped down to his athletic supporter,

Farmdale could see that sculpted physique easily. It was, without doubt, flawless. The skin was especially noticeable, the color was so pale that Joseph understood once again why so many people spoke of Alex as looking very much like a classic Greek statue.

Joseph was prepared for one of Kane's curt remarks. He'd probably just announce he was taking a shower, or else complain that something was wrong with the room. But the glint of anger in Alex's eyes wasn't from some minor inconvenience and it obviously wasn't the prelude to one of the baiting remarks that the man so often threw at Farmdale in their continuing banter.

This was much more intense and it was much more dangerous. "You've seen the paper?"

"Yes," Farmdale picked up the *Tribune* to prove it.

"I know what Theodore's doing with all of his moves here in Chicago. I made some calls before I went out this morning. I've thought through all the information and I'm sure of it, I know his plans."

"What? What could Theodore be up to? I haven't made head nor tails of it except to assume it's just an ongoing series of skirmishes to worsen the way things have been going lately for gay men."

"It's more than that. This time, it's much worse." Alex moved over to Farmdale. He stood, hesitating for a moment before he continued. "He's going to kill them. He's going to kill them all."

Joseph felt an icy shudder take hold of his body. He normally would have avoided Alex's nearly naked body, but now he reached out and grabbed hold of Kane's biceps, desperate to understand, or desperate to prove him wrong.

"He's trying to get them here for the march. It's the only thing that makes any sense. He's doing everything he can to inflame public opinion and to draw as many people here for the demonstration as he can.

"Your people called before you woke up. They reported that some paramilitary camps in the South have been suddenly deserted. There are hundreds of trained troops on the loose, no one knows where they are. They're on their way here. We have to stop them."

"But those are just grown-up cowboys," Joseph protested. "You can't expect ..."

"Those are full-grown men, many with backgrounds in the service, who hate everything we stand for. They've been duped by a group of asshole cult leaders to believe they're on a mission to save America. Usually they run off to Central America or Afghanistan or some other place like that and collect their war trophies, if they can get out alive.

"But the communists aren't the only enemies those people fear and they're not the only ones they've been taught to hate. They're on their way to Chicago, unless I'm very, very wrong. And here they're going to find thousands and thousands of defenseless gay people."

"Oh, god, no." Farmdale slumped down in his chair. "What can we do? We could never stop the marchers from coming here. It's become a pilgrimage in their eyes.

"And *why?!* Why is Theodore doing this?"

"Because," Alex said, answering Joseph's most hated question, "he hates us. He hates everything about those of us who're gay. And he hates you because you're on our side. He wants us dead. All of us. And we have no choice but to meet his challenge."

V

"All right, Scott, what gives?"

Scott Gilson was standing in front of his locker. He'd just come out of the shower and was naked except for the towel wrapped around his waist. "I don't know what you mean, Junior."

"Hell, you don't. You've been walking around this place like a candidate for the psycho ward for the past ten days. You hardly spend any time in the room, just barely come home to sleep. Something's going on and I want to know what it is."

Scott turned around and looked at the black man. They'd been in the shower together after practice. Junior didn't bother to cover himself with his towel. He was huge, well-muscled, and carried himself in a way that accentuated his strength. The first day they'd met, the day they'd both arrived on the campus of Mansford State and discovered they were going to be roommates as well as teammates, the guy had told Scott not to use his real name, Alfred. He was "Junior" to all his friends, he'd said – and to all his women, of whom there had seemed to be dozens. Scott had never quite believed the ridiculous contradiction between the nickname and linebacker's bulk.

They'd gotten along in the two years primarily because they didn't interfere with each other's privacy, and they had already agreed to keep on rooming with one another when they started next semester. In the dorm and here in the locker room, they'd seen one another naked often, but for the first time, Junior's nudity made Scott very uncomfortable.

Scott reached into his locker and dragged out his jockey shorts. He quickly stepped into them, as though the cotton fabric could give some protection he thought he needed. He pulled a t-shirt over his head and then sat down to put on his socks.

"What is it?" Junior asked again, his tone more insistent.

"Nothing. I'm fine. I just have a lot of work and ... that's all."

Junior leaned over and put a hand on Scott's neck. The intimate move made Gilson's back stiffen. "You got a woman? Is that it?"

"Come on, Junior, leave me alone. I don't ask you about your private life."

"Don't have to," the big man smiled, "I tell you all about it anyway. So, is it a woman?"

Scott stood up and took his slacks off their peg. He bent over, preparing to step into them, when Junior asked, "Or is it a man?"

Scott froze. He stuttered, trying to make up an answer that would deflect that question.

Junior had opened his own locker and had put on his own underwear. He didn't pay any attention to the awkward way that Scott was trying to form words. He took that reaction as an answer in itself. "I'm not surprised," Junior said nonchalantly.

"What does that mean?" Junior had just verbalized some of Scott's worst fears and it forced him to finally find something to say.

"Hey, don't worry, man," Junior said in a calm voice. "I don't care what kind of sugar you want to lick, so long as it tastes sweet to you." Then he winked, wickedly, Scott thought at first. But he realized it was just lascivious, a little act to show him that Junior thought his proclivities were as natural as the black man's own. "I think we should go have a cup of coffee together, Scott. Just like roommates. Time we had a little talk, don't you think?"

They finished dressing and walked over to the student union. During the walk over, they hardly spoke, making only a few unimportant remarks about the coaches and the team's prospects next year.

But as soon as they sat down at their table, Scott blurted out, "How did you know?"

"I didn't really know," Junior said. "There's nothing about you that's off, if that's what you're asking. It's just that it makes sense. Here I've been living with the one man on campus that any skirt would want to get into bed with, and he never does it. Ever! I wondered about that. I gotta tell you, so have a lot of other people. You know what they call you?"

"No." The worst and most degrading names went through Scott's mind. They had known, they'd been calling him ...

"Snowman, 'cause you never show a single emotion. You can look at a woman who's after you or a fan who worships you, and you don't give off a thing back to them. You always seem to walk through life like an icicle.

"It's fine by me if a man wants to keep his distance and his secrets. I'd always wanted to have a different kind of roommate, but you never bother me, that's for sure. You walk into the room, nod every once in a while, do your studying, never drink, never party, never cause trouble. Hell, Gilson, most of the squad isn't even sure if you're human.

"I at least knew better than that. There's gotta be something inside everyone, something that needs touching, that's all. I wondered about the men only because I couldn't figure out why you didn't respond to women. Then, there's a way I'd see you looking in the weight room sometimes. No one else can tell, don't worry," he shook his head when he saw Scott's eyes widen after he'd made the simple comment about the work-out room.

"It's just that I live with you, man, I see more. And I was out looking for answers, you see. I knew something was going on with you, I just didn't know what. I was willing to entertain any notion if it made it easier for me to understand your mind.

"Once in a while, I saw, when that Danny Fortelli starts going at it and his t-shirt lifts up or his jock strap slips a little bit, it looked like you might want to go over there and start some slurping. Is that him, Fortelli?"

"No." Scott said it quickly and adamantly at first. He was blushing. He had lusted after the school's star gymnast for a long time, but always from afar. He'd known Danny was gay – everyone did, the guy was the coordinator of the gay group on campus – and that had made him seem more accessible in a way. It'd been easy to fantasize about him because of it. Then, more quietly, Scott said, "No," again. This time he smiled. Larry Menario was a long way from Danny Fortelli.

"Well, too bad. I could picture that. I mean, Danny's one pretty guy. Probably breaking as many girls' hearts as you are in this place."

"What do you mean, you could picture that? You don't mean ..."

"No, no," Junior laughed, "not me, Scott. I am tried and true, I am single-minded in my pursuit of beautiful females. But it doesn't surprise me when a guy wants a guy. If anyone wants pants as much as I want skirts, I gotta pay attention.

"And it makes sense for guys like us. I mean, like today, you and I were in there, dressed in nothing but those skimpy shorts and jocks underneath, our asses hanging out between the straps. We worked out together, we yelled and screamed to work us through those reps, like we do every day. After-wards, we stand there and we look at each other's body and we comment on our development.

"I don't know how many times I've told you how well you're doing on building up your lats and I don't know how often I listen to you compliment me on my abs. We're ob-sessed by male bodies.

"Then we go out on the field, slapping each other's butts, and we grab hold of other guys, hugging them for dear life, kissing them when they make a touchdown for us, and burying our faces in their asses if we have to in order to keep them from making one for the other team.

"I'll tell you the truth, even though I've never had one of those thoughts in my life, I have to admit I don't understand why more of us don't jump on each other's bones after a game when we've had all that physical contact. I don't know why people can't be more honest about guys wanting to suck cock when we make such a big thing about this masculinity shit."

That hit home. "It's not a question of a piece of cock, Junior. It's different than that."

"Oh, god, Scott, don't go getting all up in arms about love and that stuff. You know perfectly well what a sucker I am for all of it. But the warm stuff you get between the sheets is one of the benefits, isn't it?"

"I don't know." Scott knew his answer sounded very weak. He'd barely whispered it.

"Scott, are you going through all this and not getting any? I mean, the reason a man loves is to make love. I know that. The feelings are fine and the romantic notion's great, but it's that touching that makes it all real."

"I haven't had it." That's all Scott could bring himself to say.

"Then we'd better have a talk here," Junior said. His tone had changed. "I'm not going to live with some stupid-assed closet case that's going to moan and groan his life away. Hell, I thought it was exciting that you finally told the truth, maybe you just discovered the truth for all I know. But I don't want ..."

"He can't have sex."

"Religion? Does he have God tying up his prick? He sick in the head that way?"

"No. It's more than that." Junior was as much of a friend as Scott had. What'd been going on with Larry had been making him crazy lately. It certainly seemed that Junior was okay about everything, that he wasn't some insane homophobe. Scott had to tell someone. This was his best chance:

"The guy's paralyzed from the waist down. *Completely*

paralyzed. He can only get around in a wheelchair. He's got real problems about that ... I can't convince him it's okay. I mean, damn, Junior. I've never felt this way for anyone. This guy's dynamite. He's got a four-point average. He reads everything. He's a whole lot smarter than I am. He's amazing in so many ways. Anyone else would have just given up after what happened to him. But he hasn't.

"And he's an athlete! He races his chair, isn't that wicked good! You know what his dream is? The Boston Marathon! Hell, most of the guys with their legs can't make it the whole course of the Marathon, and he wants to do it in a fucking wheelchair!

"And he works out. That sounds so simple, but, for him, it's a real big deal. People like you and me go to the gym every day and we don't even think about it. But he wants to stay in shape for his racing, so he has this whole thing outfitted in his room. All we do is stuff our balls in our jocks and go to it. He had to save up his money to get this special rig. For him to do a work-out takes half an hour just to get ready. He makes us look so stupid, so selfish.

"You and me, we're so used to these bodies and all we can do with them, if you took them away from us, what would we ever do? Would we have the guts to find another outlet, or would we just hang it up? I think I would. I've lived off this body of mine.

"I use this as a shield," Scott said, pounding his own chest with his fist. "This is what people see and why they like me. I do it so they never look any further than this. I've had this secret of mine for years. I've done everything I could to cover it up and to make sure that no one gets further than look-ing at what I show them and the big smile that goes with it. Because I've known what was behind it.

"So they call me a snowman, huh? Well, Junior they're right. I've worked just as hard getting that act together as I have at football.

"If you took being an athlete away from me, if you made me go out there without this stuff that people will accept because they think it's my justification for being alive, hell, I think I'd just fold it up, Junior. I'd just fold it up and fade away.

"But he didn't do that. I downright admire him. He's alive in ways that I'm not. He's got problems, of course he does, and the biggest one is this chip on his shoulder. That's his way of keeping other people distant. I've broken through it in most ways. But I can't ..."

"You scared of his body?" Junior broke in. "Is that it? Are you the one that's scared of what it looks like? What it'd feel like?"

"Leave it to you to punch the nail," Scott said. He was both frightened to have this subject come up, and overwhelmed with gratitude that Junior had spoken about the problem out loud. "What if I am turned off by it? What if we get to do something and I touch him and I can't stand it? He's never been with anyone. No one's ever paid any attention to him at all. What if I get this close to him and then, when it's time to put up, I can't ..."

"It isn't going to happen that way, Scott." Junior made the statement with authority. Scott hadn't expected his roommate to speak in such a soft and reassuring tone. "It just is not going to happen that way.

"You love this guy. You should see your face when you talk about him. You've pulled this big act of being so cold to people – they all think it's because you're the big star, I knew it was something different – but when your feelings do come out this way, man, they come out strong and loud and they are right there for the world to see them. That's 'cause they're authentic. They're real. They're you.

"You have it bad for this guy. I bet if you sat there and thought about the man's mind, it'd still give you a hard-on."

"Yeah, well," Scott blushed once more.

"'Yeah, well,' yourself," Junior said. "Now, let's talk about real stuff here. Let's get down to the nitty-gritty of it all. You are a strong healthy buck, God knows we know that about you. So you're going to want to do some things with your body this guy can't. He won't begrudge that. You know why?

Because the kind of getting off that you're telling me he can't do isn't what it's all about, friend.

"It's about touching. It's about having someone who cares put his arms around you. It's about taking away all those barriers and letting the skin mesh. So what if you're the one's going to shoot off and make the sheets messy and he won't? He's going to get to touch you and you're going to get to touch him.

"You got to think of it that way, Scott. You gotta remember, you need to feel him as much as he needs to feel you."

Scott smiled, finally, and shrugged. "Thanks, Junior."

"Hey, don't worry. Just don't come back to the room tonight, okay? You have better things to do than listen to me snore."

"Tonight? I don't know ..."

"No time like the present for doing what needs to be done," Junior said. He stood up and picked up his jacket. "Let's talk more, later. About the rest of it, okay? How we're going to handle the world when they find out the big star's got a message for them they're not expecting. But now, you forget all that. You go see your sugar, you make sure he gets something sweet tonight."

•   •   •

"Come in." Larry wasn't used to having people knock on his door – at least, he hadn't been used to it until recently. As soon as he'd heard the sound, he knew it'd be Scott.

"Hi." Scott looked different than usual. There was something teasing about him that Larry had never seen before.

"How are you doing?" Larry had been practicing sounding noncommittal. He wasn't at all sure he was ready to let Scott know how important these visits were. Actually, he wasn't sure he wanted Scott to know how important Scott was. "Did you read that book?"

Sharing things like books was as far as Larry'd gotten in this whole thing. He knew that Scott wasn't much of a reader and he probably would never know how much the books meant to Larry. But, in his own way, Larry felt some connection just knowing Scott was reading things that were important to him.

"Part of it. It's good." Scott was moving around the room, not taking his usual chair. He was looking over the walls. He'd been amazed to find a newspaper photo of himself as part of one of the collages that Larry had hung up. This creation was composed of pictures of male athletes. One shot showed Scott jumping up in the air to grab a pass; his legs were spread far apart, his jersey had lifted up and his bare stomach was visible from the low waist of his pants to the beginning of his rib cage.

It was clear that the photos Larry had chosen were a kind of private "soft-core porn". They were obviously erotic. But Larry and Scott had avoided any mention of Scott's picture being part of the collection. They'd both immediately deflected the conversation to a discussion of Danny Fortelli's photograph, showing him on the parallel bars. Even then, they didn't discuss the sexuality of the picture, only Fortelli's chances of repeating the state collegiate gymnastic championships.

Scott stood there and grinned at the collage. His hand went to his midsection and he looked down at it. He looked over to Larry next, but the smile didn't go away. "Think it's sexy, huh?"

Larry was on his bed; he'd been reading a book which he'd dropped when Scott'd come in the room. Now, just for the sake of having something – anything – to do, he picked it up again. "You're well-built." God, what a stupid statement! But what else could he say? Of course he thought it was sexy. But the friendship that was developing between himself and Scott was all he dared hoped for.

Larry's eyes were glued to the words on the page in front of him. He couldn't see a single one of them, though. He felt, rather than saw, Scott moving over towards his bed. There was some movement. He couldn't help but look over. Just when he did, Scott's shirt was being pulled over his head. There was the stomach he'd revered, made an icon of in his collage.

"What are you doing?"

"Getting comfortable." Scott laughed at his own line. Then he sat on the edge of the bed and nudged Larry over, forcing him to make room. They'd spent a lot of time talking these past few days and more than a few times, they'd held each other in various ways. But Larry'd never had to deal with Scott's bare skin before, not like this. He wanted to say something, make Scott put his shirt back on, stop this, because this was getting too difficult.

But before he could say anything, Scott's naked arm went around his shoulders and drew him close. Larry had only been held like this by nurses. They hadn't felt this way. There hadn't been the mass of this athlete's body. It felt surprisingly warm. As well-developed as the muscles were, they were surprisingly soft to his touch. Larry unconsciously turned his face towards Scott and felt his cheek rub into the other man's armpit. There was a bit of moisture there, a clean smell of soap and fresh sweat.

"Oh, god," Larry moaned.

Then Scott turned and kissed him. It was almost more than Larry could stand. There was the odor and the wetness and the warmth and then there were lips pressing against his. He couldn't help himself. He kissed back, his own mouth hungry for this new experience.

Scott shifted, lifting himself up and over Larry, bringing his chest down on top of his partner's. Then his hands were reaching up underneath Larry's shirt, a palm was pressing against Larry's own belly, then moving up to his chest.

"No, no," Larry moaned and pulled his face away from Scott's. "We can't. I can't."

"I know. I read about it. I looked it up in the library and then I went and talked to someone at the health office," Scott admitted. He was staring directly into Larry's eyes. "But we can hold each other this way. At least this way."

"The rest of me is …" Larry said. "I hate the rest of me."

To Larry's horror, Scott's hand moved off his chest and moved downwards. It glided back over his stomach and onto his abdomen, crossing that part of his body which, so far as Larry was concerned, divided the pretense of health from the fact of atrophy.

"Don't touch me there! Please!" Larry only whispered, but there was a scream in the soft tones.

"I've never touched anyone there like this," Scott said. "I don't want to touch anyone else there like this. But I want to touch all of you. It's you. It's part of you. I love you, Larry. I love all of you."

Larry lifted up his head and watched the hand as it moved down over his legs, those poles of atrophied flesh. He waited for the inevitable, for Scott to jerk away from them. But the hands just kept on moving, gently exploring that part of him that he, himself, had hardly been able to stand looking at for so many years. He stared at Scott's face, waiting to see the revulsion. It'd been there in so many other faces. But Scott didn't show it. There was nothing that betrayed any abhorrence.

"Touch me too," Scott said softly into Larry's ears. "No one's ever touched me either."

VI

Danny Fortelli stood and looked at the three other Mansford students. *Well,* he thought, *this is a surprise.* But he kept his head. One of the many things Alex had taught him was to be prepared to roll with the punches when the unexpected happened.

"Let me get this straight, Gilson," he said calmly, "you want to come to the march, and you know your being there will produce a lot of media attention and you want me to help you plan for it. But you make me come to this dorm room for the meeting. You're not even willing to walk into the Gay Students Alliance office to talk to me?"

"That's not why we wanted to meet you here," Scott said. "We couldn't go to the office because it's not wheelchair accessible. It's part of my agreement with Larry that I won't go anywhere that he can't go."

Damn! Danny was mad. After all the care that'd been put into making the group something that could be used by all the gay students at the college, he and the rest of them had been so stupid they'd overlooked the physical barriers for the guys who had physical limitations. He knew better than to just try and be apologetic. There was only one thing to do in a case like this: change things. He quickly wondered if they could trade offices with some other organization, perhaps one that had space in the new Student Union.

But there was something else going on here now. "I have to admit, Scott, this is all pretty hard to take in. You've been the least approachable person on this campus ever since I started to take classes here. I see you in the gym all the time and I've tried to be friendly. You've been rude about it. I always took it for granted that you were homophobic. Now, you tell me you're gay and that you and your lover want to go to Chicago with the rest of us. It's pretty unexpected.

"And, Junior," Danny turned and said to the third man, "I still don't get what you're doing here."

"White folks marched on Selma, Danny. It's not only gays that're pissed off by what's happening to homosexuals in this country. My parents lived in Alabama in those days and they've told me what it was like and how important it was that others took part in their marches and stood with them. I'd like to think I was a decent enough person that I'd remember those lessons on my own. But now I discover I'm living with a gay guy and have been for two years. When one of my bro's is in on the action, I can't sit on the sidelines.

"Are you saying you don't see our idea? Come on, Fortelli. Any march has to have marshals. You need some people there to help keep order and to make sure none of the bystanders get too rambunctious. Well, what more could you ask for than this awesome duo from the Mansford State College Rams? You think many people are going to mess with Scott and me? I don't."

"No," Danny admitted with a smile. He was dwarfed by the two football players and even he, he had to admit, would've hesitated before he took these two guys on. "I wouldn't mess with you unless I had to, Junior.

"And, you're right. We've been asked to help supply marshals for the march. I'm fine with it if you want to come along.

"About the publicity," Danny continued, "what exactly do you want to do about it, Gilson? What kind of help do you want?"

Scott took a deep breath. "Well, Larry and I have already talked to our parents." It was obvious from the way Gilson spoke that the encounters hadn't been pleasant. "We'll handle that flack later. I told the coach. He's not exactly pleased and we'll have to see if I'm going to play next year or not."

"You are or I'm not," Junior said with a booming voice. "That's non-negotiable."

"Junior, I don't know, there's going to be a lot of flak about it. You can just imagine what some of the guys on the teams we play are going to do once they hear."

"Well, Scott," Junior answered, "I've known you were the star of this show since the first day I saw you on the practice field. I figured all along you were going to be the one that got the glory. But I also knew that the pro scouts were smart enough that they'd be able to see just who it was that punched those holes in the opposition's lines that you got to run through. I tell you, you're my key. If I'm not playing with you, no one's going to notice me, 'cause no pro scout's going to come and look at a two-bit team like this one unless there's a big name on it.

"That's you. So, I'm warning you – and I'll warn the coach – you're on that team next fall, or I'm gone. All the way to the nearest Division I football program."

Scott was obviously delighted to hear that defense and he was relieved that Junior made it less difficult by putting it in terms of his own self-interest.

"Anyway," Scott continued, "that's all in whatever shape it's going to be, for now, at least. So," he swallowed hard, "the next thing is to figure out what to do when some newspaper reporter recognizes me.

"I'm not trying to be an asshole about it. I'm not saying that I'm such hot shit the whole thing will revolve around me ..."

"Don't apologize for that," Danny said. He understood the position Gilson was in. "Let's face it, you're one of the people the press likes to write about: The young, handsome star of the out-of-the-way school who leads his team to unexpected glory and all of it. You're only being realistic when you bring this up."

"Thanks, Danny," Scott was relieved now that he knew Fortelli understood what he foresaw happening. "I'm just not ready to stand up on a podium. I guess it might've helped had Larry and I talked about it. But this is all too new to me for that. But I'm willing to be a marshal, especially with Junior helping me out.

"I'd appreciate some help going over some simple statements, things I can say that'll sound right. I thought I'd just be ready to tell them I was there because I was gay and I was a marshal because I wanted to be a part of the march. I'm going to tell them that's all there is to it and I won't have anything more to say."

"Scott, that sounds great! Look, not everyone's supposed to be a public speaker in this thing. There are plenty of guys who're just there because they know they have to be. I respect your position fully. But I think you're trying to say more. I get the feeling you're saying it's all right to send the press to you."

"Yeah. That's it. So long as I don't have to stand in front of an audience, I'm willing to talk to anyone, in small groups or one-on-one. I want to do everything I can, now that I'm inching my way out ..."

"Inching!" Junior snorted. "Hell, three weeks ago you weren't even living, and now you got a boyfriend, you're going to demonstrations, you're having planning sessions, you're ..."

"Okay, Junior, okay," Scott smiled off his roommate's comments and put a hand on Larry's shoulder. "I guess I'm just doing what I've wanted to do for a long time. I was just waiting for the right reason." Scott moved even closer to Larry and put his arm around him.

"We're set, then," Danny said. "There's room on the plane ..."

"Plane!" Junior exclaimed. "I figured we'd be doing this in cars or else by bus. I can't afford airfare to Chicago!"

For the first time in the conversation, it seemed that Danny Fortelli was uncomfortable. In fact, the other three had never seen this handsome young gymnast lose his poise.

"Yeah, well, we've had an anonymous donation of a chartered plane. It won't cost you anything. The hotel rooms are free, too."

"Hot damn!" Junior said. "You mean, no sleeping bags on dorm room floors?"

"Hardly." Danny seemed to cringe.

"It has to be wheelchair-accessible," Scott put in. Larry seemed to be smiling up at the football player and Danny understood that the athlete's vehemence about the rights of the handicapped was a part of their personal passion. "Scott, I promise you, the place we'll be staying is anything-accessible."

Danny went over the details and then it seemed there wasn't anything more to say. But when he went to leave, he noticed that Scott Gilson made some quick excuses to leave both Larry and Junior. Fortelli knew it must mean that Scott had something more to talk about, something that called for privacy. Danny made his leave-taking linger long enough so he and Scott could depart together.

There was an awkward silence between them as they walked out onto the Mansford State campus. Danny decided to leave it alone. This was Scott's show. He'd speak when he was ready.

They automatically headed towards the Student Union. It was only when they were inside that Scott asked Danny if they could have a drink of juice together in the lounge.

"Look," Scott finally began when they'd sat down, "I'm really unsure about this stuff, all of it."

"The march?" Danny asked, but he was already pretty sure that wasn't what was on Scott's mind.

"No. I mean, yeah, that's a part of it, of course. But I mean ..." Scott was very uncomfortable. "Look, I've never been here before!" he finally blurted out. "Danny, you're sort of like me. You're my age and you're an athlete and all of it. We're from the same kind of background, too. I'm hoping you can understand what I mean and maybe talk to me a little about it. I just need to share some of this with someone."

"Of course, Scott. What's going on? What's the problem?"

"Well, I'm having to learn so much all at once. I'm dealing with being gay. I'm dealing with being in love. I'm learning how to be sensitive to all the things that Larry has to go through. That's why we agreed I wouldn't meet you at Kennedy Hall. I just feel overwhelmed."

"I bet the biggest thing is being in love," Danny suggested. "That's the most overwhelming thing in the world. Or it was for me."

"Oh, Danny, you don't know. I … wake up different in the morning. I really do. I have feelings I never knew were there. Not just the happiness, but pain, hurt, fear, all of it's stuff I didn't even know that human beings went through. It's heavy duty shit, Fortelli."

"Yeah, I remember it, that beginning."

"Is it still the same for you? Does all of this last?"

"Oh, it lasts, Scott. It just gets different. Some of the fear goes away. After a while you learn to trust that the guy isn't going to leave you and that he will be there when you have to be with him, or else, there'll be a very good reason for it.

"And the passion stays, but it alters. It just changes. Some of the hunger I used to feel isn't around anymore. It's, well, it's less dramatic. But it's good. It's very good."

"Man, Fortelli, I can't wait. I mean, I've gone without for so long and now you tell me I'm going to just keep on feeling more things! Hot shit! I mean, sometimes, like now, I just feel like I'm going to cry, but just because it's too much. I'm not just happy. I'm over-loaded."

"Scott, you're making me miss my lover, a whole lot."

"Tell me about him, will you? I want to know what people are like now. I need to know how other guys handle things. Who they fall for. I need to learn so much."

"Gilson, you're acting like a cheerleader at a pep rally. Cool down. You'll meet Alex soon enough. I promise, you'll get a chance to talk to him and I promise I'll be around so we can share more experiences as things come up. But I need to know some things about you and Larry now."

"Fire away."

"Well, tell me about him and his disability and how that's going to affect you two."

Scott shrugged his shoulders. The heated passion in his voice seemed to trail away and he spoke with a much calmer conviction now. "Larry's got a spinal cord injury. It happened when he was just a kid. He's paralyzed from the waist down. That's the bottom line."

"No sex." Danny said the words as a statement, not a question.

"That's not true. Lots of people look at guys in wheelchairs and they know that they don't get the same kinds of hard-ons as you and me and so they think they don't have sexual feelings or desires or ... well, they do." His face brightened up. "Believe you me, they do.

"Larry and I just can't have all the sex you could have with someone else. And he doesn't have the same kind of orgasm, but lots of guys in wheelchairs do, you know. It depends on what kind of injury they have or what kinds of diseases put them there. There are all kinds of sexual possibilities for all kinds of people.

"Larry and I, well, we're just into being naked together and touching a lot and massaging and he has these kinds of really hot mental orgasms, they're amazing, like his mind overcomes his body in some way.

"I ... well, I just come, like anyone else." He smiled again. "I come a lot nowadays."

"But, Scott, there are a lot of guys who wouldn't be able to say that's an okay sexual relationship for them. What makes it work for you?"

"Didn't you see his arms? They're more muscular and stronger than Junior's. It's from working on them and using them on his chair all the time. And his chest is more developed than mine is, too. So, I just focus on that part of him instead of worrying about his cock and all of the rest of it. Maybe it's because I haven't had other experiences, but I doubt that. I just get off on that part of his body like crazy.

So, it works. And, I just get off on him. That's really the thing."

Danny stood up and put a hand out for Scott. "I'm glad you're coming to the march, Gilson." Scott and he shook hands. "I'm glad you're gay, too. I really am."

VII

The caravan of three chartered buses pulled into the truck-stop outside of Champaign, Illinois. Only Spike Langer got out when the buses pulled up near the bank of pay phones. Langer was about forty-five. He wore battered clothes that'd obviously seen a lot of outside wear. He was also just as obviously tired and stiff from having spent a long time on the road.

He put a coin in the pay phone and dialed the number he'd been instructed to memorize. It had a 312 area code: Chicago. He had to remember more than the simple digits of a long distance call, there was a special sequence that had to go with it. Part of security, Spike assumed.

It took longer to go through than a normal call would have. But the voice eventually did answer. "Are you at the designated point?"

"Yes, sir." Spike had been ordered to make the call from this precise phone booth at approximately this time.

"Good. The next step is a motel on a highway just south of the city. Do you have paper and pencil ready?"

Spike did and he took down the directions. "Hope it won't be much longer on the road."

"No. You're less than an hour and a half away. Go there. There'll be more instructions in an envelope with the motel manager as well as camouflage uniforms for your men."

"Cammies in the city?" Spike wasn't used to questioning orders, especially not from this voice which'd been the brains behind the whole operation for the long time Spike'd worked for this outfit. But the situation seemed strange.

There was a sharp laugh on the other end of the line. "Very *special* camouflage, Lieutenant. You'll understand when the time comes. Your men are all with you? There've been no problems?"

"None, sir. We're all ready."

"Proceed, Lieutenant. This operation may be your finest hour."

The buses made their way up the Interstate until they pulled off it at the designated exit. A few miles from there, they came to a newly constructed motel, one whose signs said it was part of a national chain, but whose outdoor bulletin board also said it wouldn't open for business for another week.

There was a groan in the bus as the men read that announcement. This was just the kind of operational fuck-up that headquarters of any kind can do to you. But Spike hadn't been let down by this boss yet. He got out of the bus once more and went to the front door.

"You're Mr. Langer?" an officious manager-type asked after he'd run into the lobby in answer to the sound of a buzzer which rang when Spike had opened the door.

"Yeah," Spike answered.

"We're all prepared for you. The kitchen staff has a steak dinner ready. Your rooms are all made up."

"But the sign says ..."

"Oh, that. We were told by our regional manager that people affiliated with the parent company would need extraordinary secrecy. We were told that this was such a special party that you wouldn't want to be bothered by transients. We've been ready for the public for over a week. But we've kept the doors closed, just for you."

He was a really twerpy kind of guy, one of those that liked the idea of just being around a real man like Langer, so Spike figured. That alleviated Spike's uncertainty about the arrangements and left Langer feeling like he was back in control. "Yeah, well, you're holding something for me, some kind of envelope?"

"Indeed," the manager said. What a slime, you could just see the vicarious pleasure the fool got out of just being close to a mysterious operation like this one. The manager led Langer back to the abandoned front desk of the motel. He pulled out a large manila package and handed it to Langer with wide-eyed enthusiasm and a melodramatic sense of shared conspiracy.

"There are also a number of cartons of goods waiting for you. I've left them in the largest function room we had, just as Mr. Fa– ... just as the regional manager ordered me to."

"Fine. I'm going to unload the guys and get their rooms assigned. Then we're going to eat that chow you got for us and we'll see about the rest.

"The minute that meal's cleared from the table, I want this joint empty. Totally. I want you and everyone who works for you *gone.* Comprendez?"

"Of course, sir. There'll be the tightest security possible."

"You're right, there will be. Because there'll be no security except what I order myself. I've got my own guards. The rest of you, out."

The manager was obviously deflated by the command. But he wasn't going to argue. This Farmdale either had him trained, or else he was getting paid a bundle. Whichever, Langer knew he wouldn't have any more trouble from the manager. He went out to get his men situated. He wanted them settled in as fast as possible. He wanted to read the orders in his envelope. He didn't have any idea just what he was about to do.

• • •

It was a fucking brilliant plan! As soon as Langer saw what the boss had set up for them, he knew this was going to be one main ring event.

The men had eaten and they'd already stowed their gear in their rooms. They were enjoying the open bar, guzzling down free beers and booze fast enough that they'd be sure to have a hell of a hangover tomorrow. Langer knew he'd better begin the speech now.

Like most of the operation, it'd been prepared by the boss. Langer was impressed all over again when he read the talk through the first time. Not only was it written in words he could speak himself, it had all the ingredients that were sure to appeal to these guys.

Langer went up to the motel rostrum at the head of the function room. "Men, give me your attention here."

The more than one hundred heads turned to face his direction. They might be rowdy later on in the night, but these were well-trained troops.

"I've gotten our final orders for this campaign. This, gentlemen, is going to be your finest hour."

"The day after tomorrow, we are going to Chicago. We are going to infiltrate an enemy operation. The forces we oppose – the forces which would undermine the moral fabric of the great United States of America – are too great for even you, our freedom fighters, to overcome on a face-to-face basis. This infiltration exercise, however, is going to allow us to bring into play even greater power that will then be aimed at our enemies."

"Men, we've been training in the forests of Alabama for years, waiting for a chance to put God and America back into the United States. We've seen the destruction of our society and we've rebelled at it.

"The leftist press thinks we're just a bunch of cowboys, over-aged summer campers who're reliving our youth. You've seen the papers and what they've written about our survivalist programs and our lessons.

"What they haven't known is that our camps have been a cover for the recruitment and training of an elite army all along. They don't know that there are over one hundred men dedicated to the principles that made this country great. We've hidden our real strength from them.

"But now we're ready to move.

"The alliance of communists, feminists and homosexuals has been out to undermine our people's morals and our nation's dedication. We have to eliminate those forces from the face of the earth!"

There was a rousing round of applause.

"This is war, gentlemen." The cheers got louder.

"This is the moment to finally act for the sake of America!" Now the men were on their feet.

Langer waited for the noise to subside. "We've been mobilized by some of the most patriotic and most inspired leadership in our country's history. With them at our fore, we can't lose. There'll be no legislature to give away our gains." The men roared their agreement. "There'll be no courts to negate our victories." The noise increased.

"This is the first chapter in a new history!" The loudest cheers came from the men.

Then Langer leaned forward and spoke with an earnest voice as he described the outlines of the action. As the men listened in rapt attention to the details of the plan, there were occasional yells of excitement and Langer could actually hear the passion grow. There was that indescribable bloodlust building among the men. He'd have a hard time containing them tomorrow. They had to wait for two more days before they got into action. But he'd do it. Langer suddenly felt a surge of power building up inside himself. Yes, he and his boss were going to do it.

In two days, it'd be Chicago. Everyone would forget the failures of those amateurs in Philadelphia. When they were done with the Windy City, what could be next? Langer had read the histories of Mussolini's March on Rome and remembered how a ragtag band of patriots had begun their pilgrimage to the Eternal City. In every town and village, they'd picked up new recruits until, by the time they'd reached Rome, they could enter the city's gates with Mussolini at the head of an army so huge no force could oppose it.

Langer couldn't help but think of himself at the head of an army like that marching on Washington, picking up recruits in all the places in Middle America where the boss's program would find ready acceptance. But it wasn't the boss he saw leading the way when the horde was moving up Capitol Hill. It was himself. Those images of *Il Duce's* triumph had filled Langer's dreams for years. Now they were approaching reality.

By the end of the speech, as Langer stood down and walked through his troops, hands slapped his shoulders and voices were calling out their allegiance. This was his finest moment. He knew what Mussolini had felt like. But he had forgotten where *Il Duce* ended up.

• • •

Langer had a hard time controlling his glee after the speech. He'd gone to the bar and had drinks with the men who'd wanted to be close to him and wanted to talk over more of the details about the operation. He held them off, difficult as that was, not wanting to reveal the final points until the last minute.

Finally, unfortunately, the men lost touch with the novelty, and the booze started getting to them. Langer found himself nearly alone at the bar. He realized, through his blurred sight, that there were only a few other men there now. One of them was that weird one, Jenner.

There had to be people like Jenner in any combat outfit. Langer knew that. They were the real killers, the men who would act when no one else would. They were the men who approached battle acting as if they weren't worried about dying, but rather hoping they might find it.

Even a veteran of Vietnam like Langer was a little freaked by a man like this. Jenner walked around with an air about him that made you think there might not be anything inside. Even a man like Langer sometimes wondered if men like

Jenner had souls.

He knew Jenner's record. He'd gotten to know all of the men's. He'd been in Nam too. Jenner'd won more medals than most men would ever dream of receiving. That wasn't surprising, most of the men here had been battle-tried. What Langer did remember as strange about Jenner's record was the psychological profile he'd shown when he'd first entered the Army Rangers.

He'd been one of the best adjusted men in his class in boot camp. Now that was a shock. Something had happened to him in Nam. Langer wondered what it was. He looked at Jenner now. He couldn't help but notice that the guy still looked like a recruiting poster. He could've filled in for John Wayne or Clint Eastwood in one of their movies.

"So, Jenner, what do you think about all of this?" Langer finally said.

"Don't matter to me," Jenner replied, not looking at Langer, just staring at the bottom of his whiskey glass. "You want me to kill some fags, I will. You told me to off the American Legion convention, I'd've done that too. You sign the check, I do the work." He slugged back what was left in the glass and then reached for the bourbon bottle and refilled it himself.

"But, don't you think this is a great opportunity? Don't you see what could happen next?"

"Politics ain't what I'm interested in, never have been."

"But you were a hero. You performed valiantly in Vietnam …"

Now Jenner turned on Langer and his usually vacant eyes glared at him. "I told you before, don't talk to me about Nam."

"What did happen to you, Jenner?" Spike was feeling his own drinks now. The question seemed important.

But Jenner had already withdrawn into himself again.

"Look, man, I'm a soldier. Only thing I know how to do is soldier. You pay the best these days, so I'm with you. That's all you need to know."

"But what does it mean to be a soldier to a man like you?"

Jenner hesitated a bit. "I wish it were cleaner, you know that? I really do. I wish it was like in those Roman days, when a man could just go into the ring with someone else and the better man walked out. I guess I'm just out of sync with the times, man. I ended up living when the best men don't win.

"That," Jenner finally admitted with unaccustomed frankness, "was what really happened to me in Nam. I saw the best men lose. I saw the best man lose. And he lost it all."

Jenner hung his head and Spike wondered if this big oaf was even crazier than he'd thought. But he was amazed to hear any kind of confession coming from Jenner and he wasn't going to lose this opportunity see what made the guy tick.

"You think you should have been the one who lost? Is that it Jenner?"

"I know I should've. I wasn't near as good a person as him and I walked out of there and I got back here. I don't deserve that. I never have."

"You want to lose now, don't you?" Langer was moving in. He hadn't spoken loudly enough for any of the others to hear what he was saying. But Jenner heard.

"I do." Once again, the big Marine threw back his whiskey glass. "But it's gotta be like that arena. It's gotta be real. I gotta find a better man to do it. I don't quit, never. And that means it's gotta be in a fight.

"That's why you like me, Langer," the man's voice was acidic now. "I told you, I'm the perfect soldier. That's what they've been telling me for years. They told me that when I was in Rhodesia and they told me again in Afghanistan.

"I don't fear death. I wait for it to come and get me the way one of these other bozos waits for a woman to climb into bed with him. I want it. But I want it to take me. I won't go quietly.

"That makes it a bargain for you to sign those paychecks of mine, Langer. I'm a walking time bomb at your service, or at the service of whoever pays me the most. You remember that.

"You'll get your money's worth from me on this one, Langer. This one's made for me. This is the one I deserve to die for." Then he walked away, leaving Spike puzzled over just what that meant.

VIII

That same night, the Mansford State College Gay Students Alliance members were boarding their flight to Chicago at Boston's Logan International Airport. The first person on board was Larry Menario, carried in on the arms of Scott Gilson.

"Holy shit," Scott said when he'd walked into the cabin of the uniquely appointed 727. "Are you sure this is for us?"

"No question about it," co-pilot Tim Ransom said.

"Scott, please put me down." Larry's voice was full of annoyance. "This is just why I didn't want you to carry me. I've gotten on planes before, damn it."

"I just thought it'd be more efficient," Scott defended himself. He put Larry onto the front seat. "Anything you want? Anything ..."

"I'm fine, Scott." Larry bit his lower tongue after he said that. He wasn't ready to fight with Scott, but the guy had to learn to let him do some things on his own.

"Okay. Okay." It hurt Larry to hear the defensiveness in Scott's voice. He didn't want to make things worse. "Look, let me go back and be with Junior. I think he'd be more comfortable if I were with him."

Larry watched his new lover walk back off the plane and felt just terrible. He knew Scott was feeling badly about him, not worried about Junior.

"First love?" Tim said.

"Some kind of love," Larry answered. It took him a second to realize that he wasn't surprised to find out that the man was gay.

The co-pilot took the seat next to him and shook his head. "I had my problems with it too."

"I don't think you have the ones I do," Larry said.

"What, you think this is all about your legs?" Tim asked. "No way. What I just witnessed was the desperation of a man trying to figure out how he was supposed to act when he fell in love with another man. You should've seen mine when we first got started. The man's dream had been to wash someone's floor. He went at it like someone possessed, the way some other guy might go after sex!

"I knew he was deranged then, but I didn't realize it was only the beginning. I can do just about anything I need to do to get by. But, so far as he's concerned, I might as well live in a chair like yours. It's the sign of lovesickness."

"You really think it's that?" Larry asked. He wasn't at all sure about this new perspective on things.

"No question about it. The only thing we strong ones can do is get out of the way and let them work their stuff out. Though, I have to tell you, if yours is like mine, it's going to take forever."

"Tim!" Another man wearing a pilot's uniform came into the cabin. "There you are. I was worried about you. Do you have your bag? Did you get enough to eat? Are you sure you want to stay in Chicago for this march? I don't want you to get over-tired. Maybe we should just go back to Minneapolis. I think eating all this restaurant food isn't healthy. Maybe we should go home so I can cook you something decent."

Larry burst into laughter after he listened to Mike Ahern proving his lover's point. Tim couldn't hold back either and the two of them leaned into one another while they giggled. Mike didn't know what was going on and he'd learned that this was one of those times when he should just leave his better half alone in that weird private life of his that he seemed to share with certain strangers.

"Well, whatever. I guess I'll go up to the cockpit and make sure things are ready."

Larry got control of himself and finally was able to start talking again. "But I thought I only get this over-protectiveness because of my legs."

"I know how people react to limited abilities," Tim said, fighting off his own laughter. "But, really, there are some times when it's not that. There are times when we just have to live with the emotional needs of some kinds of lovers. I guess you and I both are stuck with the ones that insist on proving their love for us every day."

"Yeah. Well. Maybe." Larry was trying to slip into that mindset that would let him believe all of that. "You know. I just never ... well, I've never had anyone before."

"Really! Well congratulations!" Tim said. "How long has this been going on?"

"Not long at all," Larry admitted.

"Well, the best of luck in making it last. There's not much like it, having that one person, you know."

"Just having a person's pretty wonderful to me," Larry smiled.

"Then let him do some of the things he needs to do, kid. The worst enemy of any relationship's the kind of pride that won't let the other guy inside you.

"Now, I have to go. My friend's probably taken care of everything, but it does help if I go and sit by his side. His reward for all this, you see?"

"Thanks."

Just then, the rest of the Mansford group started to come on to the plane. Junior and Scott took the two other chairs that were clustered with Larry's. The plane's seating configuration wasn't like any other plane anyone had seen. The impression was more one of it being a large lounge.

"Leather upholstery!" Junior exclaimed as he sat down and buckled his seat-belt. "I don't know how Fortelli arranged all this, you guys," Junior continued. "But you gays sure know how to elect a mean coordinator if he can pull off stuff like this all the time."

"We haven't even attended a meeting yet," Larry pointed out. "We're hardly responsible for Danny's election."

"Well, if this is a clue, I can't wait to see the hotel room. I mean, the next thing you know, some foxy lady's going to come around with crystal glasses of champagne and tell me I'm the hottest dude she's been seeing in her dreams all these years."

Actually, the stewardess who appeared at that very moment wasn't about to tell Junior quite that. After all, her lover wouldn't have understood. But Monique was perfectly willing to bring the young gentleman his Dom Perignon, which was, of course, served in crystal.

Junior finished the bottle during the flight from Boston to Chicago, and he was so awestruck by the whole operation that he never spoke another word until they were at their hotel.

That, it turned out, was another surprise.

"This can't be the right place," Junior insisted when their cab stopped in front of the Barchester.

"This is the address you gave me, bub."

"Let's check it out," Scott said. He was just as surprised as Junior, but was beginning to assume that Danny Fortelli could perform miracles.

Scott carried Larry up to the front door of the hotel while Junior loaded their luggage onto Larry's chair. "We hardly look the type for this place," Larry said, having to admit the humor in it all.

The uniformed doorman saluted as they approached and then moved to help Junior bring the chair up the ramp that had been tastefully built onto the entrance. "I take it you are with the Mansford party, gentlemen." The doorman said in a voice that would have done justice to a Grade-B movie actor.

"Yeah," Junior said hesitantly. "That's us."

"Your room assignments will be waiting for you at the registration desk. If you'll kindly follow me this way."

When they got to their suite, the disbelief was total. "I don't know what kind of mistake was made," Junior said, "but this message says our room service bill is prepaid and I intend to make it worth the while of the person who went to all the trouble to set up the paperwork."

"I think you've had enough champagne," Scott teased.

"Hell, no," Junior insisted. "There is no such thing in this world as too much champagne, not so long as it's the good stuff."

"I don't think they'd know any other kind here," Larry said as Scott put him down on the big couch that dominated their sitting room.

"Let's just find out!" Junior declared as he went to the phone.

Larry looked up at Scott and shrugged. "It *is* our honeymoon."

• • •

It wasn't Danny and Alex's honeymoon. But that didn't mean their meeting was any less romantic than the one that was happening on the floor beneath them. Danny stood in the middle of the suite and waited for his lover to realize he was there. Alex was on the phone, yelling at someone about the arrangements for the march. He was demanding that the police department beef up their already substantial force to protect the demonstrators.

Joseph Farmdale had seen Danny walk in and it'd taken an emphatic hand signal from Danny to keep the old man from saying anything.

"God damn it!" Alex said as he threw down the receiver. "Can't anything go right around here?"

"Give it a chance. I have some ideas that might work for you."

Alex spun around when he heard Danny's voice and he froze when he saw that his partner had arrived. "Thank God you're here."

The two men didn't say anything more to one another. They walked across the floor and embraced.

Joseph Farmdale remembered all over again why their battle to be able to love one another was so important as he watched the pair of them. He didn't feel a moment's neglect or disapproval as the two moved towards the nearby bedroom.

He smiled to himself then and went to look out over the city of Chicago. There was such happiness in the world, he realized. And there were such good people.

Spread out in front of him, between their hotel and Lake Shore Drive, was an expanse of park, nearly a half-mile wide at this point. Here, the day after tomorrow, nearly half a million gay men would march, demanding their dignity, proclaiming their right to exist.

If only, Joseph thought, *people could see gays like Danny and Alex and understand that what goes on between them is so positive.* But he couldn't continue the thought. Because the one person in the world who was most responsible for that never happening was his own son.

IX

There was a final summit meeting with the coordinators of the march the next day in the Farmdale penthouse at the Barchester.

If the organizers were unused to canapés and cocktails at their events, they didn't say anything. They were actually too involved in the monumental scope of the details for such a large undertaking to notice the food.

"You've handled the coordination with the police, Kane, are you satisfied with what they're doing?" one of the men asked Alex.

"I wouldn't be satisfied unless I had every cop in the Midwest in on this deal. But," Alex admitted, "they know this is a big thing and they know the situation's potentially explosive. We have to take them for their word. Part of what I've assured them is that we'll police the march itself."

"That's crucial," the chairman agreed. "Fortelli, you were organizing the marshals."

"I've worked out a plan that seems the best possible. The marshals won't be marching, we'll all be placed in stationary positions along the route. As the parade goes by, those marshals whose positions have been passed will follow in the rear of the march as added protection. Once we get to the park, we then re-form in a protective circle around the gathering.

"For extra security, we're having all the marshals wear photo-IDs in addition to the usual armbands. They're all going through a training class tonight and they'll be on the streets by ten o'clock, two hours before the march."

Danny had obviously planned well and there didn't seem to be much more to add to the arrangements.

"We can't allow anyone's temper to flare." The chairman was obviously worried about that.

So was Alex Kane. "It's the major concern of the police. No matter what else they try to do, they can't change the prejudices of their officers. They're honestly trying to get the word out that this is to be as professional an assignment as possible. But, if some of our people get out of hand ..."

"And we know that there are some very angry faggots out there," the chairman acknowledged. "The marshals have to be at least as aware of that function – keeping that rage under control – as any other."

"I've made sure that word's gotten out," Danny said.

That was the last item of business on the agenda. The meeting was adjourned and Alex and Danny were left alone with Joseph Farmdale.

"Any more word on Theodore?" Danny asked.

"None." Alex was obviously enraged that he couldn't find out where his arch-enemy was.

"I've been following his business activities as closely as possible through computers and through my contacts on Wall Street," Joseph said, his voice betraying how upset he was as well. "There's nothing out of the ordinary going on, certainly nothing that would ever tell us anything about his whereabouts."

"Then all we can do," Alex said, "is make sure our men understand their orders and follow their instructions."

•　•　•

Following orders was precisely what Spike Langer also had

in mind. That night he was doing his best to follow them to the letter.

"Jesus H. Christ," one of his men complained, "I gotta get it all cut off? This is worse than boot camp."

The mercenaries were lining up for their haircuts. "Look, I can't help it if the homosexual fashion is short hair nowadays," Langer shot back. "We're going undercover and that's all there is to it. You," he pointed to another of the men. "That earring's got to go." The soldier had a miniature skull hanging from one lobe. "But the piercing's great. There are some simple gold hoops over on the other table. Put one of those on.

"Any of you guys with tattoos, you go to the leather clothing station and make sure you don't put on a shirt, unless the tattoo's got a woman on it or something. Gays are into those things now and it'll make your disguises even better if you show them off.

"No zippered blue jeans, Smith! I told you. You got to turn in your own and get the button-fly models over there.

"Kwaszkiewicz, no polyester! These guys act as though they're allergic to the stuff. Go get the all-natural cotton slacks over on that table."

The orders came fast and furious as he went around making sure that every detail of his men's uniforms was perfect.

He especially eyed Jenner. The big man was standing off to the side, his arms folded across his chest, his disgust with the operation obvious. But he was okay just dressed in the usual things he wore. So long as too many of them didn't go in for the military uniform slacks, the jump boots and those strap t-shirts, Spike figured it was all right to let Jenner wear his. It was a look that was on the approved list of homosexual stereotypes.

All this actually confused Langer, that gays were into the same kinds of clothes that he'd thought were the look of the real macho man when he first wore them himself years ago. But there wasn't time to worry about all of that now.

"Hey, Hernandez, I told you! Get that beard trimmed by the barber, or get it shaved off!"

Tomorrow morning they'd be ready, Langer knew. The buses would be loaded up early and they'd proceed to the staging point for the march. After that, it was going to be a piece of cake. They even had their banners all made: The Southern Alabama Gay Rights Circle. Langer smiled at that. Who'd ever try to keep a group of good ole Southern fairies out of the march?

He'd assigned Jenner the key role in the whole thing. He'd thought about that for a long time. The guy was obviously unbalanced in some profound way. But the sound of his voice when he'd promised Langer that he'd die if he needed to in order to carry out his command had reverberated in Langer's mind for a long time. He'd known, somehow, that Jenner meant it.

The probability was that whoever did start this was going to get it and get it quickly. If it wasn't Jenner, it'd have to be one of the ones who weren't smart enough to understand that probability.

Jenner did. And Jenner hadn't flinched when Langer told him how it was going to happen.

The plan was set. Victory was near. Martial music was already playing in Spike's mind.

●　●　●

Larry Menario was just as glad that he wasn't part of the marshal group and didn't have to attend their training sessions. He was almost relieved to be able to be alone and to go out and be in the city by himself.

He certainly wasn't tired of Scott already. Hardly. He'd even been able to relax about a lot of things after that talk with the pilot on the plane. The guy'd been right. There are some things that have to do with how people treat you because of what you are. But there were other times when they were acting out of something else. Larry knew he had to work at finding the distinction between the two motivations when he was with Scott, at least.

Larry was rolling up Michigan Avenue, proudly wearing his Gay March for Rights t-shirt. He'd found some pathways through the park system of the awesomely large city which had given him a chance for a good workout earlier in the afternoon. But he wasn't about to go through the parks now, at night. It was about ten o'clock and he just wanted to get out and about in the city.

He thought back to the long and fast exploration he'd had earlier. That'd felt great. He needed that, that chance to feel his own power. And he didn't want to let his stamina wear down. Not with Scott so hyper about him entering the Marathon.

They were going to do it together, in fact. They'd already worked out a whole training program for themselves. Scott claimed that running more would be good for his football stuff. Maybe. Maybe it was just a way for them to spend time together. Larry wasn't worrying about that anymore. He was still glowing a little bit inside about the fact that they simply *were.*

"Hey, hey, looks like a fag on wheels to me!"

Larry was jerked back into the present when he heard that cry. He was shocked to hear such a crude insult on the streets of the city. He was even more surprised when he saw who it came from.

The other guy was in his own chair. He was moving fast towards Larry on the same sidewalk. He was wearing a bright lavender t-shirt of his own with a slogan printed on it: GAY CRIPS FOR GAY RIGHTS.

"How's my man doin'?" The guy put out his hand for a high-five greeting when he got to Larry.

It was a new gesture for Menario, but he figured out how to do it and got a loud, "All right!" in response.

But Larry couldn't bring himself to actually say anything. He was stunned by this guy. He appeared to be about forty and he needed a shave and probably a shampoo as well, his long hair looked a little greasy. But that wasn't the point. The real thing was that Larry had never seen another gay man in a chair. Larry, to his own astonishment, hadn't even thought about another gay man being in one.

"Found the one and only hot gay bar in town that's got its shit together enough to have a ramp, just for you and me, partner. On my way there now. You wanna join up? Come on, come with Cowboy Hanks and have a beer?"

"Um, sure!"

"Wheel away into the night with me, sport, and maybe we'll find us a good old-fashioned ranch-hand to make our dreams come true!"

With that this guy named Cowboy did a hot shot move with his chair and had the thing aimed back in the opposite direction, the same one Larry had been headed in before. "Follow me, sport!"

In a few minutes, Larry found himself in the middle of a gay bar for the first time in his life. He sat there, holding the cold can of beer that Cowboy Hanks had bought him and watched as all the men moved around.

"Early yet," Cowboy said. He wasn't complaining though, that smile on his face seemed a permanent fixture. "But they'll come floodin' in here in a while. More men'n you'd ever know what to do with."

"I, um, I have one."

"Hey, hey!" Cowboy said and pounded Larry on the back for emphasis. "My man's got an every night stud?!"

Larry smiled at that. "I guess you could call it that."

"He a crip?"

"No. In fact, he's a football player." Larry tried not to react to the way Cowboy talked, but it was difficult.

"Well, good for you, sport! At least those strong ones come in handy for gettin' carried around, don't they though?"

Larry was stunned.

"Hell yes, if I was ever goin' to settle down, at least give me a stud can get me up the stairs at night. 'Course, those muscles come in handy for other things as well." He gave Larry a truly lecherous wink.

Cowboy seemed to know half the men in the bar. Larry

could only sit there and watch and listen as a whole line of them came up and seemed to flirt with Hanks who never seemed to miss an opportunity to let a hand of his rest on some other man's behind or even slip up onto the front of another's pants.

"Men, god love 'em!" Hanks said when they were alone.

"You must be from Chicago," Larry said.

"Oh, no, just got in the night 'fore last from Cheyenne. Here for the march." Hanks took a big swig of his beer and then picked out the best looking of the men who were standing at all close to them. "Hey, muscles, you goin' get a man a beer? I'd surely appreciate your savin' me that long ride." There was another wink.

Larry watched the bodybuilder check on what both of the men in wheelchairs were drinking and then go to the bar to get them refills, refusing their offers of money. It was, he'd told them, on the house. Which wasn't really true, because Larry saw him reaching into his own wallet to pay for the new cans.

When they had their drinks, and the muscle guy'd been rewarded with an obviously appreciated slap on the ass for his trouble, Larry moved his chair closer to Cowboy. He was thrilled by this guy, the wild abandon and unashamed way he came in here and acted so outrageously towards the other patrons was unbelievable and very, very exciting.

Larry blurted out: "Mr. Hanks, are you some kind of sex maniac?"

"Sport, I'm trying my damnest." Cowboy burst into laughter at the amazed look on Larry's face. Obviously, nothing was going to embarrass this guy.

But Larry did feel awkward about what he'd asked and tried to explain: "It's just that I, I never met another ... crip in a gay bar before," Larry said, nearly tripping over the slang word and not quite being honest, since he hadn't even been in a place like this.

"Oh, hell, young'un, ain't it just a good thing when that does happen?" Cowboy seemed to pick up on what was going through Larry's mind. His voice dropped and he sounded much more serious and sincere. "I got put out of commission in Nam. Now, tell ol' man Hanks just what happened to you. That's one thing you learn, sport, tell your story. Tell your story over and over again so it don't matter to you when you hear it one more time.

"Tell your story 'cause that's the thing that people always want to hear about everyone. And then, when you've told yours – 'cause let's face it, ours're gonna be worst than any of these studs – they'll be willin' to tell you their own. Get a couple guys tellin' each other their stories, and you got a couple guys got a chance of bein' friends." The leer came back, "Or maybe even somethin' more."

"No, you tell me more, first. Vietnam? What was it like? What happened?"

"Nam was bad, sport. The worst. You lost some good men there, no question about it. That I lost my natural walking sticks doesn't mean much in comparison, you know? Not much at all.

"So, that's the beginning of that story. But, sport! I want yours. You got some dirt to tell ol' Cowboy, I jus' know you do.

"Come on, sport, let's talk about big strappin' football players comin' to your bed every night. How did a tyke like you get that lucky?"

Larry let Hanks drop the subject of Vietnam and he leaped at the chance to talk to this other man about Scott Gilson and their affair.

There was something important about telling stories with Cowboy. Larry knew that immediately and he understood at least part of the reason why the others in the bar liked the guy so much. But Larry had his own reasons for taking this opportunity. This was really sharing with his own kind. This was very, very special.

It was over an hour and two beers later that Larry finished. "Oh, sport, that's wonderful!" Cowboy reached over and slammed Larry on the shoulder again. "I've always had my gentlemen admirers, I gotta admit, there's no dust settlin' on the walkway to my house and the pattern on the hallway rug goin' to my bedroom's been worn out for years from all the feet that've made the trip.

"But love ... sport, that's special. You remember love." Cowboy's mind was wandering away from Larry and from the bar. He was somewhere else. There was a much more mellow smile on his face now. Larry enjoyed watching it. That was the way he was going to look in a few years when he thought about Scott, he was sure. That look on Cowboy's face was the kind of look you got from the real thing, not play-acting.

"Enough, you'll get an ol' man reminiscin' the night away at this rate." He brightened back up to his old self again. "Now, this here march, you're gonna ride with us, ain't you?"

"You?"

"Queers on Wheels! We got our own contingent in this thing. Yes we do! Gonna push our way right down the streets of this city with our own banners and our own pride!" Cowboy lifted up his head with a mock seriousness.

"Well ..." Larry had assumed he'd march with the other Mansford students. But Scott was a marshal, so he wouldn't be there and Larry really didn't know the other gay guys from school all that well. Why was he even thinking about it? "Of course I'll be with you!" he exclaimed.

"Okay, sport, here's the plan. We got our own stagin' area at the start of the march ..."

Larry couldn't help but be happy about all of these remarkable things that were happening to him.

X

Chicago had a carnival air about it. Even if the march was a protest, the presence of so many out-of-towners produced that kind of energy.

Jenner didn't think about that. He couldn't care less about those things. He edged his way through the crowd so he could get nearer the avenue. The heavy metal pieces were slapping together in his knapsack. But no one would pay attention to those sounds in the middle of everything else. He could take his time.

A few of the people he pushed aside made the usual kinds of asshole complaints about being shoved. He sneered when he realized that at least some of them shut up when they looked at him, not because they were intimidated by his size but because they were attracted to his looks and his obviously muscular build – the t-shirt he was wearing was especially tight. He didn't mind men looking at him. He ignored the comments about his chest and didn't react when some queer made a crack about his having "major tits". Those things didn't get to him.

It wouldn't have made any difference if the words were being said by a woman. In all the places Jenner had been in the past twenty years, he hadn't had sex with another person. That part of him was dead.

The comments? No big deal, he just smiled and let the ones close to him think he appreciated them as compliments. It only added to his cover.

He stiffened his back a bit, just to make the contents of the knapsack move once more. That was his love: An automatic rifle. That was something that wouldn't leave him alone. That was something he could count on.

He was in position. He looked around at the crowd on the other side of the avenue. There he was: The mark. Just like they said he'd be: Too good-looking in an Italian sort of way with dark curly hair and a tight gymnast's body. He had a visible tag on his polo shirt. Jenner didn't know about that, but he saw the lavender armband which identified him as a marshal.

He was the one. Jenner scanned everything else around him. There was nothing unusual; there was no hint of anything going wrong. He caught sight of Langer. The asshole shouldn't try to blend in with the crowd. He didn't have the touch. Even with him going around and telling the other guys how to look like they belonged here, the leader was unsuccessful himself.

But there were so many different types of homos in this mass that he might get away with it. But then Jenner saw the mark go towards Langer. He was moving fast and he had two big guys with him, one colored, one white. The three collared Langer. Jenner had that sensation of excitement gripping his belly. He used all of his self-control not to get out the rifle parts and assemble them right away, before he was supposed to.

"What's going on over there?" someone in the crowd asked.

"A guy who's claiming to be a marshal doesn't have the right kind of ID," a newcomer who'd just raced back across the avenue explained. "They're turning him into the cops."

Jenner relaxed as soon as he saw the police take Spike away. Jenner's only concern had been that the mark might have to go with him, but the Italian kid stood his ground and kept his own position. So Langer did fuck up. Langer was supposed to have been the back-up. Jenner didn't think he'd need him. And Langer wouldn't say anything in custody and Jenner was very confident the cops wouldn't even know the right questions to ask. There was no danger in this. In fact, it was a relief to have Langer out of the way.

That left Jenner in charge. He had been, in a way, in charge all along. He was the one who'd be giving the signal. Until he moved and got the mark, everyone else was under orders not to act. This was a highly synchronized operation. Everyone was under strict discipline and had been warned not to lose his head.

Until the mark got it from Jenner, nothing would happen.

The first contingent of the parade was approaching. Applause rose from the crowd as they heard the marching bands. Once the parade was there, Jenner knew he'd only have sporadic sight of the mark. He'd wait for the one part of the march where his line of vision wouldn't be obstructed.

He snorted at the plan. The organizers had been real helpful, setting up a whole group of guys in wheelchairs. He saw the image of the mark as it occasionally became visible between the passing bodies of the marchers. That was often enough to keep track of him. When the wheelchairs came by, he wouldn't have to worry about spotting the mark. Then everything from Jenner to the mark's chest up would be open field. That's when Jenner would get him.

That's when Danny Fortelli would die.

• • •

Joseph Farmdale had the doors to his suite's terrace open. He could hear the beginning of the parade as it passed down below. What could the enemy's plan be? What could happen?

Police helicopters buzzed the crowd from above. Joseph knew that the subways and side streets, every possible entrance to the neighborhood of the parade, was being patrolled by massive police presence. At Alex Kane's insistence, the Illinois National Guard had been mobilized and was waiting in secret locations all around the route. No one would ever know the intense firepower that was here.

But could it stop Theodore?

There was a knock at the door. It wouldn't be Alex, he wouldn't knock. Kane'd been up since before dawn, looking into last minute details. He was supposed to join Joseph soon. They'd decided there was no better place to watch than this hotel room. This was one of the parade's central command units.

There was a uniformed waiter there. Joseph decided that Alex must have arranged with room service for something to be delivered, to be there when he returned. He was actually pleased that Kane would have done that. The man certainly deserved something to eat.

The man pushed in a cart covered with white linen. Joseph stood aside, expecting the door to be closed right away. But instead, three more men came rushing through as soon as the waiter had said, "Now!"

They all had automatic pistols in their hands. Joseph stared at the three gun barrels aimed at him but didn't have time to understand what was happening. The danger didn't really register.

Not until one more man followed the gunsters into the room.

"Hello, father," Theodore smiled. "Isn't this a pleasant day for a parade?"

• • •

If it hadn't been for his concern for Joseph Farmdale, Alex would have stayed on the street. But the old man had been so anxious and he'd appeared so stressed by what'd been going on that Alex had agreed to come back and stay with him during the actual parade.

That was the basic mistake. Because, when he'd come into the suite, Alex had walked into a trap. Joseph had been tied to a chair, gagged, with three guns trained at his skull.

"Make one move, faggot, and the old man's gone."

Alex didn't doubt Theodore. He knew the man would kill his own father.

So, Alex thought, *this is the end. This is how Theodore is going to win.* He thought, for the short time it took two of Theodore's henchmen to chain him to another chair – they'd come prepared and weren't about to trust a mere rope to hold down Alex – that this was all that Theodore wanted. Himself and Joseph.

Alex studied Theodore closely. He'd never really known this man, this brother of his first lover. He'd tried, at one point, to make a friendly approach. When Theodore had refused him, it hadn't been done in a very antagonistic manner. Alex hadn't pressed the issue. But he hadn't known that Theodore actually hated him either.

The man had no real resemblance to James. There were certain features – the cheekbones, the ears – which were similar, but the combination of all the parts produced a totally different image than the one Alex carried around of James.

James had been strong; Theodore was arrogant. James had been handsome; none of Theodore's parts seemed to be in proportion to the rest and the final result was unattractive. James had never had to work to keep his body in shape; it didn't look as though Theodore had to put much effort into maintaining his pot belly.

And James had never been cruel. Even in the worst of the war, James had always tried to find the ways to make that most gruesome event somehow less so – helping a peasant family whose hut had been destroyed by artillery, holding onto a sobbing infantryman who'd just fired his rifle in battle for the first time, something that never ceased to get to a man.

Theodore *was* cruel. There was no doubt about it. This man was enjoying his sadistic pleasures. Alex didn't know, though, how extreme they were going to be.

"I suppose, in an even more decadent society than ours,

that I would address you as brother-in-law," Theodore sneered once Kane's bondage had been completed. "Though, does the widow still hold that position when she's remarried? My grasp of etiquette fails me. Just one more example of my father's educational deficiencies."

Theodore went over to the open terrace door. A helicopter flew nearby, its loud rotors' sound invading the luxury hotel room. "You've done extraordinarily well in organizing this whole thing, you know," Theodore turned and said to Alex with a smile.

"I'm aware of some of the more extreme steps you've taken. What are there? Ten thousand National Guardsmen, I believe, all within a few blocks of the parade route? You brought in the police aircraft. There are police boats and Coast Guard ships off shore as well. You turned Chicago into a veritable fortress, haven't you, Alex?

"It's something that's proven very convenient, you know. I intend to use all of it."

Alex looked at him. He couldn't understand what Theodore was getting at.

"I have arranged for this operation to begin on a very appropriate note. In a very short while, your ... *lover,* that young one, is going to die, Alex. When he does, my men are going to open fire."

Alex refused to respond to the threat Theodore was making against Danny. He couldn't stand to think about it. "You haven't a chance. You've just said you know how powerfully prepared the police are."

"Oh, but Alex, I didn't explain, did I? My men aren't going to open fire on your marchers. After they get Fortelli, my men are going to attack the police!

"It's quite brilliant of me, you know. It's a form of leverage, think of it that way. My men, dressed as typical homosexuals, are hidden in a crowd of hundreds of thousands of gays. Those homosexuals are known to be very, very angry at certain events that have taken place." Theodore smiled again, a little gesture between them to underline the fact that they both knew perfectly well that Theodore had arranged those "events". "The police are on edge, aren't they? They don't like the idea of these queers, you do know that, don't you, Alex? But they'll try to do a good job.

"But they also know how angry that crowd is. Will they be really surprised when someone starts to shoot? And will they really be willing to hold their own fire when the shooting is directed towards their fellow officers?

"You know how much the police stand by one another, Alex." Theodore turned back to look out over the avenue. "There are enough of my guns out there, Alex, to make sure that the police think there's a major assault taking place. There will also be a few well-placed grenades detonated to give the impression of an even bigger attack.

"I suspect the marchers will play their own roles well, in addition. What do you think will go through their minds when they hear gunfire? Do you think they'll suspect outsiders? No. And they're not used to even considering that there might be arms in one of their events.

"When they hear those shots, those men are going to be convinced that the police have opened up on them! Some will panic, but others, the ones already so enraged, will turn on the police, adding to the impression of the assault, making the police more convinced than ever that they're the targets for all of this.

"It will be so dramatic, Alex! It's going to be such a show! And with such repercussions! Think of it, Alex. I suspect at least a few thousand people will die today. After this, what gay ghetto in what American city won't be armed to the teeth? And what police force won't be ready to respond to the slightest provocation in every one of those cities?

"Your people will lose, of course, but they will put up a good fight, I'm sure. That's one of the beauties of it all. Because a long-lasting internal battle will mean unstable markets and my father's not the only one to tell you that the rich make out very well during periods of instability.

"Of course, the other people who find success during

those periods are the political conservatives. How many news photographs of mobs of armed homosexuals rampaging through Chicago will it take for the man in the street to give up any of his hesitations about crushing gay rights? How many television shots of dead policemen in Chicago will lead others to demand revenge?

"And who better than myself and a few of my friends who understand the benefits of a strong hand in Washington to lead the country to a new step in its history?

"And," Theodore finished with a flourish, "it will all begin with the elimination of your little friend. That is our signal, Alex. That is the beginning of what will become, I assure you, the end of your despicable movement."

XI

Larry Menario had never felt so alive!

First, there was Scott.

Then, there was Cowboy Hanks.

And now, there was the entire group of them: Queers on Wheels.

The fourteen years since his accident had been a progression away from other people. He'd spent the whole time putting up his own mental walls, and he'd begun to see how very real they were, as real as the barriers that kept him from climbing stairs, entering most buildings, leading anything close to a normal life.

But, now, he was with his own kind, with what Cowboy Hanks would certainly call a "super-hunk" waiting for him, and he was coming out, gay and a crip, a real person, finally!

The euphoria was sweeping him away. After years of trying to blend into the woodwork every time he'd met a new person, he was in a parade! Him: Larry Menario! Instead of trying to divert any attention at all from his chair, he was rolling down the avenue with dozens of others, inviting people to look right at him and see him.

"Doin' some wheelies!" Cowboy yelled out beside him. Then Hanks frightened Larry back to reality as he reared up his chair and seemed to be about to fall over backwards in it.

But Cowboy was doing his routine, showing off to his admiring fans.

A yell came from the crowd on the sidelines as Cowboy swiveled around furiously and then landed back down on all four wheels.

"Come on, sport, you do one!" Cowboy yelled.

"I couldn't!" Larry insisted.

"Sure you can, sport, just do it like this." Cowboy showed Larry how to accomplish the trick. "It's all balance, sport, and you can do it."

"But, Cowboy ..." Larry was scared now, "there's no one to catch me if I fall over." There were only other men in chairs in this part of the parade.

"Hey, sport," Cowboy said in that softest, most seductive voice of his, "there's always someone to catch you."

Larry grasped hold of his wheels and felt the tension of trying something new in public. Then, finding himself with more courage than he'd ever thought he could, he performed the trick, tentatively at first, then with a sudden wild recklessness.

The crowd roared its approval once more and Larry flushed with pride and even more excitement.

"Gotta get you to the wheelchair rodeos back home, sport. You got talent."

Rodeos! *Damn!* Larry thought, *wouldn't Scott be proud of that!*

The Queers on Wheels kept on moving up the avenue. Occasionally the parade would have to stop for a moment and then Larry and Cowboy would pull their stunts. But there were also lots of opportunities for conversation with Cowboy. Larry drank it up, as though this wild man from Wyoming were some new beverage quenching a thirst he hadn't even known he'd had before.

They talked about the Marathon and training. They talked about Scott. They talked about Vietnam, the only subject where Cowboy seemed reluctant to go into details. And they talked about their chairs and what they could do with them.

"You just got to learn to think about this here equipment as a tool, sport. Forget the limitation stuff. Forget the idea of bein' disabled, and remember, this is your tool for livin'. That's the only way you can do it."

The music of all the marching bands sounded around them. The one closest was booming out Sousa marches, off in the distance, another was playing Broadway hits, still another was pounding out political protest songs.

Maybe it wasn't the best music. Maybe the different strains were in conflict with one another. It didn't matter to Larry. What mattered was that he was here. And so were so many others. They weren't going to take it anymore! That was their message. They were here to find one another and all the strength that came with that being together, all of the magic that Larry felt was a part of this march.

"Hey, Cowboy," he broke out, "there's my stud!" Larry hoped Scott didn't hear him. He'd have to break his lover slowly into this new way of talking. But he was so proud to see Gilson standing there, beside Junior and Danny Fortelli. "There, Cowboy, the one with the Mansford sweatshirt on! The dark-haired one. That's my stud!" The second time he used the phrase, it didn't sound so awkward.

He'd expected Hanks to be impressed. But Cowboy wasn't even looking in the same direction. He was staring at the crowd on the other side of the avenue. As soon as he heard Cowboy swear, he could tell from the sound of his voice that something was going wrong.

"Holy shit." It wasn't the usual way Hanks said the expression. Then Larry saw Cowboy's ruddy complexion fade, as though the man had seen a ghost.

"I just don't believe it." Cowboy wasn't even talking to Larry right now. He was off in a dream world somewhere. He wasn't even keeping up with the parade now.

What was getting to Cowboy? Larry looked in the same direction and saw too many gay men standing there to be able to pick out any one in particular. Well, maybe it was that guy with all the chest muscles, the one who was bending over to open up his knapsack. He was hot. That would be Cowboy's speed.

"Hit the wheels, sport!" Cowboy screamed. "Quick, use those damned arm muscles of yours. Ram the stupid son of a bitch. Ram him, damn you, sport!"

Cowboy was taking off down the avenue on his chair. Larry didn't even think. He just responded, the panic in Cowboy's voice sent him into automatic pilot.

He was right behind Cowboy when Hanks's chair seemed to go crashing into the crowd. Larry's subconscious was in overdrive. He saw that the bending figure had been Cowboy's target. The force of his blow had glanced off the other man, but not enough to throw him off balance. Instead, Cowboy's chair had gone crashing over on its side, leaving Larry's new friend sprawled out, helplessly, on the avenue.

As Larry put more speed and power into revolving the wheels of his chair, he could see the crowd spread out, recoiling from the sudden and unexpected violence.

Then Larry saw the gun.

The man had it in his hands and was about to stand up with it. Larry couldn't separate all of the things that were rushing through his mind – they all combined to fuel him on, making him put even more power into the hard movements of his arms as he sped towards his target.

His lover was across the street. The man had a gun. There was Cowboy Hanks on the asphalt. There was nothing but danger here.

Then Larry's chair was nearly airborne. He hit the man just as he stood, the metal footpads of the chair cut into the man's ankles. The force of the collision sent Larry flying through the air, the man beneath him. There was a sickening thud as their bodies landed together, hard.

But there was also the sound of metal hitting the ground and it wasn't near them. Larry knew, instinctively, that he had to hold the man. He had to keep him there. He had to stop him from getting that rifle back.

Take away his legs! Don't let him get that advantage!

That was the message screaming through Larry's mind. He thoughtlessly grabbed hold of the man around his thighs. His arms, the same arms he'd been building up for the marathon, were powerful, strong enough to keep the man from getting his footing, powerful enough to keep him right there.

"Hold him, sport. For Christ's sake, hold him down!"

There were brutal fists beating on Larry's back and shoulders. They assaulted his head. Larry felt blood trickle down the side of his face. The viscous fluid merged with something else: his tears. Everything hurt. Everything was in pain. But he wouldn't let the man go.

He could barely see Cowboy moving along the roadway. The other guy was using his elbows for locomotion. They were cut open with long and bleeding scrapes as Hanks rushed as fast as he could towards the rifle that sat on the road between them.

Get it Cowboy, please get it!

Larry felt his grip weaken. The pain was shooting through his whole upper torso. It would take this man, with his damned working legs, only seconds to get to the rifle that was so maddeningly difficult for Cowboy to reach.

Larry felt the man's limbs start to be able to move. He couldn't hold on much longer, he knew it. He'd have to let go. The pain was too excruciating. But he kept watching Cowboy. The second Hanks's hand seized the stock of the rifle, Larry released his opponent, rolling off him, barely conscious from the harsh beating he'd taken.

He could feel the man stand up. The legs were tensed, they were right beside Larry and he could see the man was ready to spring. Larry didn't have a single ounce of energy left to do anything about it. Helpless again, impotent once more, Larry waited for the next part of the fight.

"Jenner, you stupid excuse for a cocksucker, what the hell are you doin' and why the hell are you doin' it here?"

Larry knew he must have passed out. He was dreaming. How could Cowboy know this man's name?

"You're dead!" The voice was strange, it must be another

part of Larry's fantasy. It wasn't making a threat, the way a mugger might or a movie actor. The voice had all the sounds of disbelief in it. Maybe it was even shock.

"You're dead!" It repeated.

"Hell, I'm dead, Jenner. I'm alive enough to have this damn Uzi aimed right at your no-good balls. You want some proof I'm alive? I'll give it to you if you don't watch your step, right where the muzzle's pointed."

The man was moving towards Cowboy now. Larry was sure it was the end, even of the dream. His face was still covered with blood and it seemed right, because he was sure the man was going to kill Cowboy. No crip could really fight off anyone as strong as that.

"Cowboy!" Now the voice was strained, Larry thought it sounded the same way as his own would if he tried to talk, full of tears and ...

"Jenner, you always did have rattlesnake meat for brains. God damn, look at you, boy! Now stop that, will you stop that!" Larry'd imagined that this man would be beating up Cowboy, killing him. But Cowboy wasn't fighting off an attack.

Finding some reservoir of strength, Larry opened the one eye that he could and looked over to see the big man he'd just been fighting. Jenner was holding onto Cowboy with a desperate embrace.

"Damn, Jenner, you always did embarrass me! Too bad you had to have the prettiest cock in Nam, else I woulda been rid of you long ago. Now stop it, will you. Stop that damn crying!"

Everything had been frozen around them. The crowd had been paralyzed by the fighting. But now, with the violence evidently passed, the onlookers surged forward, trying to get close enough to see and hear what was really going on.

"Larry! Larry!" Scott Gilson fell on his lover and took him in his arms. "God! What's going on! Are you all right?"

"It's okay, Scott," Larry heard himself saying. "Cowboy just got a stud, that's all." And then Larry Menario passed out.

XII

Danny looked up at the Barchester Hotel tower. Junior and Scott were beside him once again. Other marshals had taken charge of Larry and the police had moved in to arrest Jenner. But before they took him away, Jenner, prodded by Larry's friend Cowboy, had told them all he knew about the plan.

Danny didn't have time to wonder about the strange individuals he'd just had to deal with. He had to assume that the one with the machine gun had been telling the truth. It made sense. That was the worst part of it. A mind like Theodore's was capable of coming up with a scheme like this one. To have this mass of gay men and the police turn on one another and precipitate a massacre was right up Teddy's alley.

Before the police had come to take Jenner away, Danny had carefully managed to get his hands on the Uzi. He knew, from Alex's lessons, how to quickly break it down. He'd replaced the pieces in Jenner's knapsack. He had the gun. It was, he knew now, the only thing that could keep Alex and Joseph Farmdale alive.

If he could get to them.

"Scott, I know you're worried about Larry," Danny said, his voice under the same extreme control he was exerting over the rest of himself, "but I need you, and I can't move unless I can trust you and Junior to both have your minds completely on what's going on. You have to trust the medical people to take care of Larry."

Scott Gilson gave his head one firm nod. It was the same gesture, Danny was sure, that he used when he was letting the coach know he understood the play the team needed for the winning touchdown. That, Danny figured, was as good a commitment as he'd ever get.

"Listen, your suite is directly below ours. If what Jenner said is true, then Alex and Mr. Farmdale are probably with Theodore upstairs. We have to break in there and free them. I have to be honest, guys, this is going to be heavy. We don't know how many there are and we don't know how well armed they are.

"We only have one gun between us. I'm going to try to get into the suite by getting from your terrace to ours. For this to work, I have to know that I have at least a few seconds where I won't be under fire myself. You guys have to produce a diversion and it has to be a good one.

"You might get shot. You might get killed. But you know that the alternative is that Theodore might find out that his plan's been thwarted and he might have a back-up in place that Jenner didn't know about. I can't make you take this risk. I can only ask if you'll do it."

"Don't ask," Junior said. "Just tell us. Remember, Fortelli, Gilson and I are experts at timed plays. We're just going to make believe this is a fake hand-off, Danny. Let's think of it that way. We're gonna set ourselves up for the tackles. We do that all the time. We take the licks and some other guy runs into the end zone. That's fine. That's team-work. 'Cause the real point is making sure the right side wins the game."

Scott nodded once more and, again, Danny understood that Gilson was with him, all the way.

"We have to synchronize watches. Then, this is what you have to do ..."

• • •

Junior had grown up on the streets of Boston's Roxbury ghetto. He knew what a shoulder holster looked like when it was underneath a man's suit jacket. And as soon as he and Scott got off the elevator and saw the guard standing by the Farmdale suite door, he had no doubt that's just what the turkey was packing.

The two Mansford College football players hadn't had much time to work this out. But they were used to improvising on the playing field. They'd agreed that Junior would take the lead out here in the hallway.

Thank god they had decent cover. Junior knew that no one would really look twice at the two men. Sure they were big, but they didn't look as though they'd be a part of the march outside. They appeared to be just what they were, college students in town for a good time. They'd taken off their armbands and their photo-IDs were back in their rooms.

It was only mid-afternoon, but who'd be surprised that a couple of college jocks would be a little bit high this early in the day on a weekend when they were staying in a hotel like this one, obviously on a vacation trip?

"Hey, my man!" Junior held out his palm to the guard. "Congratulate us." Junior saw the mistrust in the guy's face. But the guard wasn't going to try anything out here in the corridor if he could help it. He put a hesitant palm against the black football player's, even though he didn't know what the gesture was for.

Once the hand was in his grasp, it was nothing to throw a knee into his groin. The handclasp meant the man couldn't escape, even if he could have moved once Junior had smashed his testicles up into his pelvic cavity. But the man couldn't even speak, let alone react physically.

Junior was almost disappointed the asshole'd fallen so easily. He'd had a whole rap ready for him, sure to capture his attention and make it more comfortable for the guard to talk to a black man. The story was going to be that he and Scott'd just come from the meeting where they'd agreed to play for the Chicago Bears. *No mean fantasy,* thought Junior. Though actually he was hoping it'd be the Patriots so he could live nearer to home.

Those things were still going through his mind while he and Scott were trussing the man up tighter than a Thanksgiving turkey, using belts and the man's necktie. There wasn't any resistance, except when they dragged the fellow's hands away from his bruised groin.

"Don't worry," Junior smiled, "they tell me that sometimes it grows back."

Then he and Scott were ready. They looked at the watch on Scott's hand and knew they had another two minutes before they could act. They were both sweating, not so much from the physical exertion, as from the tension.

The elevator kept passing their floor, thank God. But it could stop. Another one of the Farmdale henchmen could come across them. Just as bad: Some innocent bystander might walk into the middle of this, whatever it was.

Junior stood there and held the handgun he'd taken off the guard. He looked at it. He hadn't held one of these in his hands for years. He hadn't fired one for an even longer time. But if he had to, he knew he was prepared.

• • •

Danny Fortelli was looking at his own watch. He was ready. The Uzi was reassembled and slung over his shoulder. He was standing, balanced on the railing around the terrace. He'd spent the last many years of his life perfecting his gymnastics. He'd won trophies and he'd become proud of his body and his prowess. But all of those meets he'd taken part in now seemed like little-boy recreations. This was the real championship.

If he could get up onto the next floor quietly enough, he'd have a chance to use the Uzi before the enemy shot him. And killed him.

His body was stiff with tension. He had to will it to relax, knowing that he needed it to be loose and malleable. He was going to ask it to perform as it never had before.

Danny didn't look down. He didn't need to. He knew the street was many stories beneath him. He was barefoot, wanting the extra purchase of his own skin for his footing. He'd stripped down to his shorts, not wanting any unnecessary garment to restrict his movements.

He'd have to jump up from this precarious stance and grab hold of the terrace wall above him. Then, much easier, he'd have to chin himself up onto the ledge. Within a single extra minute, he'd have to hit the terrace standing and get the Uzi into his hands. If he'd timed this right – he prayed he had – then the football players would perform their diversion at that precise moment.

Now. This was the moment.

Danny crouched down, tightening his legs as though they were springs. He thought of Alex and all the times Alex had saved his life. This was the big pay-back, Danny knew it. This was the all-or-nothing roll of the dice.

Danny willed his body to jump. He sprang through the air and his hands found the metal tubing of the fence. But there was a vine growing where his right hand landed! Panic surged through Danny's body as he felt that hand slip, unable to hold on. His left hand automatically tightened its grip. Excruciating pain roared through Danny's shoulder. He wasn't ready for all his weight to be tugged on that one arm. He wanted to yell in pain, but couldn't, it'd give him away. He nearly panicked when he realized the Uzi was slipping over his shoulder, threatening to fall down to Michigan Avenue.

He clung for his life. He willed himself to keep cool, to hold his right hand up so the gun couldn't slide down his arm. He didn't move for a moment, making sure he didn't make a stupid mistake by forgetting all of the tasks necessary just because he overreacted to accomplish one of them.

Then the hand went back to the terrace fence and got a handle, this time without ivy-covering. Danny stopped for another second, hanging down, hundreds of feet from the ground. Then he remembered the crucial timing element of the entire scheme. He couldn't wait. He couldn't chance anything going wrong.

With one great pull on his arms, Danny lifted himself up. He used all of his gymnast's skill to scroll his body over the fence. He landed on the concrete floor with his bare feet. There was hardly a whisper of sound.

He threw himself back-first against the wall of the hotel, out of the sight of anyone who could be looking out the suite's windows. He inched toward the opening and looked in, to see just where the enemy stood.

They were all there. He could make out Alex, chained to one chair, facing Mr. Farmdale, tied to another. Around them stood four men. One of them vaguely reminded Danny of the pictures of James that he'd seen. That must be Theodore. The rest were just henchmen.

Danny looked at his watch once more. The second hand ticked off as it made its way around the face.

Ten, nine, eight, seven, six, five, four, three, … A sudden noise erupted from inside the suite as the two other athletes broke down the door, surprising all the others who were inside the room.

Danny had memorized the position of his targets. He prayed once more, this time that they hadn't moved and that he remembered everything perfectly, the way Alex had trained him to do.

Danny swept out to stand in the middle of the window frame. The Uzi's barrel pointed inside. He pulled the trigger.

• • •

When Alex heard the sound of the door being broken open, he knew it must be Danny. He'd hoped against hope that his lover would figure out what was going on. The door seemed to have disintegrated all at once. Then two big bodies flew through the opening.

Theodore was the first one to act, but it'd taken him a second to respond to the unexpected attack. He was reaching inside his coat for his gun. Then there was an explosion from the other side of the room. The hired gunmen started to do an obscene dance as one, then another began. The two were hit by the rounds of machinegun fire which threw them off their feet, its force actually holding them up for a second as their bodies were shot through again and again.

The third henchman had ducked around a wall. He had his handgun out, and he was ready to move to face Danny. Alex watched in desperate concern, unable to move because of the chain, knowing that this man might be able to take Danny unawares.

Then a new exploding sound echoed through the room. Alex turned and saw the black Mansford student holding a smoking pistol of his own. The henchman didn't move for a moment, then he slumped, sliding down the wall, leaving a trail of blood on the white paint as he fell.

But that took just enough time for Theodore to get his gun out. He'd moved quickly to get out of the way of the deadly Uzi's aim. He was behind a table now, one that might not have stopped the machinegun's bullets, but which did deprive the marksman of his target.

Theodore didn't care about the attacker, though. His face was screwed up with hate and frustration. He cared about his revenge now that he suspected that he wasn't going to survive himself. And he was going to take that revenge. He pointed the pistol at Alex's head.

"Say good-bye, faggot," Theodore sneered.

Alex closed his eyes, ready for the inevitable. He wasn't really surprised that his only thought was how much he was going to miss Danny.

The gun fired. There was suddenly warm fluid covering Alex's body. That must be from my wound, he thought. But he felt nothing. He opened his eyes and saw that sprawled out on the floor, his head blown open by a gunfire wound lay Theodore. Beside him stood Danny, the smoking machinegun in his hand.

Danny tossed the Uzi on the floor and threw his arms around Alex and kissed him over and over again. Alex couldn't help smiling, but he wasn't going to give in to this emotional scene that easily.

"Couldn't you at least put on some clothes?" he complained.

XIII

This was the one place he felt the best. When he was in the water, he wasn't aware of his legs and he had no sense of physical limitations. He was only aware of how his well-developed chest and arms functioned to buoy him up and propel him through the New Hampshire lake.

He swam far out, away from the shore. As he moved away from the shore, it seemed as though the landscape behind him climbed up, and the mountains which were hidden from view on land by the trees were suddenly visible.

Larry stopped finally and let himself float, using his arms to provide just enough movement to keep himself from sinking into the clean, pure lake.

There was someone coming out towards him. The other body moved just as gracefully as Larry's, only a little bit faster. It was Scott. He pulled up beside Larry and treaded water, moving with his lover.

Laughing, Scott leaned over and kissed Larry. "How're you doing?"

"Real good," Larry answered. Then he took a deep breath and dove deep under the surface. Scott kept on treading water. Larry, so used to being limited by his chair, now could move around at will. His arms powered him towards Scott's moving legs. He aimed himself for the dark patch of pubic hair. He felt the cool form of Scott's cock as he slipped it into his mouth.

Scott tried to move away, but Larry held on to him by the thighs and kept up his tease for as long as he could. Finally, he had to have air and he let go of Scott and broke for the surface.

"Whew!" Scott said when Larry'd come up. "You never stop, do you?"

"Tell me when you want me to," Larry joked back.

"Never," Scott said, then he splashed water in Larry's face. "But give a man a rest every once in a while."

"That's not part of the deal, stud," Larry laughed back at him. "I've been taking lessons from Cowboy and I've learned what I got a right to expect from this here marriage thing."

They laughed some more and then, in silent agreement, made for the shore.

When they'd reached the dock from which they'd begun swimming, Larry was able to make his way up onto the platform, but then he had to wait while Scott, who'd gone straight for land, went and brought back their things. Larry felt suddenly sad, as though the touch of the wooden planks and the reality that he couldn't move on his own anymore took away something that he'd gained in the water.

But that was just a moment's downer now, not one more rationalization for a lifelong depression as it would have been just a few months ago.

Scott was beside him again. His lover sat down and began to matter-of-factly go about inserting the catheters that Larry had to use to drain his body of waste fluids. He could have done it himself, but Scott had learned how when Larry'd been in the Chicago hospital, recovering from the wounds he'd received that frightening day of the protest march.

Somehow it'd become a symbol to them both of just how much Scott had learned about and accepted Larry's physical realities. Every now and then, when it felt right, he'd perform this most basic and, maybe to others, most base task. It took a lot for Larry to let him do that. And he was pretty sure that

Scott had had to go through a lot to be able to accomplish it all without thinking too much about it.

When it was accomplished, Scott took Larry into his arms and carried him back off the dock to where his chair waited.

Junior was at the end of the pier, waiting for them. "I tell you, this affair of yours is the best damn conditioning you'll ever have, Gilson. Larry, you're doing him a favor, making him lug you around. Man's gonna have arms and shoulders to beat the band by the time this summer's done."

"Just wait till you see him after next summer," Larry answered.

Scott put Larry down in the chair and Larry began to wheel it up the hill toward the house where they were staying.

The wooden walkway had just been built. It, and other improvements on the property, had been done to make it usable for any guest, that's what Mr. Kane had said. What was the use of having a place you wanted people to visit if they couldn't do anything once they got there?

Mr. Kane was sitting on a folding chair in the yard by the house when the three Mansford students got there. He looked up from his reading and greeted them. "How's the water?"

"Great!" Larry answered. He wheeled up to a place nearby and then Junior and Scott brought over other chairs so the group could sit in a circle.

They were high enough up in the White Mountains that Larry could smell and feel a difference in the air. He'd like to have a place like this someday. Maybe he and Scott could find acreage like this, maybe even close enough that they could be at least seasonal neighbors to Danny and Mr. Kane.

The thought felt good. He and Scott were making those kinds of plans these days. He realized that a lot of other things felt good in so many other ways as well. He wasn't thinking much about his legs, for one thing. He was more aware of his chest and arms. They were going to be in pretty good shape for the marathon. He looked down at himself and moved an arm, almost shocked that he could think a part of himself was handsome.

"Have you made any decisions about next season?" Mr. Kane asked Scott.

"He sure has," Junior answered for his old roommate. "He's going to keep up that relentless march for the Heisman. And if he doesn't, I'm gonna break his legs." Junior spoke with his fake orator's voice, but then he said, in a totally different voice to Larry, "No offense, Menario." That kind of thing was getting to be a regular joke between Junior and Larry.

"I don't know what's really going to happen, Mr. Kane. I'm going to go back next season for sure. I promised these guys I would. Actually, I just think Larry wants a year of being the quarterback's sweetheart."

"Should I run for Homecoming Queen?" Larry asked Junior.

"Please! I have enough trouble dealing with all this massive gay education stuff as it is, Menario, I couldn't take too much more."

"It'd be good for you," Larry teased. "Maybe I will."

"Come on, you guys, stop it! I'm trying to answer Mr. Kane's question." Scott was smiling while the other two broke down into full-scale laughter.

"Well, I've decided to go ahead and join the team again for next year," Scott repeated. "I'm going to be the only openly gay football player for a long time, though. I hope I have the strength to make it through."

"Looks like you won't have much support from these two clowns," Alex said, but his own grin contradicted his statement.

"Well, I'll try to keep them under control. I actually think the whole football thing might become more fun. I'm really looking forward to it now that everything's out in the open. Maybe, just maybe, I can approach it the way it's supposed to be, as a game. I've used it as this crutch for so long that I lost sight of that. It became an obsession.

"Maybe I won't be as good. Maybe you had to have that drive to make it in the real big-time. I just don't know if there's going to be any Heisman in my future, if there really ever was going to be one. But I don't care. I'm doing pretty well collecting my own awards these days."

Before they could say more, a four-wheel drive tore up the road that led to the house. The brakes came on hard and the vehicle skidded to what appeared to be a life-saving stop just short of the boulders that lined the parking area.

But none of the four reacted to the stunt. They'd all seen it before by now. They watched as Cowboy Hanks got out of the truck and into his wheelchair. He did it with the practiced movements of a pro. In no time, the awkward moments of the maneuver were over and Cowboy was wheeling his way towards them.

"Hey, hey!" Hanks called out. "How they hangin' on you, buckeroos?"

"Hey, Cowboy," they answered, almost in unison. Probably none of them, not even Larry, had quite gotten used to Cowboy's flamboyant ways, but they'd come to love the character more than a little bit, each in his own way.

"How's Jenner?" Scott asked.

"I tell you, sport," Cowboy answered as he pulled up into the circle, "I'd be happy to discuss that subject, but there's this patchiness in my throat, and I swear ..."

"Hold on, Cowboy," Junior said with resignation. He'd heard all of this before. "I'll get you your beer."

"And they say young 'uns have no respect these days. Why, a more accomodatin' group of pups has never walked the earth, Mr. Kane, and I swear that's the truth."

Junior came back and handed Cowboy one of the cans of Budweiser that seemed his constant companion from afternoon on. But Larry, at least, had figured out just how much of a prop it was. That one can would probably last until dinnertime. Cowboy just liked it for his image's sake, the same way he wore his Stetson indoors.

"Well, as you were askin', that Jenner's just the same's always. Hell, and you think I'm the sex maniac! I wheel in that room of his and first thing he's doin', he's takin' off his pants.

I swear to you, those nurses are never gonna let the man out if he don't keep them on.

"Course, 'tis hard on him, bein' around someone sexy as me and bein' expected to control himself. I can understand the man's difficulties there.

"But, god! I never have seen a funny farm like that one. I don't know how you an' Mr. Farmdale came up with it, Mr. Kane, but that place is like some country club for all those oil barons and such down in Texas. I swear it's true! They pamper the old fool like he was a shah or somethin'. It's true!"

"What do they really say, Hanks?" Alex Kane asked.

"He's gonna be okay." Cowboy's voice had dropped. He was responding honestly to Alex's sincerity with his own. "Man's been through a lot. Haven't we all, though. But, he really did have his row to hoe. I gotta admit that. He surely did."

"What is the story, Cowboy?" Junior asked. "I haven't been up here as long as these two. I didn't get the whole thing explained to me."

"It's not my favorite tale, sport." Cowboy seemed to want to claim a right to be private. But he sighed and went on, "But seein' what you went through for him an' me, well, you gotta right to know it all, I guess.

"Mr. Kane here can tell you that some pretty heavy shit came down on those of us that went to Nam, son. It was pretty heavy, indeed.

"Lots of us, like Jenner, well, things happened that might not've happened stateside. Him and me were a team, partners to the end. We saved each other's lives too many times to count.

"We were Rangers, see, the Army's elite. We were the ones on the front lines all the time.

"Well, didn't take long 'fore me and Jenner were in the sack. Not the usual kinda trickin' and whorin' that a man like myself might do. This was the real heavy stuff. You know, the big L-word kinda affair.

"It was all the more difficult, and meant all the more, for a big supposedly straight stud like Jenner. Once that man tasted my lovin', well he wasn't goin' back to the skirt he was used to, I'll tell you that.

"We were young and we were full of ourselves. We had these plans, see, of goin' back to my place in Wyoming and we were gonna be cowboys for the rest of our lives, just the two of us.

"This one time, though, we got caught in a fire-fight. It was during the Tet offensive. That was hell on earth, boys. I bet you Mr. Kane can tell you a thing or two about the Tet. Hell on earth, I tell you.

"We got separated. I figured, when it was all over, that Jenner had taken the big one. I figured he was a goner. I could never find him, and the records got lost somehow, they were always fuckin' up the paperwork in Nam back then. Couldn't even get that straight, damn government!

"It was the same time I lost my legs.

"Turns out – I didn't have any way of knowin' this – that Jenner saw it all. I was runnin' to get on this Huey, we were bein' evacuated from where a bunch of us got caught. I slipped and fell, just as the 'copter was landing, havin' come back to pick me up. It'd already been nearly full.

"But, when I fell, I fell right under the damn bird's skids. The whole weight of the thing came down on me and crushed my legs, crushed some of my spine. That was it.

"Jenner, poor soul, was on that 'copter. Turns out, he was the one made them come back for me. Held a gun to the pilot's head when the flyboy said he wouldn't do it, claimed there was too much fire from Charlie.

"So, they thought they'd done me in, themselves. Jenner thought he was the one who'd caused it, since he made 'em come back. That's the demon in his head, you see, boys? He thought he'd killed me.

"Right fried what few brains the man had. I tell you, he wasn't no scholar when I knew him in Nam. Oh, he was pretty and he was ..."

Larry could tell that Cowboy was almost ready to go off

on one of his long deprecating speeches about this man he'd loved, did love. But he could see that Hanks stopped himself this time, he couldn't carry it out.

The others must have understood. They didn't challenge the way Hanks stopped his story either. They waited till he took a long drink of his beer and then let him continue at his own speed.

"Anyway, what happened: He got himself all fired up in this suicidal-like thing. He volunteered for this. He volunteered for that. Man was a maniac. He never found out that another patrol – Marines like yourself this time, Mr. Kane – was right behind us. They got me out. But it was one of their 'copters, so I went to a naval base with them. That's how my papers got screwed up.

"Then Jenner took off and became this soldier-of-fortune type. He was this big mercenary, I take it. He says he was lookin' for someone worthy of killin' him.

"That's the boy's story. Now, thanks to you, he's gettin' this special care. They think, 'cause I'm around, it won't be long before he can come out.

"Then I'll take him back home with me to Wyoming." There was an undeniable look of joy on Cowboy's face as he contemplated that. "We'll get that dream after all. We got those charges dropped for his insanity reasons. Thank God the fool didn't actually shoot anyone!"

"Man, that's some tale, Mr. Hanks'" Junior said.

"Hell!" Cowboy seemed to drag himself back into his crusty role. "No big tale there, son. Just a bunch of foolishness. Man runnin' around the world playin' soldier and all of that when he coulda been gettin' laid! Damn fool, sure as hell's got a lot of things to make up for when they spring him from the looney-bin.

"'Course, the sex is a part of it." That's when the leer came back on Cowboy's face. "Man's not had a piece in years, he says. Imagine that!" Then he cackled so lecherously the rest of them could barely stay on their chairs they were laughing so hard.

• • •

"Where did Danny go, Mr. Kane?" Scott asked while he and Alex were in the kitchen later, getting the steaks ready to be barbecued for dinner. "Will he be away long?"

Alex stopped what he was doing and looked past Scott, as though he were remembering something from long ago that had happened far away.

"He'll be back in a couple of days, I suspect," Alex finally answered. "He's got something he has to do. Something a man has to do alone."

XIV

Joseph Farmdale stood in the cemetery in Carmel, California. As usual in the morning, the fog was thick and it gave an eerie air to the undertaking. But it also gave him a sense of added privacy. He was glad of that. He wanted to do this alone.

The hearse drew up, right on schedule. Joseph reflexively took off his hat. The men from the funeral parlor went about their business with the sanctimonious seriousness Joseph had learned to expect from those in their profession.

The hole had already been dug. Joseph looked at it and then at the headstone beside it. This had been his most difficult decision, one he'd put off until they'd finally released Theodore's body to him. Should he bury him beside James?

In the end, he chose to let them rest together. Perhaps others would never understand, but now, with them both gone, Joseph only remembered the two tow-headed brothers playing with one another. They had, for so many years, loved one another. They were also, in the end, brothers.

Someone walked up beside Joseph. He turned, startled. No one else was supposed to attend but the rector of the parish who was already preparing to say the burial offices.

"Danny," Joseph whispered. "You didn't have to come, my boy. You don't need to be here."

"I had to, Mr. Farmdale," Danny answered. He put an arm

around the old man's waist and pulled them closer together. "I had to make my own peace with him."

The rector began the Anglican service. His voice was distant, not a part of their conversation, not really a part of them:

"Man, that is born of a woman, hath but a short time to live, and is full of misery. He cometh up, and is cut down, like a flower; he fleeth as it were a shadow, and never continueth in one stay ..."

Joseph put his own arm around Danny. The words seemed to be so far away, as far away as his sons were from him now. But this young man, this good young man, was so near.

He was very thankful Danny had come. He would have done everything to stop him if he'd known he'd planned it. But that wasn't relevant now. They were together, and the living would go on.

Joseph was so lost in his thoughts that he missed the moment when he was supposed to act. Finally, the rector spoke to him, "Mr. Farmdale, the earth."

Joseph reached down and picked up a bit of the ground and threw it on the casket which had been lowered into the hole. Danny clung to him even more as the rector went on. Somewhere, those most final words sounded:

"Unto Almighty God we commend the soul of our brother Theodore departed, and we commit his body to the ground; earth to earth, ashes to ashes, dust to dust ..."

• • •

"Why did you come, Danny?"

The youth was sitting with Joseph in the living room of the Farmdale mansion overlooking the Pacific Ocean.

"I'd never killed anyone," Danny answered slowly. "And, whatever he'd done, whatever I had to do, I had to face what'd happened. I owed it to him, and to myself, to at least face the reality, Mr. Farmdale. I told you: I had to make my peace."

"And have you?"

Danny nodded slowly. "Alex told me this is the worst

thing of all. He understood that I needed to be here. I don't know, actually, what I could ever have said to him. But I had to stand there. And I wanted to be with you while it happened."

Danny stood up and went and put his arms around Joseph. He'd never really understood how very old and frail the man was. Now his shoulders seemed so thin and vulnerable as he held them. "I'm sorry about your son, Mr. Farmdale."

"Danny, I'm so sorry for what we're doing to you. We're stealing your youth. You shouldn't have to be going through any of this.

"This damned world! This sorry place where we live out our lives!"

"No. Don't say it, Mr. Farmdale. Don't say that. It's not true. We'll prove it isn't. You and me and Alex. We'll prove the good people rule here yet. I promise you we will."

"I try to believe, Danny. I try ..."

"Mr. Farmdale, we're going to win. I know we're going to win."

JOHN PRESTON

Born in Portland, Maine, John Preston was an influential author of fiction and nonfiction, dealing mostly with issues in gay life. He was a pioneer in the early gay rights movement in Minneapolis. He helped found one of the earliest gay community centers in the United States, edited two newsletters devoted to sexual health, and served as editor of *The Advocate* in 1975.

He was the author or editor of nearly fifty books, including such erotic landmarks as *Mr. Benson* and *I Once Had a Master and Other Tales of Erotic Love.* Other works include *Franny, the Queen of Provincetown, The Big Gay Book: A Man's Survival Guide for the Nineties, Personal Dispatches: Writers Confront AIDS,* and *Hometowns: Gay Men Write About Where They Belong.*

Preston's writing was part of a movement in the 1970s and 1980s toward higher literary quality in gay erotic fiction. He was an outspoken advocate of the artistic and social worth of erotic writings, delivering a lecture at Harvard

University entitled "My Life as a Pornographer". His writings caused controversy when he was one of several gay and lesbian authors to have their books confiscated at the border by Canada Customs. Testimony regarding the literary merit of his novel *I Once Had a Master* helped a Vancouver LGBT bookstore, Little Sister's Book and Art Emporium, to partially win a case against Canada Customs in the Canadian Supreme Court in 2000.

Preston served as a journalist and essayist throughout his life. He penned a column for Lambda Book Report called "Preston on Publishing." His nonfiction anthologies, which collected essays by himself and others on everyday aspects of gay and lesbian life, won him the Lambda Literary Award and the American Library Association's Stonewall Book Award. He also wrote the "Alex Kane" adventure novels about gay characters. These books, which included *Sweet Dreams*, *Golden Years*, and *Deadly Lies*, combined action-story plots with an exploration of issues such as the problems facing gay youth.

Preston was among the first writers to popularize the genre of safe sex stories, editing a safe sex anthology entitled Hot Living in 1985. He helped to found the AIDS Project of Southern Maine. In the late 1980s, he discovered that he himself was HIV positive. He died of AIDS complications on April 28, 1994, aged 48, at his home in Portland.

About ReQueered Tales

In the heady days of the late 1960s, when young people in many western countries were in the streets protesting for a new, more inclusive world, some of us were in libraries, coffee shops, communes, retreats, bedrooms and dens plotting something even more startling: literature – highbrow and pulp – for an explicitly gay audience. Specifically, we were craving to see our gay lives – in the closet, in the open, in bars, in dire straits and in love – reflected in mystery stories, sci-fi and mainstream fiction. Hercule Poirot, that engaging effete Belgian creation of Agatha Christie might have been gay ... Sherlock Holmes, to all intents and purposes, was one woman shy of gay ... but where were the genuine gay sleuths, where the reader need not read between the lines?

Beginning with Victor J Banis's "Man from C.A.M.P." pulps in the mid-60s – riotous romps spoofing the craze for James Bond spies – readers were suddenly being offered George Baxt's Pharoah Love, a black gay New York City detective, and a real turning point in Joseph Hansen's gay California insurance investigator, Dave Brandstetter, whose world weary Raymond Chandleresque adventures sold strongly and have never been out of print.

Over the next three decades, gay storytelling grew strongly in niche and mainstream publishing ventures. Even with the huge public crisis – as AIDS descended on the gay community beginning in the early 1980s – gay fiction flourished. Stonewall Inn, Alyson Publications, and others nurtured authors and readers ... until mainstream success seemed to come to a halt. While Lambda Literary Foundation had started to recognize work in annual awards about 1990, mainstream publishers began to have cold feet. And then, with the rise of e-books in the new millennium which enabled a new self-publishing industry ... there was both an avalanche of new talent coming to market and burying of print authors who did not cross the divide.

The result?

Perhaps forty years of gay fiction – and notably gay and lesbian mystery, detective and suspense fiction – has been teetering on the brink of obscurity. Orphaned works, orphaned authors, many living and some having passed away – with no one to make the case for their creations to be returned to print (and e-print!). General fiction and non-fiction works embracing gay lives, widely celebrated upon original release, also languished as mainstream publishers shifted their focus.

Until now. That is the mission of ReQueered Tales: to keep in circulation this treasure trove of fantastic fiction. In an era of ebooks, everything of value ought to be accessible. For a new generation of readers, these mystery tales, and works of general fiction, are full of insights into the gay world of the 1960s, '70s, '80s and '90s. For those of us who lived through the period, they are a delightful reminder of our youth and reflect some of our own struggles in growing up gay in those heady times.

We are honored, here at ReQueered Tales, to be custodi-ans shepherding back into circulation some of the best gay and lesbian fiction writing and hope to bring many volumes to the public, in modestly priced, accessible editions, world-wide, over the coming years.

So please join us on this adventure of discovery and rediscovery of the rich talents of writers of recent years as the PIs, cops and amateur sleuths battle forces of evil with fierceness, humor and sometimes a pinch of love.

The ReQueered Tales Team

Justene Adamec • Alexander Inglis • Matt Lubbers-Moore

Mysteries from ReQueered Tales

Sweet Dreams / Golden Years
John Preston

The Alex Kane Missions, Books 1 & 2 – Meet Alex Kane. In Vietnam, the only lover he had known had been killed by a homophobic coward. With his physical prowess and the financial backing of his former lover's family Kane's sorrow turned to action, and he is resolved to fight back against anyone, anywhere who dares to challenge the dreams of gay men.

In *Sweet Dreams*, someone was daring to mess with young gay men in Boston. Danny Fortelli, a high school senior and superb gymnast, gets caught up in a drugs-and-prostitution ring exploiting gay youth. Boston's South End had become the epicenter of violence driven by a corrupt elite. Enter Alex Kane to alter their plans forever.

In *Golden Years*, Joe Talbot, long retired and now widowed, dreams of an easier life in a gay retirement community that sounds too good to be true. But when his young friend Sam, left behind in New York, begins to suspect the "golden agers" are being mistreated, the news reaches Alex Kane's financier. Kane jumps into action, gaining the support of a local cowboy plucked right out of the Old West. These evil doers won't know what hit them when Alex Kane and his Cowboy ride into town!

"The first of what is to be a series on the adventures of gay avenger Alex Kane is both fun to read and uplifting. Any culture needs richness of mythos in order to grow. Preston's story is a step toward filling a deep need for gay dreams."
— *The Advocate*

A celebrated series of superhero adventure stories written for a general audience by bad boy John Preston whose journalism and fictional writings brought leather and bondage scene mainstream. This new edition includes a foreword by Philip Gambone (*As Far As I Can Tell: Finding My Father In World War II*).

Deadly Lies / Stolen Moments
John Preston

The Alex Kane Missions, Books 3 & 4 – Meet Alex Kane. In Vietnam, the only lover he had known had been killed by a homophobic coward. With his physical prowess and the financial backing of his former lover's family Kane's sorrow turned to action, and he is resolved to fight back against anyone, anywhere who dares to challenge the dreams of gay men.

In *Deadly Lies*, Kane knows politics is a dirty business, filled with dirty lies. The dirt becomes deadly in Minneapolis/St. Paul when rampant political smearing and corruption turn toward unscrupulous politicians' easiest targets: gay men. With his lover and sidekick Danny Fortelli, Alex comes to protect the dreams – and lives – of gay men imperiled by the lies and deceit that threaten to tear them apart. Together they can generate the heat needed to burn away the political trash in Minnesota – and anywhere else it endangers the dreams of gay men.

In *Stolen Moments*, a malicious newspaper editor targets Houston's evolving gay community in a cynical power play. But he never counted on the resolve of Alex Kane, a proud and fearless man devoted to the defense of gay dreams and desires everywhere. Alex and his lover Danny take the Texan head-on.

> "It's here that John Preston brought together his talent as a genre writer and his lifelong commitment to healthy, fearless gay pride. Read these novels for the delicious entertainment and for a reminder of how far we have come as a queer tribe."
> — Philip Gambone

The Alex Kane Missions are a celebrated series of superhero adventure stories written for a general audience by bad boy John Preston whose journalism and fictional writings brought leather and bondage scene mainstream.

In the Game
Nikki Baker

A Virginia Kelly Mystery, Book 1 – When businesswoman Virginia Kelly meets her old college chum Bev Johnson for drinks late one night, Bev confides that her lover, Kelsey, is seeing another woman. Ginny had picked up that gossip months ago, but she is shocked when the next morning's papers report that Kelsey was found murdered behind the very bar where Ginny and Bev had met. Worried that her friend could be implicated, Ginny decides to track down Kelsey's killer and contacts a lawyer, Susan Coogan. Susan takes an immediate, intense liking to Ginny, complicating Ginny's relationship with her live-in lover. Meanwhile Ginny's inquiries heat up when she learns the Feds suspected Kelsey of embezzling from her employer.

"The auspicious debut of a black writer who brings us a sharp, funny and on-the-mark murder mystery."
— *Northwest Gay & Lesbian Reader*

"An entertaining assortment of female characters makes Baker's debut promising" — *Publishers Weekly*

"It has adventure, romance, and some of the best internal dialogue anywhere." — Megan Casey

Nikki Baker is the first African-American author in the lesbian mystery genre and her protagonist, Virginia Kelly is the first African-American lesbian detective in the genre. Interwoven into the narrative are observations on the intersectionality of being a woman, an African-American, and a lesbian in a "man's" world of finance and life in general.

First published to acclaim in 1991, this new edition features a foreword by the author.

The Always Anonymous Beast
Lauren Wright Douglas

A Caitlin Reece Mystery, Book 1 – Val Frazier, Victoria's star TV anchorwoman, is Caitlin's newest client. She is the victim of a viciously homophobic blackmailer who has discovered her relationship with Tonia Konig. Tonia is a lesbian-feminist professor, an outspoken, passionately committed proponent of nonviolence. She is enraged by her own helplessness, she is outraged by Caitlin's challenge to her most fundamental beliefs, and by Caitlin herself, whom she considers "a thug".

As Caitlin stalks the blackmailer and his accomplices through the byways of the city of Victoria, she uncovers ever darker layers of danger surrounding Tonia. And she struggles against a new and altogether unwanted complication: she is increasingly attracted to the woman who despises her.

> "A very accomplished first novel, which is distinguishable by an elegant flair for description and an obvious love of the language." — Karen Axness, *Feminist Bookstore News*

> "Douglas' book is snappily written, peppered with wit and literary allusions, and filled with original characters."
> — Sherri Paris, *The Women's Review of Books*

Douglas's debut novel in 1987 began a six part series for Caitlin Reece. This new edition includes an introduction by the author and a foreword by legendary Katherine V. Forrest.

And don't miss ...

Ninth Life: Caitlin is hired by a woman code-named Shrew, to pick up a package. Caitlin is sickened to the depths of her being by the contents of the package: a blind and maimed cat, and photographs of animal experimentation. And now Shrew is dead. As a member of the militant animal rights organization Ninth Life, she had infiltrated Living World, a cosmetics company. The other members of Ninth Life suspect she was betrayed by someone within their own ranks and murdered because of what she learned.

A Body to Dye For
Grant Michaels

A Stan Kraychik Mystery, Book 1 – Stan "Vannos" Kraychik isn't your everyday Boston hairdresser. Manager of Snips Salon, which is owned by best bud (and occasional nemesis) Nicole, Stan thought this day was an ordinary one. A delivery van backed into the salon's rear driveway and accidentally spilled gallons of conditioner, leaving Stan and hunky Roger) embracing in a gooey mess trying to staunch the flow, with little success as they slid and slipped with Nicole watching on with rolling eyes. Later Roger is found murdered.

Stan's client, Calvin Redding, who owns the apartment where Roger's body was found, can't explain why the body is dressed in little more than bowties. Enter Lieutenant Branco, dark, muscular, Italian, (straight) of Boston PD Homicide who immediately suspects everyone, especially Stan. In an attempt to clear his name, Stan travels to California, takes up mountain climbing, eavesdropping, spying, schmoozing, and a little bit of schtupping, all in an attempt to find the truth.

Grant Michaels' zany series of adventures starring Stan Kraychik garnered multiple Lambda Literary Awards including a 1991 nomination for Best Gay Men's Mystery. For this new edition, Carl Mesrobian reminisces about his brother Grant in an exclusive foreword, and Neil S. Plakcy provides an introduction of appreciation.

And don't miss ...

Love You to Death: Stan visits a chocolate factory after a patron drops dead at a chi-chi cocktail party

Dead on Your Feet: Stan's new boyfriend, choreographer Rafik, is accused of murder

Mask for a Diva: Stan nabs a gig as wig master to a summer opera festival but the final curtain for one star comes down early

Time to Check Out: Stan takes a holiday to Key West but a dead bodies turns up anyway

Dead as a Doornail: In the midst of renovating his new Boston brownstone, Stan becomes the (unintended?) murder target

Sunday's Child
Edward O. Phillips

A Geoffry Chadwick Misadventure, Book 1 – Lawyer Geoffry Chadwick is 50, Canadian, single, gay and, after a brief struggle with a hustler who tries to shake him down, a murderer. Herein lies the device for this macabre, funny, first novel. Although Geoffry must dispose of the body – which he does by dropping off sections of it around town at night – the trauma of the murder affords him the opportunity to reminisce and ruminate: on the recent termination of his affair with a history teacher; on the not-so-recent deaths of his wife and daughter; on the alcoholism of his mother; on growing old; on being gay. The visit of a nephew and the New Year's festivities only serve to intensify his thoughts. Although Chadwick is abrasively disdainful early on, he is fascinating when he loosens up. Phillips keeps the reader hopping with throwaway quotations from Donne and scatological references and puns.

First published in 1981, and a Books in Canada First Novel nominee, this new edition contains a foreword by Alexander Inglis.

And don't miss ...

Buried on Sunday: "One of the problems with weekends in the country" says Geoffry Chadwick's genial host in *Buried on Sunday*, "is that people feel free to drop in unannounced." And sometimes that includes criminals on the lam: forget the hors d'oeuvres, everyone is now hostage. Winner of the coveted Arthur Ellis Best Novel Award from the Crime Writers of Canada.

Sunday Best: Geoffry gets roped into planning a wedding for his niece Jennifer, but the groom has closet issues and a sexy latino chauffeur has a mixed agenda. Then there is widowed Montreal socialite Lois, mother to the groom, who casts her net for Geoffry ...

Working on Sunday: Geoffry Chadwick has a stalker. But between avoiding Christmas parties, gift shopping, moving his mother into a senior living facility, handling his recently widowed sister, and dealing with the loss of his long-term boyfriend Patrick, Geoffry Chadwick does not have time for a stalker.

Let's Get Criminal
Lev Raphael

A Nick Hoffman / Academic Mystery, Book 1 – Nick Hoffman has everything he has ever wanted: a good teaching job, a nice house, and a solid relationship with his lover, Stefan Borowski, a brilliant novelist at the State University of Michigan. But when Perry Cross shows up, Nick's peace of mind is shattered. Not only does he have to share his office with the nefarious Perry, who managed to weasel his way into a tenured position without the right qualifications, he also discovers that Perry played a destructive role in Stefan's past. When Perry turns up dead, Nick wonders if Stefan might be involved, while the campus police force is wondering the same about Nick.

> "*Let's Get Criminal* is a delightful romp in the wonderfully petty and backbiting world of academia. Well-drawn characters make up a delicious list of suspects and victims." — Faye Kellerman

> "Reading *Let's Get Criminal* is like sitting down for a good gossip with an old friend. Its instant intimacy and warmth provides clever and sheer fun." — Marissa Piesman

Originally published in 1996, the first book in the Nick Hoffman Academic Mystery series is now back in print. This edition contains a new foreword by the author.

Death Trick
Richard Stevenson

A Don Strachey Mystery, Book 1 – Don Strachey isn't exactly the most sought-after private eye in Albany, New York. In fact, this gay P.I. has gotten to the point of having to write checks to pay his tab at the cheapest lunch counter in town. And he isn't sure that the latest one, for the grand total of two dollars and ninety-three cents, is going to clear.

Surprisingly he's hired to locate Billy Blount, the gay heir to one of Saratoga Springs' upper-crust families. On top of that, Billy, a young and outspoken gay activist, is wanted for the grizzly murder of the man he slept with on his last night in Albany – a man he'd never met before that night.

"Sassy and sexy ... Don Strachey is a private dick who really earns his title." — *Armistead Maupin*

"This murder mystery, recounted with sassiness and wit, is full of true-to-life details about contemporary gay existence. Stevenson uses the yarn to poke fun at straitlaced parents, homophobic cops and greedy gay bar owners ... This is a great lazy-day read – and politically correct, yet!" — *The Advocate*

Written just before the onslaught of AIDS, *Death Trick* is a time capsule of gay life as it existed in smaller towns in America. A foreword for this edition by Michael Nava (Henry Rios series) is included.

And don't miss ...

On The Other Hand, Death: An elderly lesbian couple thwart the plans of a mega-mall developer ... then killings begin.

Ice Blues: The body of the grandson of the godfather of Albany's political machine in P.I. Donald Strachey's car.

Third Man Out: Queer Nation activist has been outing closeted gay homophobes and now he is found dead.

Simple Justice
John Morgan Wilson

A Benjamin Justice Mystery, Book 1 – It's 1994, an election year when violent crime is rampant, voters want action, and politicians smell blood. When a Latino teenager confesses to the murder of a pretty-boy cokehead outside a gay bar in L.A., the cops consider the case closed. But Benjamin Justice, a disgraced former reporter for the Los Angeles Times, sees something in the jailed boy others don't. His former editor, Harry Brofsky, now toiling at the rival Los Angeles Sun, surprises Justice from his alcoholic seclusion to help neophyte reporter Alexandra Templeton dig deeper into the story. But why would a seemingly decent kid confess to a brutal gang initiation killing if he wasn't guilty? And how can Benjamin Justice possibly be trusted, given his central role in the Pulitzer scandal that destroyed his career?

Snaking his way through shadowy neighborhoods and dubious suspects, he's increasingly haunted by memories of his lover Jacques, whose death from AIDS six years earlier precipitated his fall from grace. As he unravels emotionally, Templeton attempts to solve the riddle of his dark past and ward off another meltdown as they race against a critical deadline to uncover and publish the truth.

> "Wilson keeps the emotional as well as forensic suspense up through the very last sentence. The final scene is not only a satisfying explanation of the crime, but a riveting study of the erotic cruelty of justice." — *The Harvard Gay and Lesbian Review*

Awarded an Edgar by Mystery Writers of America for Best First Novel on initial release, this 25th Anniversary edition has been revised by the author. A foreword for the 2020 edition by Christopher Rice (*Bone Music*) is included.

Murder and Mayhem
Matt Lubbers-Moore

An Annotated Bibliography of Gay and Queer Males in Mystery, 1909-2018.

Librarian and scholar Matt Lubbers-Moore collects and examines every mystery novel to include a gay or queer male in the English language starting with Arthur Conan Doyle's "The Man with the Watches". Authors, titles, dates published, publishers, book series, short blurbs, and a description of how involved the gay or queer male character is with the mystery are included for a full bibliographic background.

Murder and Mayhem will prove invaluable for mystery collectors, researchers, libraries, general readers, aficionados, bookstores, and devotees of LGBTQ studies. The bibliography is laid out in alphabetical order by author including the blurb and author notes, whether a hard boiled private eye, an amateur cozy, a suspenseful romance, or a police procedural. All subgenres within the mystery field are included: fantasy, science fiction, espionage, political intrigue, crime dramas, courtroom thrillers, and more with a definition guide of the subgenres for a better understanding of the genre as a whole.

A ReQueered Tales Original Publication.

ℭ𝔰

If you enjoyed this book,
please help spread the word
by posting a short,
constructive review at
your favorite social media site
or book retailer.

We thank you, greatly,
for your support.

And don't be shy! Contact us!

For more information about current and future releases, please contact us:

E-mail: *requeeredtales@gmail.com*
Facebook (Like us!): www.facebook.com/ReQueeredTales
Twitter: @ReQueered
Instagram: www.instagram.com/requeered
Web: www.ReQueeredTales.com
Blog: www.ReQueeredTales.com/blog
Mailing list (Subscribe for latest news): https://bit.ly/RQTJoin